"Richard Dean Buckner is just the hero for our modern world: a righteous killer who can step outside convention and right the wrongs; and Sayles is just the writer to drive his story. This is how I like my fiction: unrelenting prose and kick-ass justice."
—Joe Clifford, author of *Lamentation*

"The brutality is in the prose. Course and violent, Sayles writes like he is seeking vengeance against the world. It's 21st century noir. Mickey Spillane on meth."
—Tom Pitts, author of *Knuckleball*

"As subtle as brass knuckles to the face. Buckner is a classic and Sayles is one to watch."
—Eric Beetner, author of *Rumrunners* and *The Year I Died Seven Times*

"...Richard Dean Buckner left me wanting more. He is a breath of fresh air in an antiques shop. A biker in a museum. A chaotic, reckless anomaly. You know I'm enjoying something when I deliberately slow down my reading pace to enjoy the novel longer. The Subtle Art of Brutality is a ridiculously strong first novel, starting the new darling of the P.I novels legacy."
—Benoit Lelievre, blogger and reviewer at Dead End Follies

"Gut twisting detective fiction done the way it is supposed to be done. RDB makes Dirty Harry seem a little soft."
—Todd Morr, author of *Jesus Saves, Satan Invests*

THE SUBTLE ART OF BRUTALITY

ALSO BY RYAN SAYLES

Richard Dean Buckner Mysteries
The Subtle Art of Brutality
Warpath (*)

Other Works
That Escalated Quickly!
Goldfinches

(*) Coming Soon

RYAN SAYLES

THE SUBTLE ART OF BRUTALITY

A Richard Dean Buckner Mystery

Down & Out Books
3959 Van Dyke Rd, Ste. 265
Lutz, FL 33558
www.DownAndOutBooks.com

The characters and events in this book are fictitious. Any similarity to real
persons, living or dead, is coincidental and not intended by the author.

Cover design by Eric Beetner
Cover photo by Jason R. Photography

ISBN: 1937495965
ISBN-13: 978-1-937495-96-1

To my wife Donna, as all things are.

To Brian Lindenmuth, who took the leap
with me and changed my life.

And to my father.

1

"The worst thing about a contact shot to someone else's head is getting their brains, hair and skull fragments washed off my face."

I cock the hammer back. He sobs harder. "If you've never tasted a man's grey matter tinged with gun powder and revenge you have an inexperienced palette."

The man is on his knees before me, facing away, hands tied behind him, crying, .44 Magnum squeezed against the back of his skull as tight as a waterproof seal.

"Then of course, you have no idea what diseases the guy might have had." I blow smoke. It crowns his head. "But the money is good."

Smoke drifts off my cigarette, lazy and weaving in the air. The souls of dead soldiers rising from a battlefield. I drag and watch ruined ashes flutter off the cherry-like leaves from a long-dead tree, tracing spirals through the night down to their deaths before my feet.

Winter in Saint Ansgar might as well be winter in Anchorage, if Anchorage never fully woke up from a nightmare. The sun is shining, eyes are open, but every corner is razor-sharp and every shadow has gritting teeth.

Here, outside on the street, frost dances in the predawn hours like devils of ice cavorting around a fresh kill. We're south of the river that cuts Saint Ansgar from west to east in a beltline of ice floes and estuary water. Here, in these half burnt-out urban developments, the graffiti and the chalk outlines, people know where they are by the police crime scene tape and stained concrete.

Street lamps keep vigil over the empty traffic ways. Aged guardsmen cast from ironworks during the Great Depression that have seen these streets constructed and then turned over to scum and felons. Here, outdoors, we're alone as far as the eye can see. It must be extra cold kneeling on frigid concrete.

"Please mister...I have a wife. She's a worrier anyways and I—you'd love her. She's blonde and hilarious and and—oh God...my wife is gonna be wondering where I am soon and—"

"Your wife will find out from the police where you have been. Or you can tell me where she is and you can go home right now."

"Tell you where *who* is? My wife? She's at home like I—" He shuts up with a stern whack from my iron.

"Who? For Christ's sake *who?*"

"Alisha McDonald." I say.

"No, no nono—"

"Yes, Francis. *Her.*"

"No, I had nothing to do with—"

"Missing nine weeks now."

"No, you sonofabitchno I—"

"Alisha McDonald, age seven, sandy blonde and brown, four-foot-one, last seen—"

"Fuck you, pig, and fuck your mother I am—"

"*With you.*"

"I didn't do nothing—"

"You went to the shopping mall—"

"I was cleared!"

"You saw her last. Before she vanished off the face of the planet."

"I was cleared—"

"Your wife's family lined some pockets."

"That little girl is with somebody else—"

"Pocket lining doesn't *clear* shit. Death does."

Desperation and vindication both: "I told her stupid fucking old man I had nothing to do with that little girl! I told him as soon as I turned my back some pervert must of

2

took her! I didn't even wanna go to the mall! Her old man was probably banging her out himself and then hired some junkie to shut her up! That's why he asked me to take her to the mall instead of doing it himself! A set-up! He was always dog shit like that! It's just that the people around him never knew! He hid it well!"

Francis. Like a scorned woman crying to the police about her boyfriend hitting her.

But his next words...those he says with contempt. And worse, honesty. Flat pulse honesty: "Fuck that girl and fuck her old man for pointing the finger at me."

I let the last bit sink into the air.

"Her old man always points the finger at me." Like a spoiled child.

"He pointed the finger at you, Francis, because you did it."

"I didn't do nothing—"

I strike his head and he collapses forward. Sees stars. Hell, I can see them dance around in his eyes like old cartoons. He groans. Growls. Had enough. He rolls and leaps up. Teeth bared at me.

Unfortunately for him my left cross is just short of a freight train. I bury my fist into the crumpling structure of his mouth. His eyes roll back to white.

No time for unconsciousness.

My cigarette rubs a burnt ashen sore on his forehead. Francis wakes with a searing startle. I shake the sting of a good punch out of my hand and lift him up by the hair. I turn him to face a silhouette waiting in the shadows. His eyes adjust to the contrast of dark on darker. He sees what the shape makes out. *Who* the shape makes out. Recognition. Horror.

"This is how I see it played out, Francis," I say. "The girl's mother trusts you. And why not? She knows you. That is what you want. The girl's dad knows better but he doesn't tell his wife for obvious reasons. Something inside is hungry. I know the type. Maybe you've been starving it since the incident when you were a child."

He looks to me. Wants to ask how I know but won't. To ask how I know is to admit it's real.

"Your brother told me, friend. But maybe you've been feeding that hunger all these years. Maybe after I gore you out, I could dig up your back yard and find a slew of four-foot tall skeletons still with some baby teeth lining their jaws."

A single tear freshens his cheeks.

"But whatever that hunger is, you give in this time. You plan a nice day at the mall, just you and Alisha. Buy her a soda and a stuffed animal. Listen to the music in her laughter, you cast your smile down onto the little girl. Your next meal. You don't take her home. You take her someplace else, do whatever it is you do, and stash her away for later use.

"Or you dumped her corpse." I twist his hair until I feel clumps tear out from his scalp. More squealing. Thrashing.

"Of course you're the prime suspect. No security videos, no eyewitnesses. Nothing to prove you *didn't* do it. Your wife and her nouveau riche family bought your freedom. I checked. The D.A. owes your father-in-law a blow job or two for all the campaign money, the fund raisers. They release you on your own recognizance; shake down a few convicted child molesters to make everybody else feel good. Slowly loosen the squeeze on you. Just let it slip from memory. You get away scot-free."

"No!" Clawing at my fingers as I tighten my grip.

"Yes. Too bad I got the case."

The silhouette walks forward. An apparition appearing before us. The gray of the evening, the jejune bleakness of the situation paints the new man with its sad brush.

Washed out, defeated and hollow. His eyes say it all: he just wants an end. No matter how ugly. Or truthful. He wants his little girl in whatever remaining condition she may be found.

Francis takes it all in. The fistful of hair shudders in my fist. Small at first, becoming more pronounced. Francis becomes afraid, ashamed. Dirty. Ignominy and consternation flood about. He becomes a little boy, he pisses his pants and has the demeanor of a beaten dog. Making progress.

"Say it." I yank his head in a staccato whip. "I know you think you are a man, so be big. Be strong. Say it." A whisper to his ear.

"I—I never—I mean, *oh God...*"

"Do not think God will intervene on your behalf," I say, a snarl. "He might not like me *per se*, but I have noticed He stays out of my way. God is in all things, but not this street alley. Not tonight."

Francis starts crying again, his shame surfacing. Our every word a cloud of ice dying in the freezing, rank air. Every one of those clouds containing secrets.

Another whisper: "Her old man told me you did something like this before." The heat of my breath against his ear must be like a dry breeze from Hell.

Eyes light up in humiliation, the way a boy looks when somehow his mom finds out he's been sneaking peeks at her clothing catalogs and stuck the pages together. A seedy, pervert breed of humiliation.

He begins to cry harder. Good.

Another breeze: "Little Francis, not straight, not queer, just deviant. Your mom used to babysit kids? And you were what? Fourteen?"

He does not want to hear. The truth of one's past always has a way of haunting, and where there are ghosts hidden the guilty can only hope they go un-resurrected.

Another whisper: "You called it *tickling?*"

His sobbing is so messy and intense he cannot speak using vowels. Blubbering. A whole minute, his throbbing eyes focused on that silhouette. I smack him good and hard. "Speak it, before I lift you off the ground by your deranged cock."

Through his blubbering and his punch-broken mouth he stumbles out: "Back then I—I just...I wanted to figure it out is all; I had such strong urges and no one to talk to. I didn't mean to hurt—"

"What you *meant* and what you *did* are two different things. Your brother told me that kid's name and I looked him up. Dead. Three years into college. Suicide. His boyfriend said he talked about getting molested as a youngster. Happy now? You did that to a kid your mom was trusted to babysit and you barely escaped with a hair on your ass. And now, all grown up, decades later, and this."

Our eyes meet. "Alisha McDonald."

My gun goes to his forehead, plugging into the round wet cigarette burn. "Where is she?"

He stares at the silhouette in the shadows as it grows tense, antsy. Agony.

"Or," I ask, "did her old man really bang out his eight-year-old, kill her and frame *you* for it?"

In the shadows Kenneth McDonald cries like a lost soul who has now just realized he is in Hell, and the concept of permanence brings with it a new definition. His child molester brother accusing him of fucking his own kid.

Francis McDonald. One of the thousands of reasons God blessed me with brutality.

"Oh..." Gun to his head. I can hear his diseased heart break. Exposed. Family ties severed. Some things you cannot take back. He stares at his brother in the shadows, crying himself.

At last: "Ken, please forgive me," he says. Defeated. This is where I want to be. A broken man will squawk. Confess. Plead. Beg and negotiate.

Alisha's father walks into the buzzing light from the street lamp overhead to face his sibling.

"Where is my little baby?" Ken McDonald asks. His voice quiet, grave and betrayed.

"Forgive me, please."

"I don't know what to forgive you for."

"Forgive me and I'll tell you. I promise."

Ken looks on as Francis mumbles something about giving in to temptation. The words come out through wet tears and all-consuming fear, like the speech itself was something hiding from predators and is poking out to see if the coast is clear.

Ken, so softly: "When we were kids you promised that if I lied to Mom about what happened you'd never do it again. How do I know you won't lie again?"

"Christie knows. She'll—"

"My own sister-in-law knows? *She knows what you did?*"

"Yes, but—"

"And she has said nothing?"

"To protect her family name! They have an image! Jesus, Ken! You *know* that! She caught me burying Alisha—" He cuts off, swift and permanent as the gallows.

Burying. It destroys Ken. His little girl. I know he had expected to never have his baby again, but the finality, the reality, is never the release people think it is.

"*I'm so sorry.*" Blabbers. "I just—I just—I've had to sleep on the couch ever since she caught me and she broke all my things and she was screaming about forcing me into therapy or chemical castration and—"

"*Shut up. You. Shut. Up. Now.*" No longer his brother. It's in his eyes. Their family name is the same but from

7

two different levels in Hell now. He croaks out the words like they are sand and he is underwater. The cold distance, the irrevocability of this godless situation creeping in his voice.

The soulless countenance of Ken McDonald changes. His demeanor changes. Becomes alien. Gone cold now. Never fear a man more than when his callousness emerges and you didn't see it coming.

I squeeze the gun tighter against Francis. "Where?"

"Promise my forgiveness," the pervert says, so low the dirt hears him better than we do.

After a breath as long as God's, after he can retrieve his voice since hearing the word *burying*, Alisha's father speaks. He does not look up.

"I forgive you for your sins against—" but he cannot finish.

"Thank you." Such relief.

"Where?" I say. The only word I can insert into this gunpoint conversation.

"Under the new herb garden we planted. The marigolds mark her headstone."

Ken starts to cry. But he bares his teeth as well.

So desperate now, rooting for mercy anywhere it may be dug up: "She loved marigolds, right? I thought they'd be a sweet gesture, a nice thing for Alisha—"

"*You don't speak her name. Ever,*" Ken says through teeth that must be carnivorous now.

I don't want to ask if they have cooked with those herbs. If they have trimmed the flowers and put them in a vase on their kitchen table.

A diseased man in Francis. A terrible accomplice wearing the mask of a soulmate in his wife. Their own niece, entombed unceremoniously in their yard. Hidden. Cast off.

How many other children? I make a note to look up his previous addresses.

"Let me go now," the molester asks. "Let me go. I did my part here..."

Ken looks with a galvanized fury. It makes my heart warm.

"Alisha sends her best." An arctic tone. "You are not my brother. I want you to hear that from my mouth. I will cut your name in two.

"*I will cut your name in two.*"

He turns around and begins to walk away from us, bathing in the shadows that line this neighborhood. "You'll understand that when I said I forgave you, I lied."

Alisha McDonald's broken father strides away from us to go unearth his dead child to give her some dignity. I told Ken as soon as he hired me the answers would come, but not without a price.

Ken steps up and off the street, past the lights and into the gloom and darkness. But then he stops. Stands bolt still.

All that emerging callousness doing its work. Ken doesn't fight it; just welcomes it. It's armor. The best kind. Transforms his core just past the edge of shadow where the light cannot reach him.

Eventually Ken turns back towards us. Walks forward from the shadows a different man. Just like that. Flashes of his little girl and whatever horrors his mind played for him, flashes of his kid brother and the sins Ken committed to protect Francis, coming back now to stab him in the back. Betrayal lodges deep. Past bone and into the soul.

The decision Ken has just made, bathed in the ink from a night here in country that God has overlooked, he becomes someone else. Some*thing* else.

He walks up, holds out his hand. Now we're talking.

I pull a drop gun I took from a gang-banger months

back. He didn't need it anymore; he was quite dead. The drop gun goes to Ken's open palm, then it goes to Francis's head and my .44 doesn't have to worry about being traced.

A gunshot later and I am heading home to wash the brains off of my face. Contact shots are bad about that kind of thing.

2

My name is Richard Dean Buckner.

People call me either Richard or Mr. Buckner. No one calls me Dick.

No one.

3

An overflowing ashtray.

The air is blue with so much smoke. I crush another butt into the glass dish after using it to light a new cigarette. Two old, yellowing cigarette carcasses shift in the pile like demolition rubble. They almost cause a landslide. I drag deeply, exhaling through my nose like a raging bull snorting heat into a crisp morning.

I rub my neck where several years ago I was assaulted with a hypodermic needle loaded with a lethal dose of the Big Fry. Hit attempt. To kill an elephant you have to hit it with a missile. I guess I'm something more than a typical elephant because the missile failed. Not without cost, though.

The PD called me *unserviceable*. I think that bitch Flemming picked the word on purpose. The PD retired me unceremoniously with a pension check just big enough to legally argue they gave me something.

Black and white photographs are scattered across my desk and ink blots like square leaves falling off a zebra tree.

My desk's far edge is lined with origami. Two swans, with their flat heads and triangle beaks, tread water on the wooden surface and swim without moving an inch. A sailboat with so many imperfect folds it would do better as an anchor. It sails in the empty sea along my desk, prow facing the swan, invisible waves rolling and hitching it to nowhere. A paper rose, a table with two chairs. A whale. All so imperfect.

A half-dead fan spins above me. Two dim bulbs dangle from it, casting light in search beacon fashion. It, being tossed around by the fan's wobbly spinning, jumps and bobs and dives and swings, throwing light here and there and back here again. Trying to read by the lone fan's erratic behavior gives me headaches.

The blinds behind me are drawn loosely, allowing grated, wedge-on-top-of-wedge blocks of waning sunlight to fall over the room. A fake plant rises out of a cheap, wicker pot and leans into the corner; a drunk using the wall to hold himself up while he searches for his next step.

I blow smoke rings up at the fan and watch them get thrown about and torn into thousands of small gray strips. I rub my face and sandpaper lining my jaw grits under one palm.

The phone rings.

"Hello?"

"Richard?"

"Hello, Abe." Abe Baldwin is my main man. He is a terrible trial lawyer who has a crusader complex bigger than a movie star's ego. He spent a few years in the city's district attorney's office, but he is horrible at research and even worse at arguing. The sign of a good cook is if they are fat. If Abe were as bad a cook as he is a lawyer, we would have lost him a long time ago.

The writing on my office door says I'm a private investigator. In between jobs for Abe I take pictures of rich housewives banging the pool boy, rich husbands banging the maids, dirty cops taking pay-offs, blah blah blah. The usual, *makes-ends-meet* fare. There's plenty to go around.

Abe will call me with a special case every now and then, and I look into it for him. He called me a few weeks ago about Ken McDonald and his daughter.

"How did it go?" Abe asks.

I sip my bourbon and coffee and say, "His brother did it."

"Francis? He confessed?"

"Yes."

Abe sighs with relief. "Good. Because Ken McDonald went to his brother's house last night. He made a huge scene. Cops and media huge. Smacked around his sister-in-law."

"I saw on TV."

Abe keeps on anyways. "Fucked that house up like he was a bull on 'roids. He pummeled every square inch of that house."

TV had some on this morning's broadcast.

"Dug up his kid," Abe said.

"Saw it."

"They'll be looking for Francis, you know."

"Yeah, I know. Dubberly was the investigator on that one?"

"Yes."

Detective Mickey Dubberly is a fat, shining example of the police department's inability at quality screening. Dubberly is about as dirty as a cockroach trudging through pig shit, and what I really need to do is just plug him full of lead.

The one thing about scum cops: if they are given a way out that doesn't involve something ugly, they'll take it. No doubt Dubberly, the head detective on the missing Alisha McDonald case, was the one taking the biggest cut from the pervert's in-laws.

"Dubberly can be dealt with easy enough," I say without a true worry.

"You think?"

"Yes. Dubberly is a squirmer. He'll run straight to the captain and blabber on and on about how he always thought Francis was the real threat...blah blah blah. He'll pass the buck."

"What if they find Francis's corpse?"

"They'll see that his brother shot him. If Kevin hasn't already confessed everything."

"Do you think McDonald will talk?" Abe. Cautious. Worried about his ass.

"Not about us."

"You sure?"

"We shook hands on it if that means anything anymore. He said what he wanted. He got it. He pulled the trigger. I doubt he'll talk." Abe breathes in and out from his nose. I know Abe; that's his nervous breathing.

"But, just in case I took the usual precautions." Cash. No paper trail. No phone records. "All he could prove is he called you for help. When we first met he told me he spoke to several lawyers that day. You'll be lost in the shuffle. Deny. Stick to it. You're out of any real trouble."

"Just deny it? What about the girl's body? How'd he find it then?"

"Just because the police let go of their prime suspect doesn't mean McDonald had to let go of his as well. Alisha was last seen with Francis. The brand-new garden planted the same time his kid disappeared, probably as big as a child's coffin. McDonald also knew his brother had hurt another kid. It all adds up to him solving this on his own."

"I hope so. I don't need that kind of heat right now."

"Pussy."

"You know, I like that—" and I can't hear Abe's words because the colors smear in my mind, running like a fresh oil painting drenched in water. Red cascades down and peels away to an orange which becomes yellow before my brain seizes for just a moment and I know my teeth grit so hard it's audible. The last runner of liquid horror traces down across my vision and my skull clears up.

Just like that. Why I am unserviceable. Big Fry Smear.

My voice groggy and choked up: "I said I'd find his kid, not have his back later."

Abe said, "Anyways, I sent a guy your way. Friend of a friend of a friend."

"You don't have friends, Abe."

"My wife keeps saying that. Friend of a friend of a friend of a former client. He needs you to look up his daughter."

"Great. Another father-daughter case. Is he legit?"

"Sure he is. Why not?"

I installed a light outside my office door for one reason: security. There is a panel of frosted glass in my door, shoulder height. The light limns anyone who shows up knocking, and the glass frames their heads in case I answer the door with a gunshot.

It's been known to happen.

A man's silhouette appears from the murky grayness of the textured glass and I say to Abe: "I'll call you back."

Abe says something about having me over for dinner, and before I can tell him I won't eat the slop his English-immigrant wife cooks, my doorknob turns.

The man walks in unannounced. That will get you killed around here. He looks distinguished by way of his IQ or academic accomplishments. He is rather unremarkable, but the snooty air about him immediately puts a bad taste in my mouth. I do not like being around people who think they are better than me. I do not like it at all, Sam I am.

Under the desk, my revolver comes out and aims in his direction. If he knows he's covered by a large bore revolver he doesn't act like it. My eyes go to his hands. Without patience: "You knock first."

"I do apologize, sir."

"Don't apologize." I say. "Knock."

"Mr. Buckner, may I call you Richard?" He says, smoothing the front of his suit jacket.

I say nothing. After an uncomfortable minute he takes

the hint, nods like a spoiled child and walks back out my door. He stands there for a second, clearly not used to bending to someone else's will. Knocks. Hard.

"Come in." I say, pleasantly enough. I do not re-holster my iron.

Irritated: "Mr. Buckner, how are you?"

"Oh, just fine. What were you saying?"

"Well, I—" He stares at my swans and sail boat. "Your origami are...unique."

"The good ones are at home."

"Your mother must be very proud of you."

"Even if she were alive I wouldn't give a shit."

"Hmmm. Well, anyways." He looks around. Smoothes his jacket again. "Is it Mr. Buckner or Richard?"

"Depends on who's addressing me."

"A paying client?"

"Well, anything but Dick. Do *not* call me Dick."

"Understood. I am Dr. Windslow, and I need you to find a certain young lady for me."

"Your daughter?"

An uncomfortable chuckle. Then, "Absolutely not. As it were she was a...mistress."

"Abe send you over?"

"No. I don't know an Abe."

"Why do you want the mistress?"

His eyes slink about. Serpent. His throat clicks at the speed of light. He needs to think of something. If he is going to lie he should have concocted it before now.

"To rekindle, I suppose."

"Marriage not work out?"

Incredulous: "I beg your pardon, but you cannot seriously—"

"Yes or no. Has your marriage failed?"

"Why must you assume I am married? I have no wedding band. I am not fat as so many married men are. I—"

"Only a married man has a 'mistress.' Single men have girls, girlfriends, bitches, baby mamas. A distinguished man like you uses the correct label for everything. It would be an insult to your superior self-perception to do otherwise."

Angry. Seen-through.

"Very well. My marriage has ended. Quite abruptly."

"Because of your affairs?"

"None of your business."

So yes.

"And now you want to rekindle an extramarital affair? Correct? Why did the affair end in the first place? Wife find out?"

"The wife and I spent our time in therapy trying to salvage our marriage. Now it is over and I want my old girlfriend back."

His throat clicks again. A tell.

"Why?"

"Why what?"

"Why do you want her back?"

"So we may continue, as I stated earlier."

"Does she want to be found?"

"What do you mean?"

"Well, why do you need a private detective to find a woman whom you think will still want to be with you? If she's that in to you she shouldn't be hard to find."

"Will you take the case or not?" Cut to the chase.

"What's her name?"

"Denise Carmine. White female, age thirty-two. Brown and blue. Five-foot-eight, one hundred and thirtyish. Divorced, no children. Drives a white Toyota sedan."

Impressive. And dangerous.

I lean forward, one elbow on the desk. That hand I rest my chin into, the other hand still holds him unwitting, inches from death. "Let me tell you about a common theme running through my office."

"Very well." Impatient red rising up his collar. The throat clicks. I already know my answer.

"I need to make this clear. Dudes come in here asking me to find the ex-girlfriends they've been hiding from their wives. It happens. For some reason man will court a woman, spend money on her, make plans with her, propose to her, marry her, live with her, make children with her, and then cheat on her and risk everything. Much like yourself.

"Some of these guys get away with it. Some don't. But they all hide their affairs. Some want to hide them deeper than others. Those are usually the guys who have something to lose and they decide that whatever it is, they don't want to lose it. So they come in here and hire me to find these girls.

"Once I found a married dude's mistress. I told the guy where she was. He left my office, went to her place and beat the fuck out of her for talking about their affair in a bar."

Dr. Windslow begins to shake his head in denial.

"So this mistress, it'd been few years since porking this married dude. She got drunk in Steamy's Pub and blabbed that she slept with a guy who had a membership to some country club. I'm sure she bragged about him, said his name, the whole nine yards. The married dude must have had a friend in the bar, because it got back to him. How, I have no idea. Don't care. She needed four reconstructive surgeries afterwards. I don't know what she looked like before. But now, wherever in the world she goes she's the ugliest thing walking down the street.

"I guess the married dude thought there was a quiet

understanding that the mistress was not aware of. The affair was a secret, and she wasn't being secret anymore."

Dr. Windslow still shakes his head, but as an act. A knee-jerk response. No real reason behind it. Another tell.

Our eyes meet, mine dig into his. "No. I will not take your case." Firm. Stolid. "But I will be keeping an eye on you. If Denise Carmine, white female, age thirty-two, brown and blue, five-foot-eight, one hundred and thirtyish, divorced, no children, drives a white Toyota sedan turns up beaten or dead, I'll remember *you*."

The good Dr. Windslow smoothes his jacket again and looks very uncomfortable. I should kill him now and spare Denise Carmine the looming threat.

"*I do not hunt women for angry, jealous men.*"

"You are mistaken about me, Mr. Buckner. But I can see there is no turning back from this point—you believe my motives are soiled—so I bid you farewell."

I cock the hammer. He takes notice.

"I will be keeping an eye on you."

His throat clicks again, but this time because he is swallowing hard.

"I do not sleep. And I see everything."

He walks out.

I do not hunt women for angry, jealous men.

4

"I really 'preciate this, Mr. Buckner."

Through tendrils of smoke I say: "It's not a problem."

Elam Derne sits before me. Abe's referral. Mr. Derne: late fifties, early sixties. Bottle cap glasses. Coarse beard the color of bleached sand. A gentle air about him despite his hefty build. Thick. Stocky. He could have been saddled and pulled a cart in his youth. Maybe even now.

"Elam?" I drag. "Biblical, right?"

"Yes it is. My mother was extremely Baptist."

"Catholic myself." One hand goes to my Saint Michael the Archangel pendant. "Dated a Baptist girl once. She was a huge bitch."

Avoiding my last comment, Derne clears his throat, then: "My mother was Evangelical. You can tell my by name, and I have six brothers and sisters. Jonah, Adam, Bethel, Daniel, Eden and Zachariah."

"Impressive."

He looks uneasy. Not the same way Dr. Windslow looked. I crush out my smoke and grab my notepad.

"Tell you what, just start at the beginning."

"Sure. Here goes." He says and readjusts in his seat. Breathes in. Exhales. Even across the desk I can smell the cigarette on his breath. Takes his glasses off, puts them back on.

His narrative: "Let's see, I guess my wife and I bought the house on Madison back in...oh, '71 or so. Nixon still had the office when we signed for it. Maybe in '76 was when the Boothes moved in across the street. Newlyweds. Beboppers. Nice couple; the wife especially. Darla, her name. The husband, Benjamin, good enough fellow but he had a stand-offish quality I never trusted. Still childless at the time. Belinda was born first, not too long after they settled in. Maybe a year or two. Before Ronald Reagan anyways.

"About two years after Delilah came about Benjamin just got up and left. This must have been in '82 or '83. What a piece of shit, if you don't mind me sayin' so. Piece of shit. I told Anne as soon as we met them—I said, *Anne, watch that guy. You can tell by how he keeps his car and his yard he ain't too keen on responsibility.* And damnit I was right. A wife and two little girls depending on Benjamin Boothe and *poof!* Just leaves. I heard he was incarcerated up north of here some ways, but I never did ask much about it. Between us, I think he was queer.

"Anyways, it was like Delilah was like our own little girl. Anne and I—bless her soul, my wife is very ill these days—we had our two boys and our daughter but Delilah...she was just something special to me. Out of the three of them left in that house, Delilah—even at age two—took her daddy leavin' them the hardest. Sonofabitch.

"So I stepped in. Anne too, now. Kind of grandparents. I tried as hard as I could to be their father as well. Anne, she watched the girls while Darla worked. Darla didn't have no skills, not any great ones. But she could wait tables or work a cash register. We'd have the girls and see 'em off to school and get 'em when they came home. Feed 'em.

"Belinda graduated school with honors and got picked up by the Naval Academy. She's off on some huge boat somewheres now. I think she's a Lieutenant Commander. She missed her father's bullshit responsibility gene. Good for her.

"Delilah was so precious. She was more into the popularity in school than her sister was. Delilah was there every mornin' 'cuz it was social hour. She had a lot of friends. But you know how that works after high school. All your buddies peel away the day after graduation. Delilah squeaked by. She needed night school for a math class her senior year but she took it, passed it. Graduated.

"She bounced around for 'bout year, came in and out of our lives. Each visit was a snapshot. I could see she was maybe learnin' the wrong things with every drop-in. Every snapshot was somethin' a little concerning. Not so wrong that she was gonna be some hardened dope dealer or nothin', just livin' life a little fast is all. She was older than she should have been. We were sad.

"You know the type of thing. Bad boyfriends. Late nights. Maybe came to drunk a time or two wonderin' what happened to the night. Probably smoked grass. She got her father's bullshit responsibility gene.

"But then one day clear out of the blue she shows up. Says she's been through the ringer and now she wants what Belinda's got. Education. Career. Turning over a new leaf. Fresh start-kinda thing. Said she heard some commercial on the radio from a school sayin' they'd teach you that IT stuff. In demand here in the city. In demand everywhere I suppose. I got my dad's auto shop when he passed away—stroke—when I was in my twenties. I never stepped foot in no college but she wanted to in a bad way.

"I asked her 'bout scholarships and loans and all that. She said her credit was shit. Belinda told her there was no way the Navy Academy would take her but she could join up as a swabbie and get some education benefits. Delilah didn't want to be a squid. If you ask me she just didn't want to be in the military. Too much discipline. Strict rules, responsibility. She was bad about it. She'd have to wait her four years and then go to IT school. She never wanted to wait for nothin'.

"So, in the end, I gave her tuition money. I did with all my children. She was no different. I woulda done it for

Belinda too, but the Navy beat me to it.

"I set up a plan with Delilah, an agreement. The IT school was a four-year degree from college, it wasn't nothin' specialized. No tech college. She didn't want that either. She wanted a *degree*. Somethin' her mom never had. But, bless her heart; Darla Boothe always would complain her employment choices and troubles were rooted in the fact that she didn't have a degree. Benjamin did. Piece of shit.

"Delilah must have figured she could avoid those same problems with education. So our agreement stated she spend two continuous, full-load years at a community college. Then two years at the university over in Dunkirk getting her IT degree. And by God she buckled down. Must have drained every ounce of hard work and good judgment from her.

"She worked nights four days a week waiting tables at some chain restaurant in the suburbs. Lived with her mother. Cut her bills down to the bare minimum.

"She struggled, made C's in everything mostly. Some B's. Had a steady boyfriend by the name of Ted something for two years before she found out he had a steady girlfriend at his job and a third one over in his home town about two hours away.

"Got her degree from the university and Anne and I were never so proud. Our own kids did their accomplishments; we loved them and cheered them on. It just seemed Delilah had more adversity to tackle. I'd be lyin' if I didn't say we were proud even more because she was—let's face it—a financial risk and we had our necks out.

"Right away she got a good job downtown. Some medical company."

Mr. Derne huffs the kind of sigh an old pack mule will the moment it knows its heart is exploding. Giving it up.

"And then it started spiraling down.

"She saw a house over on Carolina, near Mason Avenue. For sale, nice older couple. Moving to a retirement pad. She just loved it. Not too big. Well-kept. I had no idea Delilah was even entertaining buying a house. She was sneakin' Anne and I a few bucks here and there to pay us back for the education costs. I didn't care myself—I never made Elam Jr., Tommy or Angela pay us back—but Delilah insisted. So we set it aside for her. She didn't know.

"And Delilah wanted the house so bad. She could afford it too; but her credit was ruined worse than she ever told us by those years between high school and college. Apparently she got in a few of those triangle pyramid schemes—whatever—and took a bath. She got behind on her credit cards, floated checks, bounced checks, you know the deal. Took a bath. And another bath. And another bath.

"Well, that's not wholly correct. Banks will lend to anybody these days so she *could* buy the place but the APR, closing costs, all that. She couldn't afford all of it. Not with her blighted credit and non-existent bank account.

"Anyways, she asked for help.

"We bought the house for her. She paid me for the mortgage, insurance, all of it. I paid the companies. It didn't help her credit, but we talked about credit cards, a car loan, that sort of thing. Steady payments, all that. Delilah started trying to be responsible.

"Then, she met Pierce White. Rat bastard. Some senior client rep over at the medical company. He was married, of course. Two kids. Naturally they start an affair. They couldn't control themselves in the office and gossip started. They get asked about it; they say they were dating. The company's image came first. I guess every employee of that place signs some agreement sayin' if they have an office romance it's gotta be disclosed, yada yada yada. People cheatin' on spouses in office romances will not be tolerated.

"Pierce and Delilah got fired. Pierce had to go home and explain to his wife. His kids. Delilah broke up with him. She said he was flamin' pissed off about losin' his job. Called her somethin' horrible like a *sport fuck* and Delilah said she felt so trashy and used, she just stayed depressed for months. Come to really think of it, I believe all this started goin' really downhill then.

"Delilah went through the rigmarole of life: woke up, eventually got out of bed. Smoked a cigarette for breakfast, lunch and dinner. Drank coffee. Missed a few months' worth of bills. Interviewed at another place for half the money. Got hired on.

"Then she met James Dobbins. Married, no kids. His wife, however, was a great white shark. Jesus, what a bitch. Delilah started seein' this guy. It was a short romance before they both got fired but I'll give it this: she started eating again. She wore make-up. Dressed in something other than sweat pants. You never knew she was so low until you seen her out of it.

"Anyways, she says they got caught kissin' in a break room or somethin'—she didn't wanna talk about it—and for whatever reason it was against the rules and she was canned. Dobbins too. He flipped out. His shark-wife took him for a ride in divorce court. I guess as soon as he told her what happened she was in a lawyer's office. Fast-tracked his ass to the poor house.

"This was a little over a year ago. Delilah hadn't made a payment on the house since. Anne and I moved into a new place about three years ago and while I can do some extra every month, I don't have the bones to pay two mortgages. I kept tellin' Delilah this but she never...never got back on her feet. Decided to rot in that house. Throwin' parties, wakin' the neighbors. Botherin' the cops. They'd get called there so often they looked the property owner. Found me.

"I got calls at work and home. The cops thought it was a rental property. Finally I said to Delilah: *Look, you've got to get a job and get back payin' for this house. I don't care if you wait tables, if you paint buildings or if you drive a semi through the Rockies. Get back on your feet. Or else...or else you're out.*

"I hated putting the ultimatum out there, but I had to. It was hard. No way would she dare to lose the house. But I'll be damned. She called my bluff. I guess it's fair to say she's not used to hearing *no* and having it be firm. Real. She always gets more chances.

"She never did go find work. She asked to borrow more money. I said no. She begged, cried. I still said no. It was time to be stern. Tough love. She borrowed from her mother, her sister. Her friends, maybe. Never paid no one back that I'm aware of.

"I went over there one morning and found four strange people drunk, passed out in the living room. Car parked in the damn front yard. She was in the bedroom, some shitbird asleep next to her. Both naked as newborns. I woke her ass up and demanded to know what kind of spring break crash pad I was footin' the bill on. We got into a huge fight. Huge. Said things we shouldn't have. Can't take back. She was cryin', throwin' her arms about, yellin' at me for not doin' enough. I was blown away. *Not doin' enough.* She cussed, she broke a damn window.

"I left. Didn't speak to her for almost a week. Anne was goin' to be gettin' the results from her biopsy that week so I had other things on my mind. And when my wife said she was dyin', well, I felt the clutter in my head greater than I had ever before. I needed to clear some space. And for some reason, sellin' that pit over on Carolina was the single best thing I could do.

"I called Delilah and told her she had thirty days to vacate. Period. Done. I told her mom the same thing. Belinda too. My daughter-in-law, she's a real estate broker. She fixed me up with friends of hers who were in the market for a home. They saw it, liked it. Even with Delilah's mess all over it—I told her we were showin' the place and to clean up but of course she didn't—they just liked it.

"She was gone August fifteenth of this year. Moved back in with her mom. Up until the very end she thought I'd change my mind. Right up to the very last day.

"And not a month later, Darla calls me. Screaming.

"Said she come from work one evening and the house was abandoned. Delilah left. I wouldn't be surprised if Darla was missin' some jewelry though. Darla said she called and called and called but Delilah wouldn't answer.

"Gone for two days before Delilah emailed her mother. Here, I got a copy for you."

Mom, leaving town for a while. Scared out of my mind. I'll call when it's safe. Love, Delilah.

"That was two months ago. Mr. Buckner, I ain't got no earthly idea what scared her like that. The police said she's an adult and adults can go where they like, when they like, tell or not tell anybody they like about it. I need her found. Her mother needs her found. Her sister. My wife, too.

"Anne ain't got but this year to live, and she wants to see Delilah home safe. Mr. Buckner, what'd I do throwin' her out like that?"

5

I get Delilah's information and say goodbye to Derne.
He leaves. I dig.

6

The next day I hit the streets.

Derne said Delilah had a car. There are three tow truck companies in the city. I know folks at each. I'll call and see if there's something in their inventory matching her wheels. I'll also get ahold of a guy I know at the PD who can check their records for me.

Then it's the usual canvass protocol: truck stops, hookers and the check-cashing stations. Carefully canvass the women's shelters. A lot of the shelter workers know me from my cop days, but there's no guarantee a new one won't see a rough, gritty man with a neck tattoo and shoulders wider than the Pacific cruising their "safe" place and freak out. I could easily be mistaken as an abusive husband trawling for his battered wife.

Jane Doe checks at the area hospitals, emergency rooms and morgues. Check her on the usual social media websites. I find profiles but they're set to PRIVATE. I use a fake profile of mine to send her friend-type requests. I doubt it'll pan out. She might be a complete moron and still post about every last thing she does, but if she really wants to disappear she'd have abandoned those things as soon as she decided to drop off the face of the earth. Hours of dull but necessary legwork that almost never pays off.

The snow is coming down in blankets; crisp virgin flakes of sheer white fluff pouring out of the sky like the angels were sobbing in frosted cotton.

Saint Ansgar, my hometown, my double-edged mistress, my living coffin.

In the foreground is a major modern city, skyline complete with goliaths of architecture and stunning views.

In the background, a seedy maze of cracked streets where nightmares are given free reign about the neighborhoods. Separated north and south by a river flowing east to west, the city of Saint Ansgar flourishes on the top and rots on the bottom.

Composed of Germanic elements, *Ans* means "God" and *gar* means "spear." Our namesake was a Frenchman born in 801 AD. He lived his pious life and died sixty-four years later. Somewhere in that lifetime he tried to convert the Danes and the Norwegians to Christianity.

His life parallels our city. Originally founded on the southern shore in the 1880s, the city of Saint Ansgar quickly fell to scoundrels in the early twentieth century. The saint himself founded the first Christian church in Sweden, only to be run out by pagans. He lost most of his earnings for the church to them and the pagans burned his house of worship to the ground.

It seems that good does not prosper where that saint first set foot. The northern shore of our metropolis is alive and well with business and culture, while the pagans still burn and roam unhindered on the southern, original side.

Sports: an arena football team, major league hockey team, triple A baseball team who won their pennant two years in a row and a woman's basketball team that is top notch though no one in the city cares.

The ocean borders us to the west. The shore is a thin mountain range, cut in half by a single inlet. The inlet flows from the ocean into the large Fissure Bay, which separates the mountain range from the city proper.

Fissure Bay is wide and deep oval, reaching from east to west almost ten miles. From north to south it is just over thirteen miles long. At the northern tip it opens into a small waterway known as The Funnel that broadens into a smaller, tighter body of water called Shrouded Bay. A treacherous series of spits—finger-like ridges of sediment that extend from the shore out into the water line—span the northern coast of Shrouded Bay and protrude southward about two hundred yards.

Police are always finding dead bodies in the shallow strips of water between the spits. The mafia here, a weak but viable presence, will dump the few people they feel the urge to kill in those spits. I have deposited there as well. A convicted but paroled child molester fell to my hand cannon and was found six weeks later, anchored down in the shoals between spits. Eventually he was positively identified and, as it should be, no one cared.

A river flows from Shrouded Bay easterly and it crawls east-northeast up into the state. The river, known simply as The Fjord although it is not one, thins out and finally breaks up into a series of deltas about thirty-five miles into land.

Just south of the midpoint of Fissure Bay is Landcaster Island. Back during the turn of the century, developers tried to form the island into a ritzy, posh living space. The idea never caught on, largely because no bridge from the mainland was built. It'd be miles long, and not even to this day will someone undertake that.

Eventually fisherman bought up the island. A small nugget of land a few hundred yards off of Landcaster's northern coast is where the fisherman and their families, settled there for the better part of a century, have buried their dead. Littlecaster Island is not much more than an overstuffed graveyard, creepy at dusk. The fading sun throws just enough backlight over the old, ornate gravestones to create a tense and foreboding ambiance.

Fissure River flows dead east from the middle of Fissure Bay, cutting Saint Ansgar in half. The river is broad and straight, a deep swath carved from the earth. The northern shoreline is adorned with a three-mile long boardwalk and expensive, trendy shops and restaurants. Northward of that shoreline, the newer section of Saint Ansgar thrives.

The southern shoreline is a work in progress, and remains mostly a broken down series of docks and refineries. The refineries still stand, gutted and burned out from a deadly and massive fire in the 1920s. The remains hold themselves against the horizon like the skeletal remains of great beasts still not swallowed into the ground. Southward of that, the old section of the city is a haven for evildoers and the economically destitute. The Burrows exist there.

The two western peninsulas that define Fissure Bay and the state's western border are solid mountain ranges. Spotty areas of flat, grassy fields scattered throughout the strips of mountains are protected as state parks and no industry has ever befallen them.

Both peninsulas are thin, only a mile or two wide. The southern peninsula measures almost six miles in length while the northern extends down almost four. Their tips, missing touching each other by a mile-wide mouth that was never bridged, each have a lighthouse that serves the waterborne traffic entering the bay.

The lighthouses are named The Sirens because of their duel foghorns, sounding in a call and answer. Their shrieks, as low-pitched as a tuba with silvery, sharp and tense edges to them, are common background noise here. Landcaster Island is almost perfectly between the two when looking into the bay from sea. Boat navigators line up the Sirens like sights on a handgun and steer directly at the Landcaster lighthouse. The light tower itself heaves out of the island's central hill almost two hundred feet into the air, providing a three hundred and sixty degree blast of white light.

I have thrown a man off the walkway on top of that beacon.

On the easterly shore of the Funnel leading into

Shrouded Bay is Eastman's Light, a squat box-like structure close to the ground. On the southern-most point of Fissure Bay is Ansgar's Light, a candy-cane colored tower at the center of the only decent park in south Ansgar. I still wouldn't go there at night.

The city. Her streets welcome me. The day is bleached out by the overcast and it all looks like an eclipse. I light a smoke and step out into my hometown. Another day.

7

Because of me, Darla Boothe's phone starts ringing.

Walking along the street, snow has stopped. I pause by the public library because it has WiFi and I get good reception.

"Hello?"

"Hello, Ms. Boothe?"

"Yes, who is this?" Her voice, tarnished with absolute concern and worry. Those few words paint her picture: bags under weary, bloodshot eyes, aged ten years in two months. Lips drawn in a perpetual look of sorrow. A brunette despair.

"My name is Richard Dean Buckner. Mr. Derne hired me to look for Delilah. I was hoping you could help."

"He said one of you people would be calling me, I guess. I get so lost now after...all this. So, a...what are you called?"

"I'm a private investigator, ma'am."

"Right. Like Dog the Bounty Hunter."

"No. I have much better hair."

She laughs, mostly hollow.

"Have you heard from her, ma'am?"

"No." The worry creeps out of her voice and slithers across the phone line. She says with a defeat so absolute I am taxed to hear it: "Bring my baby back to me." Little words. She begins to sob quietly.

A brilliant sun cascades down through skies as azure as the waters in Lake Tahoe. The thick sheets of snow and ice coating everything rob the light of its warmth and life before reflecting them back up into the world. Beauty, but only skin deep. The allure of the glowing day turns to fangs of icy bitterness as soon as I step into its grip. An empty dazzling.

"Ma'am, do you drink coffee?"

"I do."

"There's a place called Raoul's Mexican Cantina that serves breakfast. If you like chorizo this is the place. How about we meet in a half hour?"

"Okay, I guess."

I give her directions. Hang up. Raoul's loves the police. Without us they'd have no business before noon. Their coffee sucks so I hope Darla Boothe hasn't pinned all her hopes and dreams on the Joe I offered. But their chorizo really is the best. I'm hungry. And, I can drink bad coffee.

We've been in Raoul's now for a half hour at least and Darla Boothe smokes.

The snow has driven construction workers inside here from a site across the street. They'll spend the day eating hash and eggs and smoking cigarettes, watching the crummy TVs tuned to the local news and making fun of the female anchor who is twenty years past her face-for-TV.

"I hate to trouble you but I just smoked my last cigarette," Darla says, eyeballing my smokes.

"You're welcome to share mine," I say, nudging the soft pack across to her. "Beware though. They're heavy."

"I've never heard of these." She examines the pack, taps one out. "Rum Coast cigarettes, huh? Do you buy them online or at an Indian Reservation or something?"

"South of the river. Any convenience store with bars on the windows and the clerk inside a bulletproof box will have them."

Rum Coast is my brand of coffin nail. For ditch weed tobacco, they're stout. Darla's first inhale, she hacks as if that one drag gave her cancer. I can see the look on her face as she contemplates trying it again, but her eyes say that one more drag and she'll be choking back vomit. She crushes it out.

"Sorry for the waste," she says, her voice a swirling mixture of rasp, worry and a gentle smoothness that must have been erotic if I heard it lying next to her back in her prime.

"You're not the first to reject my brand. No worries," I say, enjoying my smoke. "So, this is Delilah?"

Darla brought a shoebox full of photographs. Each picture tethered to the next by the presence of Delilah Boothe. They're all jewels on a necklace that is the timeline of a little girl's growth into adulthood. I flip through the pictures and Delilah Boothe becomes more human than search object.

"This is my little girl," Darla says, sipping coffee. "She was ten in this one; that was the first year I planted Foxglove in the front yard."

She taps her finger on a picture of a dark-haired girl looking bold on a pink bicycle. Where the drive meets the walk to the front door is a small patch of white Foxglove, a flower that sends a long, thin stem upwards adorned with rows of bell-shaped and freckled flowers.

They are also rather poisonous.

"Where have you already checked?" I ask, take a bite of my chorizo burrito. Lazily roll ash off my smoke.

Darla thinks. Gears turn behind her eyes, rust in their cogs from all her tears. She exhales and I can hear the flutter in her lungs born from being emotionally drained.

"I think if she wanted to come home she would have."

"Excuse me?"

"I know Elam cares for her; he's the only father she ever had. But, Delilah follows her heart everywhere, even to places she damn well knows she shouldn't go. If her heart isn't aiming back here, she won't come."

"Ma'am, you've spoken with old boyfriends, friends from work, school, maybe checked her old places of employment—"

"Delilah's heart is guided by a wayward compass," Darla says. "For a time I dated a man who loved to sail. He used to say something about deviation with compasses. I get it all confused now but he said it interfered with how a compass could read north. Delilah's heart is guided by a compass that cannot read north."

This is how people answer questions that they do not want to answer.

"Elam said after high school Delilah went off on some crazy adventures before she came back around and went to college." Darla's eyes slowly close and she nods. She does not re-open them. "Is there a possibility she's off on another adventure?"

"I guess," she says under her breath, closing her eyes for a long while. She opens them suddenly and shakes her head as if she were asleep and startled awake.

This is going poorly.

Redirect. I drop a fingertip on a photograph and slide it out from the bunch. "Tell me about this one."

Darla focuses on the photo, reads it with her memory. Smiles. "Christmas," she says. "1992, I think."

The picture is of Darla and her two daughters, all wearing matching Santa sweaters that screamed early '90s. Even Darla's hair was still feathered with ridiculous bangs; the '80s fashion mistakes hadn't had enough time to bleed away before this picture immortalized them.

"Yes. 1992. That was the year we had these sweaters," she says, a small bit of life seeping back into her. "I wanted it to be a tradition but this was the only year we wore them." She huffed a dry laugh. "Fashion. What a fickle bitch it is."

"This is your oldest daughter?" I point to a girl fully cloaked in the awkward development of adolescence. Glasses, braces, teeth much too big for her mouth, pimples so clustered it's as if she was being punished by the gods.

"Yes. Belinda. She's an officer in the Navy now."

"Okay. A military officer, huh? Did she attend Annapolis?"

"Yes. Graduated in the top half of her class. Economics major. She says the Marines tried to steal her somehow—they'll steal anything—but she wanted to drive huge boats. Be a captain one day. She always loved pictures of the sea."

I won't mention I was a Marine. We Devil Dogs didn't steal "anything."

"Did Delilah ever talk about joining the service?"

"Belinda practically beat her over the head with it but Delilah...she just—well, it's not in her genetic make-up to be so...pinned down. Delilah will just take flight when the mood strikes her. In high school she lost virtually every job she had because she just never showed up. She would follow that heart of hers. Hell, one time she took a four-day weekend and left the state. If she had a cell phone back in those days it might have eased up on my heart a little bit to know that she and some friends just went on a joy ride and it turned into some teeny-bopper version of *Thelma and Louise* without the weird suicide thing at the end."

"When she left this last time, there was no note? No phone message?"

"No."

"Email?"

"No."

"What happens when you call her?"

"Voice mail. My emails go unreturned."

"Any friends or family heard from her?"

"No. Unless they're lying."

"When she did this before, she just dropped off the face of the planet?"

"Yes."

"What does she do for money?"

"I know a few times when she's taken waitress jobs here and there for a few weeks at a time to make ends meet. She bums."

"Does she have a credit card with your name on it?"

"No."

"Does she have her own credit card?"

"I don't know. I assume so."

"Did she ever go to a payday loan place?"

"Oh, I'm sure."

With the way Derne made Delilah's credit sound, she'd have a low limit credit card that wouldn't go far.

"What did she take with her?"

"Oh..." Darla drifts off. Finally, "Some clothes, I guess. She left most everything. Jewelry, her laptop. If she kept cash around I never knew it."

"So you came home and Delilah was just *gone*. Correct?"

"Yes."

"How did you know she wasn't coming back?"

"It was just in the air, I suppose. She's done it enough over the years that I have a sixth sense for it. After a few days, well, the writing was on the wall."

"Where did you think she'd gone?"

"At first I thought she'd run off with a man. But she hasn't talked about any guys for a while. Usually she mentions whoever she's dating at the time in casual conversation. She'd say things like *I'm going out with Chris tonight* or whatever. Usual stuff. She hasn't done that for a while I guess."

"Any boyfriends?"

"The last two steady ones she had you know about. White and what's-his-fuck. God I hated that last guy."

I search my memory. "Dobbins."

"Yes, him. White, I could see why she was ~~with him. It~~ wasn't until it was over did Delilah mention he was still married. But he was clean-cut, handsome, sophisticated. I thought for sure she'd landed a movie star. My Delilah always had the looks to draw in Hollywood-quality men."

If anyone labeled me a *Hollywood-quality man* and thought it was a complement I'd correct that in the ugliest way I know how.

"Delilah didn't need a degree from Annapolis hanging on her wall. There are two types of women, Mr. Buckner. Belinda was one, Delilah was the other. Belinda wanted to show the world there is nothing a man can do that she cannot do. Delilah was happy having men clamoring for her."

So I need to focus on the men.

"But you don't think she left with a guy?"

"No. I can't put my finger on it, but no."

"With a girl?" Darla smirks and coughs out a half-laugh. "Maybe not romantic, but even a friend?"

"No. Maybe. I don't know. She—she hadn't kept tight friends for some time. Just a lot of tenuous connections. Delilah was pushing people away even if she didn't know it. I think her life was crumbling a piece at a time but she's so inured to folks coming and going and hard times that she probably doesn't see it."

"So she left on her own for no discernible reason?" I ask, wondering why I'm here.

"I don't think so."

"Why not?"

"I know my daughter. Something pushed her away."

"What?"

"I don't know."

Frustrated: "She's an adult. She's free to leave and not tell anyone. Why even hire me to look then?"

Before she can answer her cell phone rings. A single moment of blabbering and then silence. I crush my cigarette into the tray and take one more bite from my burrito. I'll find the girl because people are paying for it but this is the kind of shit that is a waste of time. Delilah didn't want to be here anymore so she left. Case closed.

"Mr. Buckner..." Darla says. I look up. She's scared. She points to her phone and mouths something at me.

"I can't make that out." I say. Then she says it and it makes total sense.

"It's Delilah." She says as she closes her phone shut. Tears carve fresh lines down her cheeks. "She says she's pregnant."

Darla looks down at the table and touches her cell phone, an insignificant object that held her to her daughter on a silk thread for a fleeting moment before it was cut off.

"Delilah says someone is trying to hurt her."

8

Darla Boothe hasn't breathed since I don't remember when.

Sitting there, her skin slowly drains of color like death is creeping into her veins, bleaching her life to a waxen nothing. I drag from my smoke and watch her. She methodically, somberly closes her cell phone and sets it on the table before her. She stares at it, sadness dropping like a veil across her eyes. Examines the mundane details of the phone as if inscribed in there somewhere were the answers she needs.

I reach out. Take the phone. Hit REDIAL. Nothing. Voice mail. I do it again. Voice mail again. Over and over.

Finally: "What did she say?"

Quiet, so quiet: "She said she was scared and she was being threatened. She said she was pregnant."

"Why would she call, tell you how scared she was and then just hang up?"

"You'd have to know her..." She exhales so wearily it sounds like she were a starved and frozen soldier in some long campaign and for months now there has been no sleep. Just terror. Just a quiet hell.

"Delilah is impulsive. Sinfully so. She'll get in these moods and just start to confess a secret or lay her troubles on you and then just as sudden as the wind will change she just catches herself and thinks better of it. I have *always* hated that. It's like she had some terrible secret she needed to tell me and she just couldn't quite get it out of her mouth. Belinda was always just silent. Contemplative. Delilah would do this start-stop thing."

"So you think she called out of momentary fright and then thought better of it?"

43

"I wouldn't be surprised, Mr. Buckner."

"Do you think someone else made her hang up?"

"Who knows?"

"Would that not surprise you either?"

"No."

"Did you hear another voice in the background?"

"No."

"What about any noise at all? Cars? Boats? The sounds of daily living?"

"I didn't pay attention. This is the first time I've heard her voice in months. She was being threatened."

"Did she give an example?"

"I don't know she just said—"

"Call the cops but listen to me first. Ready?"

"Oh..."

Probably not going to hear a word I say. Outside, the daylight passes from us in an instant. It might as well be Darla's soul. Gray.

"Without something specific to go on, something like Delilah saying John Doe tried to punch her or a note from John Doe saying he is going to hurt her, they can't do much. So—"

"Can't do much? *Much?* My damn kid is being *threatened* for Christ's sake! What does that sound like to you?"

"It sounds like a girl who, according to her own mother, runs from everything. The word 'threaten' needs to be quantified. Her just saying it means nothing. It's not illegal to be crazy. Or act crazy. Or make bad decisions. Or fuck up constantly. Or be a drama queen. Are you listening?"

"No..." She begins crying. Head-in-hands crying.

"Call the cops. Tell them what she said. They can put out notice to other agencies. Check the welfare. That means if they see her they'll stop her. See if she's okay. And they'll notify our PD."

"Can they form a, a...like a manhunt or something?"

"No. Not on this."

"Will it be a missing persons case?"

"Maybe. For a missing persons case there needs to be some evidence that she went missing *against* her will. A crime was committed. Call the cops. Call her back. Leave a voice mail saying you need to know where she is, who is threatening her, who the father is, anything."

"Why do you need to know the father?"

"He might know where she is. He might be threatening her. A child from an affair can be a serious problem. When was the last time he slept with her and where gives us a date and time of her location. Call the cops. Call me with anything."

"Okay. Okay, I'll call and call and call."

"Alright."

I consider the possibility that, for who Delilah Boothe apparently is, the words that come out of her mouth need to be dialed down a notch. Finding out she is pregnant is a great motive to run away. If Darla raised her girls to get married before they got pregnant, and Delilah went against it, I can see her doing this.

But if she really is knocked up I want to know who the father is. Dad equals suspect. Bigger than shit.

With the sun tucked safely away behind a cloak of pregnant clouds, the wind feels confident enough to dance outside. It conjures dust devil patterns which snatch up crystalline grains of snow, swirling in angry frenzies.

"Mr. Buckner?"

"Yes?"

"Do you think they could trace this call if I asked them?"

"No. Again, as far as the police know, this adult

woman left to enjoy the freedom America provides and she just called home to check in with her mother."

"It's just that...she won't answer her phone or anything."

"That's not a crime. The police will tell you the hard truth just might be she doesn't want to talk to you." More crying. Sorrow. "You said it yourself: you don't want to be part of the life Delilah left behind."

I look Darla in the eye. She looks away. "But you might be."

The only thing I hate worse than listening to an innocent woman cry is listening to a child cry. Darla shuffles through her box of pictures for a while. She singles a few out. Even smiles at one through her tears.

"Darla?" I say. Her name shatters the moment and her smile is stolen by the demons of her predicament. Sniffles. Breathing deep and jagged.

I ask: "Why would she not want you to tell *anyone?*"

"I have no idea."

"Who would you talk to enough that would make her not want you to let them know?"

"I talk to everybody. *Everybody.* My baby girl has gone missing. Who wouldn't I talk to?"

"I'd advise you against telling anyone."

"Why?"

"Let's assume she's in trouble. She doesn't know you've been talking to 'everybody' since she left. She just knows who you normally talk to. Whoever they are, don't tell them. Play it safe."

"But what if a friend or a relative hears from her? Knows something?"

"*They'll tell you.* I'm going to question everybody through the course of this. Now, call the cops."

"You said they won't help."

"I said this isn't a crime. There's a difference."

"But you'll help?"

"That's what I do."

"Find my baby girl, please. This is all my fault and I do not want her paying for my mistakes."

"Don't blame yourself." I crush out my smoke and eyeball the bitter conditions outside. The sun has not been resurrected yet. The wind had become emboldened. I tighten my coat against its machinations and lay cash on the table.

"I'll be in touch," I say with finality.

"Where are you going now?"

"I'm going to shake down Pierce White."

9

A note on the Vietnam War: not too long after Walter Cronkite told America and ostensibly the world that the Tet Offensive in Vietnam had failed when it hadn't, the war drew to a close.

Seems our New World Benedict Arnold cast quite a wake. People listened. It's all ancient history now. I was a sophomore in high school then. With the falsely preached abysmal failure of the Tet Offensive, the politicians running the war quickly lost their intestinal fortitude. Which is why generals are supposed to conduct war, but don't tell Congress that. A month or two later, troops began to drift in back home, being peeled away from the frontlines in thin but consistent layers. It took America almost eighteen months to call all her boys home.

They stopped drafting when the first soldiers were recalled. When the last shipment came home to one degree of humiliation or another, to spitting and protesting, to joblessness and insults, I was a senior in high school.

The timing was a thing of unique coincidence.

A note on *my* war: the continent of Africa is nothing if it is not embroiled in dispute. Governments of nations constantly trading hands—many times through a blood spill—inhospitable conditions, violent seasons, thousands of miles dominated by nature and her fangs, broad groups of people who refuse to get along.

There's nothing like a superpower nation broadcasting its failures over the news to invigorate its enemies. With ample footage of stupid hippies smoking dope and fucking one another in the dirt and rain, protesting the military with cart blanche, a small rebel army in the northeastern corner of African decided to strike while the fire was hot.

Think the Rwandan Genocide. Same thing.

They were a half-militarized band of tribes, trained in part by Soviet defectors turned mercenaries and even some Arab military. They were collectively held together in part by religion, but mostly by a need to feed their power thirsts. It seems any third-world gang of monkey-fuckers will wear the same color beret, pick up a machete or mostly-functional AK-47 and begin slaughtering one another over some ancient blood feud or tribal rivalry.

Mostly they want to rape and pillage and butcher those who didn't belong. So the enemy scavenged what munitions they could from the Soviets and started their death-mongering.

The new U.S. administration was eager to show the world it could still smash an opponent. The black eye left by Vietnam was still grotesquely swollen. This would be a quick fix. It would save face. And it was fine with me; rapists and child-murderers never warranted much beyond a horrific death as far as I was concerned. It's all ancient history now.

I barely graduated high school on my eighteen birthday; the last Friday in May. Come Saturday: my draft notice. Marines. Boot camp started up the following Tuesday. Seems like the war machine issued one too many DD214's between Vietnam and the African Conflict. I was infantry. They needed a lot of those guys.

It lasted for seven months, one week and three days before we had pummeled them into submission. It was never hard, per se, but there were so many of them.

I took two things from the war. One, since our enemies were plain clothed and looked just like everybody else, I got used to the idea of hunting for prey in a pack of lookalikes. It's the same on the street: criminals don't wear uniforms and march in order. They look like the very people they rape and rob.

Two, I learned that killing a man who is asking for it is only as hard as pulling the trigger.

Both have served me well.

First, I need a car.

The snow is a prizefighter: won't quit and laying it on thick. By the time I wind up at the rehab clinic my feet are numb. I stay outside; I just lit another cigarette. Waste not, want not.

Cell phone out. I dial the number.

"Hello?" the receptionist says. Looking through the front window, I can see her behind her small desk. Red hair, bold green dress and just, in general, rather hideous. Her tone huffs, annoyed. She sounds extremely thrilled that her life led her to answering phones in an addiction rehabilitation clinic in a bad part of a bad town.

"Jeremiah Cross, please."

"One moment."

The hold music is New Age jazz done on synthesizer. Instead of relaxing me it stokes a deep, stomach-acid fire of annoyance. I almost hang up. Twice. I hear Jeremiah paged over the speaker system, while on the phone some retard with a basement and a jazz dream flits his fingers over plastic ivories as he maims bar after bar of some lost 8th and Vine song.

God I hate New Age anything.

A note on Jeremiah Cross: while there is a broad range of burnouts in the world, my personal favorites have to be burnt-out medics.

No one comes close. Think about it: a burnout on an assembly line starts not putting things together right. They don't tighten their bolts, they intentionally forget their gaskets. They make a game of risking their customer's lives in poorly constructed vehicles.

A burnt-out 911 operator takes nothing seriously. Kids call and request help and the operator demands to speak with a parent. They refuse to believe that the parent is dying and the kid is trying to save mommy.

But a burnt-out medic? Why, they wave severed limbs to gawkers driving by, slowing down to catch a glimpse of the wreck. They steal dope from their drug kits. They steal prescription pads and write their own medications. They're the ones who make saving your life a funny little game in the back of a cramped ambulance while you're racing down a bumpy road.

Jeremiah was a paramedic in Savannah for years before he went over the edge. He said it was one hell of a thing. "Richard, it was the kind of thing that, when it's over and the dust settles and you're lookin at all the bridges you've burned, you realize you're not in prison, on skid row or dead and you get the fuck outta Dodge. It was *that* kinda thing." That's all he'd say about the event that ended his career there.

Over beers one night he did tell me about how he wandered from city to city, paying the fees to get his EMT license reinstated. Eventually he realized the burnout followed him from ambulance to ambulance, no matter where the city is located. Macon, Chattanooga, Gulfport, Fort Worth.

Demons are like that. When they find something tasty they'll follow the scent wherever the tasty thing runs.

So he wound up here, in Saint Ansgar. Far west from where his demons where born.

"Yeah?" Jeremiah says.

"Hey. It's RDB."

"What's up! RDB. You never call anymore. You just use me and go somewhere else!"

"I know. I should send you a flower bouquet or something."

51

"More than that."

"Listen, I need something. And fast."

"I know better than to get involved with you again, but you had me at hello. What is it?"

"Two things," I say, staring through the glass at the redhead. I decide she might look good naked. "Number one: stop talking to me like we're homos."

"Okay, okay."

"Two: I need your car."

"Sorry, I'm busy right now." I can hear him start to hang up and I shout to keep him on the line.

"C'mon. My car is in the shop and I'm on a case."

Quiet, quiet. Then: "So?"

"So there is a time limit involved. Missing persons case."

"Then what you need to do is go consult a genie or a palm reader or something. My Auntie Janel found a baby she put up for adoption twenty years ago with the help of a palm reader. There's this Indian chick—Indian with a dot, not Indian with a feather—who works about three blocks from here that screwed me out of seventy bucks but I swear she knew things about me that no one would—"

"Drop what you're doing and hook me up, please."

"What I'm doing right now is administering medications and spraying shit out of the seclusion room."

"So a break would be nice," I say. "A *smoke* break."

"No."

"Yes."

"No. Tell you what, you fight some coked-out bitch who needed a damn spit mask and restraints and enough Halidol to kill a horse and then see how generous you feel. Then, that coked-out bitch took a shit all over the—"

"Do it, Jeremiah. Tomorrow you'll get a new junkie forcibly incarcerated and he or she will get the DTs and shit all over the seclusion room just like whoever did it today. What's the difference if you hook me up now?"

Silence.

"GIVE ME THE FUCKING KEYS," I say, loud enough for an echo to repeat me. "PLEASE."

Jeremiah sighs. Quiet. The wind blows icicles down my back and I drag off my smoke just to replace the warmth inside the breeze is stealing away.

Eventually Jeremiah says: "Fine. But I barely put helping you out above spraying a garden hose on human feces."

"You're the best, Jeremiah. Where are you?"

"Sixth floor." I step under the window I know he's near.

"Near the break room where you guys open the window and smoke?"

"Yes."

"So just open the window and drop the keys. I'm under you. I made it convenient."

"Oh, well thank you. Tell me why, though."

"I told you. A case. I'll need the car for an hour, tops."

"That's not much of a case."

"Okay, I'll probably need it all day."

"Tell me why."

"Sorry. Client/detective confidentiality."

"Goddammit, RDB, why—"

"I got you out of a drug rap. Give me the keys."

"That was almost ten years ago when you still had juice with the department—"

"Keys."

"I swear, if there is a dead dude stuffed in my trunk when I get off work tonight—"

"I wouldn't do that to you, Jeremiah."

"You already *did*, motherfucker."

"I meant I wouldn't do it *again*. I forgot about the last time."

"Whatever. You forgot until I smelled the dirty bastard and surprise, surprise. RDB at work."

"I got rid of it. I don't have time for this."

"What if I got pulled over? How would I explain that?"

"You didn't."

"You're an asshole. I don't know why I get involved with this shit."

"Yes. Now drop them."

The phone clicks off and I hear the window yank open. It wrenches with a creak the way a medieval tomb would. The keys fall down, landing right into my hand.

10

Pierce White's office placard bears only three words beneath his name: *Assistant Regional Manager.*

The company Pierce works for has a large complex in downtown Saint Ansgar but White's office is located in a satellite building ten miles north. From the outside, the single-story building is non-descript, the way business parks that don't rely on foot traffic are: neutral earth tones, subtle landscaping, glass and store front signs designed to label as opposed to advertise.

I walk up to the receptionist and say: "Pierce White?"

She looks up from her Hollywood gossip rag and says, "Who? Me?"

"Which way to his office, sweetheart?"

She looks to her left and stammers. I just start walking that way. Corner office. Vertical blinds opened behind floor-to-ceiling windows that flank his closed door. Pierce White, *Assistant Regional Manager.*

I knock. See him through the glass. He stirs. Looks up. Perplexed. Thinks about not answering his door.

Pierce White: white guy, spends time at the gym but he's not hard. That much is obvious by how absolutely beautiful his hands are. Dark, thick hair. Fat black slashes for eyebrows. Wire-rimmed glasses that say, *Hey, I'm studious.*

I stare at him. His eyes dart away. I knock again; a ram on a castle door. A picture falls from his inside wall. Two heads poke out of cubicles. He gets the message. Stands. Spends a long moment behind his desk, weighing options. Finally he subconsciously adjusts his tie one-handed and comes around the desk. Opens the door.

"Yes, Mister ...?" He adjusts his glasses with his left

hand. Shiny wedding ring on the third finger.

"Boy, you bounced back after Brandy Medco." Shove past him. Tour the office space. Smells like Pledge and Old Spice. I whistle and pretend I'm impressed. Weasels like him always bounce back.

"Excuse me, but I don't know what—"

I turn and square up to him. Imposing. "When was the last time you spoke with Delilah Boothe?"

"*Who* do you think you are just barging in here—"

"My name is Richard Dean Buckner. I'm a detective looking for Ms. Boothe. Now answer me."

"Hold on a minute now, do I need my lawyer?"

"Will he take an ass-beating for you?"

"I—uhhh...*no*." Leary. Guarding now. His body language shows he's afraid. Good. He leans back, half-cowering over his desk. Making distance.

"Then I don't see what help he would be to you."

He straightens up. Tries to be big. It doesn't make him any manlier.

New angle: "Married again?" I point to his hand. "Moved on past Janet?"

"How do you know my ex-wife?"

"I am looking for the woman that caused Janet White to revert back to her maiden name. Richley, right? Janet Richley?"

Sweating now. Looks about.

"When was the last time you saw Delilah Boothe?"

Calm. Too calm: "I haven't seen Delilah in quite some time."

"You blew up after she squawked about your affair at the wrong water cooler?"

Straightens his tie again. Red rises in his neck and ears at the mention of his old catastrophe. Then: "I was justifiably angry when the girl I was sport-fucking told every blabber mouth in the office of Brandy Medco that one day she and I would be married. I never said I cared for her, let alone love her. Let alone *marry* her. Whatever delusions that split-tail conjured up while I was wasting time with her...they're her own business. But, she made them *my* problem.

"Yes. I got just a tad angry." He rolls his shiny new wedding ring around and around on his finger while he says this.

Read on Pierce White: Grade-A cocksucker. He's scared of me, but he's also sure he was slumming with Delilah and assumes everyone else thought so as well. And since he's slumming, there should not have been repercussions like a divorce and getting fired.

"Married? Again?" I say.

"Yes."

"That makes twice now?"

"Yes. A total of two, yes."

"Why so bitter and spiteful towards Delilah?"

Cocky smirk. "You know, she just has a way of bringing it out in me."

"Threatened her, right?"

"Now hang on. Are you police? You said 'detective' so I—"

I step into his personal space the way a bear does when the last thing you see is it swiping down. His breath is tinged with evergreen mint and the metallic smell of adrenaline. Fear. Fight or flight.

I stab a finger in his chest. "The last time you have seen her. Tell me now or I will knock that high-dollar nose job of yours right back to ugly-as-fuck."

He actually touches his fingers to his nose, caresses. It's as rare as Haley's Comet to find vanity running this thick through a man who likes pussy.

"I saw her a few days before Halloween."

"This Halloween?"

"Yes."

A week or so before she went AWOL.

"Go on."

"We...met at a hotel. Spent the night."

Really.

"What hotel?"

"Boulevard Grand. You know the one, correct?"

"Pool on the roof and the restaurant that rotates?"

"Yes. Such a beautiful view of the skyline."

"When she left where did she go?"

"I assume back to her new place. She said she was living with her mother again. Truth be told, I wasn't paying attention. I just wanted one last taste before I blew her off forever."

"What's that mean?"

Distasteful and uncomfortable in his self-awareness: "Let me rephrase that so it doesn't implicate me in any wrongdoing: I wanted to sleep with her one more time before I stopped talking to her. Completely."

His eyes smile. "I mean, I *was* getting married to my new wife the following week. Now or never, right?"

"You're one serious motherfucker." I say, lighting a smoke.

"You can't smoke in here."

"*I* can."

"Well..." looks around, flabbergasted. Defensive, getting irritated. "You know, she fucked up my entire life. Fucked up everything. Do you know how much I pay in alimony every month? Let alone child support."

"Actually, I do know how much you pay. Speaking of your ex-wife, did she ever threaten Delilah?"

His eyes twinkle. A tell. Conniving. Revenge. Opportunity. "All the time."

Boil that down, burn off the obvious enthusiasm: Janet Richey cursed Delilah's name when White came home and explained what had happened.

"Specifics then," I say, blowing smoke at him.

"Janet blamed Delilah for everything."

"Not you?"

"We shared the burden. I paid for it."

"Keep going."

"Well, she blamed Delilah for all kinds of things. Ruining our marriage, making Janet a *divorcee'*, the extra hassle with picking the kids up, dropping them off, moving, all of it. But, Janet also knew that Delilah was sexier than she was. Even when she dabbled in drugs too hard for me she just had this...*way* about her. It was in her ass. The way she shook it. Janet saw it just as well as I did. Plus, Delilah was the last affair Janet would tolerate."

I smirk. This guy couldn't ooze jackass anymore if he was John Edwards' used car salesman brother.

"Did she ever look Delilah in the face and threaten her? Not call her names, not blame her for anything, *threaten*."

"She said she could kill her for what she'd done, so yes. Threats."

"Did she really say that? Or are you making up shit?"

"It's in the divorce proceedings. She said she could kill Delilah for her part in ruining Janet's life. The judge stopped her, had the court reporter read it back. Janet threw a fit, said she meant every word."

"Where is she now?"

"Up in Knoll Hill. Lives by the lake. Want the address?"

"Why else would I ask where she is?"

"Fine."

He digs through a Rolodex, writes it down. I pocket it.

I stare at him for a moment. A punk with traces of a skittish animal in him, wrapped up in a designer suit. Looking for a reveal: "Wear a rubber?"

"What do you mean?"

"The last you slept with Delilah, did you wear a rubber?"

"Why? Did she give me something? Oh my God you're—Oh my God."

He has no idea what I'm talking about. A baby daddy would react, even if it were just a flick of the eye. I turn to leave.

"Wait! Is it AIDS? Oh my God what will Amy think? Oh Christ, not again! Every time I fuck that scrawny tramp I have to confess it to my wife!" Whining. Gushing forth. "Oh what if I gave it to her? To Amy! We've been trying for a baby..."

The door shuts as I hear him ask: "Did Delilah give *you* something?"

11

The war was a success in the sense that there was a vermin population and we eradicated it.

There was no hope for the continent or its nations; as soon as we cleared their streets of the current threat, we were shunned in the very towns we kept from being burnt down. Oh well. I wasn't into nation-building.

I returned home to the same fanfare the Vietnam vets did. Fine. Shitbird hippies and protesters were waiting when we got off the plane, screaming that we didn't get enough in 'Nam and there were more babies to kill. More women to rape. Some fool in the crowd actually held up a small child and asked if we were going to come over there and murder that baby too.

Then someone spit. Protest signs hit us. We soldiers were like rodents in a Whack-A-Mole arcade game walking through the crowd; our heads popping up and down as signs chopped at us. I got about halfway through the throng when a goon with a flavor-savor and blue-tinted glasses bitch-slapped me. "Be ashamed," he said.

I punched him so hard his nose folded flat and I could feel his jaw crack in two underneath my knuckles. His glasses crumbled off to the side and all the soldiers around me started giving the hippies their rightful due.

Ten seconds later and all us soldiers were clearing the crowd with little more than spit dribbling down our faces or shirts. Our knuckles chewed up, our teeth gritting. The hippies all on the floor, writhing and cradling broken arms or faces. Or both.

I left. I needed to get my discharge and start my life.

My high school girlfriend was two years younger than I. I came home in the late winter. She graduated that spring.

She developed cancer at eighteen. We married in the middle of her lost cause chemo because I'd rather be joined to her for all eternity as she withered away than to not have her at all. She died. I protect her memory from the soiled life I lumber through and keep private her name and all I love about her.

Just for me.

James Dobbins lives in Three Mile High.

I'll take the rail tomorrow. Three Mile High is nestled into the mountains a few hours away. For right now, I go looking for Delilah's old camp.

Delilah Boothe used to live on Carolina Avenue. It'll be a drive coming from White's office. Jeremiah's sled squeals in all the rank, gritty slush. Bad for winter driving.

On the way I call Derne. I've got about three miles to go before I reach her old place. This will kill time. I can hear him inhale on a cigarette as he answers. "Hello?" I can almost smell the mentholated smoke as he exhales with that word.

"It's Buckner. How are you?"

"Gotta smoke outside now, Mr. Buckner. The wife, she's on a tank. Oxygen. Some green bottle she takes everywhere. It has replaced her damn purse, only there's no pocket in it to put my smokes. What has my life come to?"

"Sorry to hear."

"Oh. Thanks," he says. I cross Maple parkway. Two miles now. "Any word?"

"Well, Pierce White said he's seen Delilah recently."

"*Recently?*"

"Yes. Said they had seen each other for a few days. A loose kind of dating thing. Then she took off."

"Good God. When was this?"

"Right before Halloween."

"So before she disappeared."

"Yes. It's not quite a lead but hash marks on a timeline always helps."

"That's what you're goin' for? A timeline?"

"I'm trying to find an adult who is free not to be found. Knowing she was with Pierce White a few months back might not sound helpful, but it lets me know where she laid her head for a night. Who else has she visited since?"

"What? Are you goin' just knock on all her ex-boyfriends' houses and trace her one night stands like a trail of bread crumbs?"

"Yes I am." I cross Revelation. One mile left. There's a great little Italian place on the corner here.

"I see," Derne says. A deep, long inhale. I can hear the paper burn he drags so hard. "Well, I hate to know you're havin' to do such a thing to find her, but if it gets her safe...I just want her safe."

"Every clue is forward motion, Mr. Derne."

"Of course."

This is getting old. "I'm going to jump off here, Mr. Derne. One more thing. Do you know the folks who bought Delilah's house?"

"My daughter-in-law did. I met 'em, but that was all really. I was glad to see they wanted the place."

"Remember their names? Anything?"

"I used to. Haven't thought of it in a while."

"Okay."

"Thank you, Mr. Buckner." He hangs up. Hmmm. Genuinely bothered by a girl he knows is promiscuous, is a drug user, is a flake...heartsick to go back to her old flame.

Carolina is a decently long street, segmented into bite-size lengths by cross streets. It runs through a residential area composed of several quaint neighborhoods. An elementary school is a few houses down from Delilah's old address; a middle school only a few blocks away. About a mile east is a Catholic parish with its own school. So much education.

The neighborhood is quiet. Lined by elms and oaks and walnuts. Just enough yard to where everybody has space. The homes are old enough to have avoided the cookie-cutter look of newer neighborhoods. These residences might have been built with pride and lasting value as opposed to the hustle of recent homes stamped out to be filled ASAP.

Delilah Boothe's old residence is boxy. A skirt of brick lines the base of it, siding going on up to the roof. Wooden deck in the front. Single car garage. Spots for gardens, now all layered in sparkling snow. I park. Rub my face and get out. Make the cold call.

The husband answers the door.

Around thirty, brown and brown. Big guy. The type of dude that if I were arresting him I'd jump his ass with a sap when he wasn't looking to make sure I didn't have a fight on my hands. Side note: fights against perps are only fun when you know you'll win. If ever any doubt, white knuckle and cheat it out. The reality of it is, if you find yourself in a fair fight your tactics suck.

But as it is, the husband seems rather pleasant.

"Hello. I'm looking for Delilah Boothe." I say.

"I'm sorry, sir, but she no longer lives here." Braces, gives me his full width. The kind of stance someone takes intuitively to fight. It's the body's way of squaring off to the target. A tell. Two, actually.

One: I'm not the first dude to come knocking and sniffing for our little princess.

Two: whoever came before me didn't leave without a brawl.

A different angle: "I've been hired by a man named Elam Derne to look for her. Got a minute?"

He calculates the situation and I understand. It's all in his eyes.

"Your name, sir?"

"Richard Dean Buckner."

"Would you mind waiting in your car for a moment?"

"No." Clear direction on where he wants me.

He steps inside, shuts the door. I walk back to my car. The blinds in the front windows are drawn back; I see him with one eye on me, cell phone in hand. Checking up. Good man.

I smoke two cigarettes back to back before he comes to his door. Waves me in. The home's warmth washes over me like relief.

"Mr. Derne's daughter-in-law sold us the place. I called her, she called him, said you were legit." He says. His stance is much more relaxed.

"I appreciate your candor." I look around. The walls are off-white, tipping towards a very creamy, extra light brown. The baseboards are painted, chipped. Hardwood floors, scuffed here and there. One or two cigarette burns stick out like bombed craters in an aerial photo.

"Complements of Ms. Boothe, I'm sure," he says, looking at the burns also. Looks to me, meets my eye. Sticks his hand out. "Tyler Bellview." We shake hands. "And this is my wife, Abigail."

She enters the room from what I presume is the kitchen. The aroma of baking cookies follows her like an escort. She smiles and waves; looks slightly uncomfortable at the stranger in her house.

The wife: white female, black and blue, thin, busty. From down the hall a toddler-aged girl comes running to us, mismatched socks on both her feet and hands, a cowboy hat cocked off to the side on her head and about three pounds of costume necklaces around her neck. Big blue eyes with high cheekbones. Beautiful and radiant as only an innocent child can be.

She sees me, halts, runs back the way she came. Abigail turns to go for the child.

"How can I help you, Mr. Buckner?"

"Well, Ms. Boothe hasn't checked in for a few months, and Mr. Derne asked me to kick over some rocks looking for her. I don't suppose you've seen or heard anything living here, have you?"

"Oh yeah." He says, shaking his head. "Tons of shit. Jesus, that gal leaves a mess in her wake, let me tell you."

"Please do."

"We're still finding evidence of how much she partied. Obviously we toured the house before we bought it. She was still living here. Mr. Derne said he asked her to tidy up but she didn't listen. Had her bras tossed over the bedroom door, piles of dirty clothes everywhere, I swear she was trying to turn us off of the place with her squalor. I was surprised we didn't find a used rubber sloughed off into a pile in the corner or something.

"She left streaks of various colored paints up and down a wall in the back bedroom, like she was checking out several colors. Trying to see what fit, I dunno. Never decided on one. Just left the streaks. What she did manage to paint entirely was moody, like she was trying to express her inner...angst or turmoil or whatever."

He guides me down the hall to a freshly painted room. "I haven't gotten the time to do this one yet," he says, showing me a second bedroom which is painted in black and depressing purple vertical stripes. Even the baseboards are black.

I want to tell him to burn it down and start over but decide not to.

We get back to the living room and he offers me a chair. Continues his tale. "Looked like she was coming out of something bad. Had self-help books lying around, little inspirational sayings posted here and there, all themed around recovering from personal catastrophes. I saw a couple of phoenixes on book covers, the word 'survivor,' phrases like 'new day,' 'start again,' 'start fresh,' 'start anew.' You get the idea.

"When we were putting in the gardens out front, I couldn't move a stone or stir the grass without a cigarette butt or beer bottle cap surfacing. Found a couple of doobie roaches also."

I smirk. "I know the type."

"Yeah. When we first moved in I put my drum set down in the basement and went to both the neighbors. Apologize in advance for the noise. The woman living to the south of us there, Mrs. Franklin, she said the drumming would be welcome after the late-night noise and carrying on Ms. Boothe was known for."

"Obnoxious parties?"

"The neighbors made it sound like it was all the time. She said the cops were called at least once a month." He shook his head and his face fell. "One day a couple of buddies brought their guitars over and we played downstairs. The basement is unfinished and I never thought to search the house for dope...but I'll be damned if we didn't find it."

"Like what?"

"Glass pipe. The guy who sold the house to Mr. Derne was originally going to make the house his retirement home. Before he finished it he and his wife bought something down south they liked better. Waterfront, I think. Anyways, he installed thin wooden slats along the beam ceiling to hang a drop-down ceiling from and just never got around the ceiling itself. Delilah had sheets stapled to the slats; the place looked like an opium den.

"But anyways, I guess her or one of her friends stashed

a pipe and lighter in the ceiling, wedged between the rafters and the AC ducts. When my friends and I played, the bass tones literally just rumbled it out. Fell to the floor and shattered. We didn't hear it because of the noise from playing. Abigail, the baby and I were down there the next day and the little girl saw the glass, ran to it.

"Abigail stopped her right before she reached that crackhead bitch's dope pipe. I was fucking furious."

"I would be too. Still have the pipe?"

"No. I just tossed it."

Obviously he is glad to have this vent about Delilah. Some people just clam up when they're asked to speak about someone they don't know. Other folks are quick to dump everything they've seen or heard. The latter helps out better. "Anything else?"

"Now that I think of it, she grew a lot of morning glory flowers out back. Probably tripped on the seeds."

"Could be. Or she liked flowers."

"Maybe. I think it was for the dope."

"Alright," I say. Look around. "Got that real estate agent's name, by chance?"

"Tabitha. Tabitha Derne. Over off of Highway 8. Works for Hoffman Real Estate."

"Thanks. Anything else?" Always ask more than once.

He searches for a moment. Then his eyes light. "Yeah. About a month ago it happened. Some car pulled into our driveway—we could hear the bass coming a mile away— and I figured it was just somebody turning around. With the school practically next door a lot of parents will do that. So, initially we didn't think much of this dude parked there."

"Friend of hers?"

"*Something* of hers."

"Can you describe the car?"

"It was wine red with gaudy gold-spokes in the wheels.

'80s model sedan, four-door. Had a ridiculous license plate that read BMPIN." He spells it.

"This state?"

"Yup."

"You took good notice."

"Thanks. I did a tour as an MP. So anyways, then he shuts his engine off and now I'm wondering what he wants. We get door-to-door salesmen all the time. They show up whenever the kid's asleep and ring the doorbell. We've got a Jehovah's Witness church a few miles away and they stop by. Same thing with convicts selling magazine subscriptions, all that stuff. I went out to the porch to meet the guy."

"Ballsy."

"He was white or Hispanic; either way he didn't have an accent. I'd put him at five-eight, one-seventy. Looked like a punk. His hat was off to the side with a flat bill, baggy pants. Shifty. He asked if Delilah 'still stayed here.' I said no. He looked in the windows as he left."

Bellview shifts his gaze to Abigail. "He saw my wife."

Now that he mentions it, his wife has the same stats as Delilah; color, build.

"He think you were lying?"

"I think so."

"Your wife, seen through a window in passing, bears a resemblance to Ms. Boothe."

"I guess so. Because he came back."

12

"The same day?"

Bellview smiles and rubs his scalp. "No. A few days later."

"Still asking for her?"

"I wasn't here."

I look to Abigail. "What happened?"

She's holding the little girl. The toddler favors her father's look but has her mother's dark beauty. Abigail hands the daughter to her husband and looks at me. Pleasant.

"Well, that ghetto douche who thought I was that drug addict, it gives me chills."

I can see faint, ghostly traces of the jeopardy she felt then. They surface as she brings the memories forward. Peruse any women's shelter and see. Abigail's traces aren't bad by comparison.

"Well, it actually wasn't much which is why we didn't think too hard about it. Tyler went to the store, and while he was gone this guy shows up and bangs on the door. I didn't know what to do but I didn't want to be...oh, we were still new in the neighborhood and I guess I didn't want the cops to come screaming to our house, lights blazing. I called Tyler and told him to hurry. Then I answered the door."

"No cops?" People do stupid shit like this.

"No. Well, I should say I cracked it just enough to tell him I called the police—I'm so stupid, I know. I just didn't think. The man, he looked drunk or something and he just barged into the house. I tried to shut the door but he was just so sudden—I screamed and he looked at me like he was trying to figure out who I was or something. I ran back to the baby's room and that's when Tyler got home."

I look at him, he nods. "I called the cops on my way home. I pulled up, got out. I came inside and went right up to him. I recognized the car. On the phone, Abby said he was beating the front door so I just drilled his ass. Best punch I've ever thrown. He was out like a light. Then the cops came. An ambulance. He refused treatment. He looked like my slug sobered him up. He said he used to date Delilah and she cut off contact and he thought she still lived here. Thought I was her new man and I was lying to him. Thought Abby was Delilah."

"Arrested?"

"Yeah. Disorderly conduct and some kind of possession by intoxication. I think they found a smidge of weed also. I heard the dispatcher come back with a warrant, but I missed most of it. They looked into burglary but the state law requires something that they couldn't prove so they let it go."

State statute defines burglary as entering or staying on property with the intent to commit a felony or sexual assault. There's more to it, but if they couldn't prove he barged in to rob, beat or rape Abigail it'd be a lost cause. And with him being intoxicated, it would be a defense that he, not in his right mind, thought Delilah was opening the door for him. It might not be a good defense, but it would be a decent kernel of doubt.

"He knew for sure Abby wasn't this Delilah gal and he knew I could throw a punch. I also own a .40 caliber and a shovel."

"I'd kill him next time," I say. "One story: yours. You can make it whatever you want that way."

He chuckles, maybe thinking I just made a joke. I did not.

"Catch his name?" I ask.

"Benny. Benny something. Last name was Greek, I know that."

"Anything after that?"

"No. All quiet."

"You've been a big help. Really."

We exchange numbers and I roll out into fresh sheets of wind-driven frost.

Benny Something.

13

I joined the Saint Ansgar PD in 1974.

I was a patrolman, a corporal and then a sergeant. In 1982 we were blessed with a new chief *and* a city manager. With both of those worthless, spineless fucks came a shift from the '70s beatdown-style to more professional stuff. They wanted folks with four-year degrees. They wanted folks who would write detailed reports instead of settling things. One of the first things they did was take away our saps. Then they changed the policy to forbid striking an active, aggressive perp with a flashlight. What kind of world were we coming to when you couldn't beat someone with a four D cell flashlight?

I became a detective shortly after that. There was no room on the street for me anymore. I had the tricks I needed to get away with doing what I always did; but the microscope placed on us was something I could never get over. I was a detective for eight years. Partnered with Graham Clevenger for the last two.

In the car I call Graham Clevenger. The best man I know. The only man I know left in this city that has honest intentions about anything.

He was a rookie detective and he was placed with me for one reason: I was the best. Now, all these years later, *he* is the best. God bless Clevenger for it, someone needed to take my place.

He answers on the third ring: "Richard! How's it been?"

"Good. I'm on a case. Wannabe missing persons. Can you do me a favor?"

"Sure."

"Can you scrounge up any reports taken on a Boothe, Delilah L., white female, date of birth August 29th, 1983? Reporting party is a Boothe, Darla K., white female, date of birth March 6th, 1954. Should be dated about two months ago."

"Leo, huh? White girl, blah blah blah. Darla her mother?"

"Yup."

"Not a problem." I wait. We pass the time in silence the way we did for countless nights in the detective's car. The hushed inhale and exhale. All of it fathomless.

I turn north, then east. I pass a spot where back in the '80s there was a damn good home cooking buffet. The owner torched it for the insurance and was caught later in the year. His lies were terrible but his fried chicken and mashed potatoes were unequaled. The old place sat at the corner of 90th and Clemmons, which means I have five blocks to go until I hit the interstate onramp.

Navigation by food.

I feel the familiar freeze rolling up my spine and whip the car into the nearest parking lot, whose entrance is mercifully only a few feet in front of me. My foot mashes the brake and then everything blossoms to red in my vision. Blooms of crimson with burnt speckling like fire to celluloid bubble up and run to orange. The orange glows with hatred and yellow flares at their ends. Cold colors creep in as they always do; greens and blues and sharp daggers as runners of color cascade down across everything I ever knew.

Then one by one they go away. Moment by moment it clears up.

"Richard?" Clevenger's voice comes from deep in a well a thousand miles away.

I clear my throat. "Yeah? Go ahead."

"All right. Mom upset that her adult child took off into the night?" Clevenger asks.

"Yeah. She called her once since then—today—screaming about being pregnant and afraid of something."

"You think she's crying wolf?"

"Who knows. I told Darla to file a new report, but there are no specifics on any threat, just general yelling and whatnot."

"Oh, okay."

"Can you also run a plate for me?"

"I *can.*"

"*Will* you?"

"Sure."

"Thanks. The plate is our state, vanity. Reads BMPIN. B-M-P-I-N. Belongs to a Ben something. Last is Greek."

"Anything else while I'm digging?"

"Yeah. The Ben something was involved in a forced entry and an address over on Carolina." I shuffle through a pile of papers and give the street number. "Can you send me a copy of that also?"

"I'll take the rest of the day off from the murder investigation I'm on. No problem. Do you want a coffee also?"

"Yes. Black. With whiskey."

"Fuck you."

"Graham, you're the best partner I've ever had."

"It wasn't hard. All I had to do was not report you to IA. Unlike every other partner you ever had."

"Tell Molly I said hello."

"Yeah yeah. Good luck. I'll call when I have the reports. Your BMPIN car is registered to one Benjamin Kolokios, 12298 Grantham Boulevard, apartment 18D."

"Thanks."

"Priors on possession, B and E and misdemeanor theft, failure to appear, DUI, assault, assault, possession, public intoxication, failure to appear, DUI."

I hear Graham click and shuffle through the online rap sheet. Looking for details. Then, "His charges...dope is all Big Fry-related."

"Big Fry?"

"Big Fry."

"Alright. Grantham Boulevard here I come."

"If you're going to kill him you better make damn sure this doesn't get traced back to me. Got it?"

"They never trace anything back to you. You know why?"

Graham laughs, a dry but warm sound. "I know, I know. Because you're *one of the good guys.*"

"Exactly."

We say goodbyes. Grantham Boulevard is south of the river. In the Burrows.

14

A note on the Big Fry: AKA delicious freak, delicious fry, DF, BF, the dose, demon dust, demon, the devil, capital D, Jimmy Hoffa's teeth, speed cunt, gray matter detonation, the virgin drop, the red-eyed stare.

The drug that, for a time, experts feared might just push both meth and crack out the door. It was designer, came about back when I was still on the force. Half speed, half hallucinogen. All horrible.

It's similar to meth in that is causes a brain dump of dopamine. The brain never dumps like that again after the first chemically-induced time, which is why addicts get a taste for it so quickly. They chase the first high and will never re-achieve it. They spend the rest of their short lives ingesting harsh chemicals and sweating out solvents.

It's similar to LSD in that another chemical in it causes hallucinations. They are not as intense as LSD-induced hallucinations, but still fairly constant.

It comes in a pill form and must be ingested that way. The hallucinogenic compounds, like LSD itself, are too sensitive to heat to be smoked. So someone has to press the pills. Pill presses are regulated here in the States by the FDA, so clandestine operations have to build their own or raid a pharmaceutical lab. Ecstasy producers in Europe pressed the Big Fry for a time. Eurotrash cocksuckers got the ball rolling and then ditched it when it became obvious the drug was a one-way street. No return business.

Gangs in Mexico picked up the slack. Every year during Spring Break the States get a big influx of date rape drugs—which are produced legally down there—and the Big Fry.

Why some shitbird clandestine chemist thought about

mixing speed with tripping I'll never know. But, then again, dopers do that shit all the time. It's called polydrug use. Ask a cop qualified as a drug recognition expert; they'll explain it.

The bottom line for this new Frankenstein's Monster: cash. A new drug properly distributed brings with it a new cash flow.

It hit the streets. Cheap. Easy to find. Easy enough to make. Made the rave circuit. Corrections began pulling baggies and balloons of it out of inmates' assholes upon entry. Schools started finding kids as young as seven whacked out on the shit.

Swept the nation. A-List dope, the Hollywood Oscar winner of drugs. Not so hard you'd be stigmatized as a serious junkie if you used it, not so light as to be some Mickey Mouse shit.

Then stories started surfacing. First a few, eventually a flood. People started calling it 'demon dust.' Then just 'demon.' Then 'The Devil.' Capital D.

Here, in our backyard: an elementary school teacher south of the river realized she issued a bathroom pass to some goofball fifth grader who never showed back up. Some female student, walking the halls with a pass saying she could hurry and take a piss and get back to class. Oh, the horror. The teacher wanted her back.

Teacher-lady got up to go fetch the kid. Later, when she was capable of speaking again, she said she was fully expecting to find the absent student dealing with her first menstrual period. Teacher-lady went in to the nearest little girls' room. Teacher-lady started screaming.

The ambulance said the girl had suffered some kind of massive, internal-cranial hemorrhage. Maybe a freak stroke. The Perfect Storm of strokes, to be sure.

In the narcotics bureau we called it *gray matter detonation, GMD.* Like a lot of cop lingo, gray matter detonation weaseled out of the squad rooms and onto the streets. It seemed like just a few days before we started hearing criminals using our jargon.

Stroke or GMD, either way the little girl's eyes were so bloodshot nothing else was recognizable. The red-eyed-stare. No response to stimulus. Shallow breathing. Low heart rate. Still clutching a bathroom pass in one arthritic claw of a hand. She went in to dose herself. A fifth grader, dropping the Big Fry.

Her body was on autopilot. Reflexive. Emptied. Ruined. Forever.

The thing about the Big Fry is this: it works with brain chemistry in such a way that some folks genetically predisposed to a bad high would...get *fried*.

Permanent. Scramble. The drug, with the right genetics, will turn the unlucky user into a vegetable. Irreversible.

The lucky ones: stiff, six feet under. Unlucky, the red-eyed-stare. In between are some who don't die or become vegetables. Any new user pins all their hopes on being in that elusive third class of folks. *The smeared*, we call them. The smeared have a bizarre brain chemical reaction that foils the drug's ability to kill instantly. Instead, like acid flashbacks, the drug pops back up here and there. Just in bursts. Smears.

When I was assaulted, the hit was an overdose of Big Fry.

I'm not dead.

I'm not a vegetable.

I'm smeared.

Word on the street said it was a freak accident. The little girl OD'd. Could happen to any retard taking too much. That's why fifth graders shouldn't dose. But then other folks started getting the red-eyed stare. Became a spreading, not-so-isolated phenomenon.

The Big Fry.

It lost a lot of sex appeal after it became commonly known to hose certain users, even after only one dose. The virgin drop, they call it. See if it wants you coming back for more or if you only rated a GMD. I saw a lot of unworthy users in my time.

Serious: I saw a junkie's bulldog with the red-eyed stare once. Dead as the ideals of the old Democratic Party.

Still the drug persists. Cheaper labs, inexperienced folks cooking it up. Killing more. It has a rep worse than crack back in the '80s.Worse than meth does now. It was a rep no one wants but still people risk it. People like this Benny Kolokios. So be it.

I have been heading south this entire time. Hammett Parkway all the way to fifth, right a block and then a left—southbound again—onto Regional Avenue.

Regional Avenue continues south and when I get to the Saint Ansgar River it becomes the Mannasmith Memorial Bridge.

Mannasmith Memorial is kind enough to take whoever is foolish enough to cross it into the mouth of the Burrows.

Because of its elevation and terrain, south of the river has a slightly different microclimate than north of the river does. It's hotter. The prevailing summer marine layer helps. South of the river's soil is much heavier in clay than north. Glaciers, deposits, ice ages. Whatever. The clay acts like pavement and absorbs the sunlight.

The way the faltering dusk carves its way through every brick and building down here gives rise to an image of what Dante and Virgil saw as they crested Limbo and entered Hell proper. A spread of land, studded with vile undergrowth and human beings who have been drawn here to suffer. Their own hands violating themselves or others. Sometimes both. I hate this place.

Business takes me here a lot.

But I light a smoke and exit off the bridge.

With the sun growing a deep orange to the west out over the bay, the Burrows is being fed another vehicle and its lost-soul driver for dinner tonight.

15

This is a mouth lined with jagged teeth, and I am stepping inside it.

The area of town known as the Burrows is just the gutter for another area of town known as Little Haight. As in Haight Street, San Francisco, California. I'll explain.

During the '60s San Francisco's Haight Street was romanticized by the hippie movement. The Grateful Dead, Jefferson Airplane, Janis Joplin, they immortalized the street as a whole but especially its intersection with Ashbury. Therefore, it attracted that culture. Hippies, dirtbags, dope heads, shitbirds and the general free-loader class of humanity.

Now, decades later, the street is littered with bums, a new generation of wannabe hippies or authentic hippies so old they have no idea that their time is gone and over. So, essentially, just the bottom-of-the-barrel dregs of society. Outside of a deviant record store, a tattoo parlor or a sex paraphernalia shop these freaks would not be employable.

The area of Little Haight is the same thing, transplanted from San Francisco to fester here in Saint Ansgar. The Burrows are the streets, about thirty blocks tall and eighteen blocks wide where cops do not respond and wholesome people do not venture.

It earned the name the Burrows because it is where the rodents dwell in ramshackle hovels and clapboard fire traps. Groups of young and angry boys, teenagers on up to early twenties adorn the streets like fleas will crowd into spots on a mangy dog's back. Most are high school-aged because once out of even a small excuse for a classroom, these punks find their way into prison or a six-foot long pine box.

Down here was the only affordable area to live in right after the Great Depression. North of the river was barely developed, and what was developed mostly belonged to the super-rich survivors of the crash or farmers. Now it is a bustling metropolis, but back then it was almost no help. So the poor and wretched packed themselves in down here. Eventually those that could move out did so, and what was left still exists today. And that of course forms the hive of villainy that is stretching its claws up around me like the devil's fists reaching up through a crack in the earth.

I venture on into the slums. Jeremiah would be pissed if he found out I was taking his car down here again.

Last time someone stole his stereo.

Grantham Blvd is a major artery running through here; not hard to get to. It winds for miles; widens in some parts and contracts in others. The apartment complex unfolds on the east side. Dilapidated. Fit for rodents and cockroaches. Or a wrecking ball.

I park in an open slot next to a burgundy ghetto sled with gold spokes in the wheels and a license plate reading BMPIN. Out of Jeremiah's car. Gritty, dirty ice underfoot. I crush out my smoke on the BMPIN windshield.

A stern knock on the door and somebody stirs. Answers.

Read on Benny: front line dealer, thug punk, bully only because he has bigger guys standing behind him to push the threat, basic drug-addled shitbag. His meth mites must be biting; his forearms are covered in scabbed sores.

"Benny?" I say, looking over his shoulder. Listening.

"Yeah?"

He must deal out of his place. Anyone in this neck of the woods who, with a stranger knocking, doesn't get alarmed must have a *lot* of strangers knocking.

"You alone, Benny?"

"What?" He is. I know it. He gives all the tells.

I punch his face and hear his jaw crack, shut the door behind me.

16

I clamp Benny's groin to the floor with my foot.

When he comes to, he doesn't react well to being cock-pinned. He screams. Thrashes. Heels dig up carpet fibers and his fingers are nothing more than claws as they rake the floor. He loses a nail in the ridiculous ordeal.

Pointing the .44 Magnum at his face sobers him up.

"Where is Delilah Boothe?"

"What?"

"You've been sniffing around for her. Tell me where she is."

"I mighta been sniffin' but I ain't fuckin' found the bitch! Swear!" Good. I figured he'd lie about knowing her for just a minute or so; as long as he could take the searing heat crawling up from his balls into his abdomen. But him just spilling makes this easier.

"Why even look?"

"She rolled my homie on some dope! Jesus, my damn dick is turnin' blue! Get your fuckin' foot offa me!"

"No. What friend?"

"Oh, Jesus!"

"I doubt Jesus Christ is hunting Delilah Boothe over drugs." I cock the hammer back. Benny's eyes turn red and glisten at the sound.

"Nicky! She owes Nicky!"

"Spill the deal and I'll let you keep your twig and berries. Otherwise I'll start popping."

"I don't know much of anythin'! Swear! Nicky just said I could pay him back for fuckin' up back in August—I got bounced for possession! I was ferretin' for him! So I tried to pay him back! Fuck me, that's it!" Mental note: get that report as well.

"*How*? How did you pay him back?"

"He said the bitch hosed him on a deal and I ain't got no idea about the deal at all! None!"

He squirms. I lean in. He screams, cries.

"Get offa me motherfuc—"

My foot comes off. My heater swings so hard into his left knee I feel something give under the skin. My foot comes back down on his cock.

Rage: "Answer me, motherfucker! How did you pay up?"

Blabbering: "I went to some address! I asked for her and some douche told me she ain't stayin' there no more but I swear I saw her through the window so I told Nicky and he said get her so I went back but it wadden't her and the douche shows up outta nowhere and fuckin' decks me! Swear! Pigs swarmed the place! Swear!"

I lean off. His nuts have breathing room. He cuddles with his knee. Palms his junk. Digs his face in the carpet and tries to stop blubbering like a bitch. Consider this setting a scene. I'm working up to something here.

"Where is Nicky?"

"Over on 11th and Elm. Apartment 2B. Swear."

A tell. Big time.

"You let Nicky know Delilah owes *me* bigger than shit, and if he puts his hands on her before I get my shake I will fucking ruin him. Got it?"

Quiet, between wet sobs: "Yeah."

"I will fucking *ruin* him."

"Okay."

His wallet, keys, cell phone, smokes, lighter and meth pipe are all on an end table next to the door. A small ghetto-quality 9mm also. A small amount of Big Fry in plastic baggie. I pocket the pea shooter. I smash his cell phone and knock the table over.

I leave. Make for Jeremiah's car fast. Before Benny can

work up the intestinal fortitude to move from the carpet. It could be a good while. I get the car, relocate. Vantage point. I sit there and steam for a minute about how guys like Benny can use the Big Fry and survive, while guys like me get the short dick. I resolve to beat him a good one just for being better genetically predisposed to the drug than I am.

I smoke three cigarettes before I see him leave his front door. No cell phone to call Nicky; he's got to go see him.

Benny's tell: the Venetian Apartments were located at 11th and Elm before they burnt down last year. Nicky doesn't live there.

Benny's tell: a lie. Even to the end. It's all about posturing. Probably just stupid; the rule of the street is to be arrogant and foolish above all else. He probably doesn't even think about it anymore. He just does stupid shit, even in the face of death. Bangers are like that. Retards demand respect from perfect strangers and then go out of their way to disrespect everyone, everywhere. It's all about posturing. Benny lies.

Benny's tell: coffin nail.

17

Falcon Ridge Apartments.

Northwest side of the Burrows. The kind of place that has the dumpster right next to the pool. The dumpster is overflowing; the pool is drained. An old bloodstain makes a small, brown and rust-colored splatter pattern in the deep end. Trash has blown inside the pool, half-covered in snow.

The scent of nail polish remover in the air is redolent of a clandestine lab. The complex is small; there might be ten cars in the single lot that serves the place. A mile over is the newest landfill. As long as the breeze is coming in off the ocean it'll blow that trash stink through here. Cover up the drug-cooking stink. Not today, though. I smell the complex.

I throw another glance at the dumpster. Coffee filters. Empty jugs of solvents. I kick a discarded propane cylinder. The nozzle is tarnished. Blue, corroded. Propane doesn't do that. Anhydrous ammonia does. I leave it. Someone's operation here is either sloppy enough to be an industrial accident in the making, or worse, brazen enough because no one cares or is too afraid.

Benny had parked and limped as quickly as he could down to a secluded office nestled in the guts of the small, still-as-a-bone-yard complex.

Ghost town. Litter and dilapidation are the twinkles in this complex's veneer. One hand on my iron. I follow Benny; good distance.

He knocks on a door, waits. The door talks to him, he shouts through it. Voices muffled; he says it's an emergency. In short order the door opens enough for a hand to yank him inside.

I walk down the flight of creaky, rotted steps to the door. All by itself. Near the laundry room. Says MANAGER.

This door is not stock. It doesn't match the others on the surrounding apartments. Replaced. Drug house door. Faux gold on the door's hardware, boiled up in spots with rust. That means there is a decent chance that the folks inside this apartment, while not expecting a raid, are prepared for one.

MacGyver drug dealers will rig wires and guns to their external doors. Some will keep loaded, cocked, locked and ready firearms within arm's reach to snatch up when the door comes shattering inwards. Some will have nine deadbolts. Then again, some won't do shit.

Curtains closed, shouts from inside. Chaos. Distractions. A prepared dealer isn't reaching for a loaded, cocked, locked and ready gun when he's fighting with some jackoff like Benny instead of paying attention to who's busting through his door. Surprise.

Entry Music.

I step back, breathe in deep. Hurl one foot into the door next to the handle. Knock, knock.

18

A shower of splinters and dry wall dust announce my arrival.

A deafening blast of shattering wood fills the room, and before anyone can really compute what's happening, I take a big step inside. Eye contact with Benny.

He's being manhandled by a thug with a lazy eye. A more effeminate man is a few feet away. I have to assume he's Nicky.

In the blink of an eye: I close the gap and my arms propel to Benny's head like pistons breaking free mid-pump. Right palm heel strikes his chin; pushes it away. Left hand grabs the back of his head. With a fistful of hair yanks it towards me.

The thug can't comprehend Benny's death happening. Poor Benny probably doesn't understand either as I appear from nowhere and snatch his head. His neck breaking gives one staccato *snap* into the room. He crumples. One more step and I'm in the thug's personal space. Elbow to the eye socket. He's cradling his dangling lazy eyeball in one palm because the bone that used to hold it in place just doesn't work as well broken into pieces.

He starts to scream but I clock him square on the head with my sap. Goes down. I'm pretty sure he lands square on the eyeball.

I look up at the girly-man and say: "Nicky?"

"Oh shit..." He turns around and starts to run.

He doesn't make it far.

19

Bathroom.

Before I shoved Nicky's head into the toilet I saw the water had a yellow tinge.

Getting information from someone the Arab terrorist way—that is, horrendous mutilation and slow, punishing torture—doesn't work. Ask anybody except for an Arab terrorist. When your testicles are being sawed off you'll say anything. I guarantee.

The PD teaches the newer guys all about how to gather information, define a suspect, interview the suspect, ask various types of questions such as open-ended or close-ended questions, leading questions, ask what they call baiting questions and just gather, gather, gather. Develop themes to use as a noose later. Develop hooks. Get them to commit to a story. Lock it down. Then you leave the room for a moment. Make a battle plan. Figure out your hooks and themes. Where to place the squeeze. Come back in and lay it on thick.

Of course, I am not a cop. Not anymore.

One part question, one part violence, one part threat of greater violence. Easy enough. Sniff out a nerve and press down hard. Hawk eye for hinks, tells. Jitters, hesitations, moments where lies are being concocted. I don't have all day to ask questions, gather and maneuver.

There is very little the correct, strategic application of brutality won't get you.

When people fear worse what will happen to them if they *don't* cooperate than what will happen if they *do*, people usually cooperate. Benny lied some, but that happens. You can't fix stupid, and stupid people do stupid things for no better reason than because they are stupid. In the end he gave me what I wanted.

What I know about Nicky: early thirties, rail-thin, calculating look in his eye. He's got a tattoo of a ring on his left ring finger. He's got to have *some* intelligence because he's apparently got something of a business going on here in the apartment complex. A small manufacturing gig. It's like any other legitimate business: you have production costs, distribution, supplies, labor, a schedule to keep, in-flow and out-flow, hours of operation.

If Nicky is the brains behind this he's got to be squared away at least in that sense. A clandestine lab requires management. If he has Benny and the lazy-eye thug as his enforcers, he might have others I haven't dealt with yet. I'll keep that in mind.

Nicky has been face down in the toilet for almost a minute now. Timing method: how many drags off my cigarette I've had. I know he's still alive because he hasn't stopped struggling. Good enough. I pull him up, and as he gasps for air I exhale into his face. It's always good for a laugh.

"Jesus Christ, what the fuck is going on here?" he screams between hulking intakes of air.

"Let's make this simple. Delilah Boothe. Talk."

"I don't—"

He hinks. Bingo. I bounce his face off the porcelain rim. The spot above his teeth and below his nose is...out of alignment. His teeth just red flecks in his mouth.

"Fuck you!" Before he spits I crank his head and his gob of blood-tinged slobber paints the wall crimson. Back in the bowel. Out. In. Out. I hover his face over the rim again, the threat of more pain sinking in.

"Talk and you won't be drinking piss and blood."

"She and I used to date a little bit so I just wanted to know if she was still into me. That's all."

"Lie."

Back into the bowel. The yellow becomes orange with mixing blood. Out.

"Why send the punk to check up on her then?"

"Restraining order for a fight—"

"Lie."

Back into the bowel. I light a new smoke. Out.

"Come clean or we will move on to worse things." I turn his head towards the old wooden toilet plunger beside us. One foot kicks his ass, X marks the spot. He eyeballs the chipping paint, the splinters on the plunger.

"I swear I swear—"

Bounce again. Back in the bowel. Drags. Exhale, making leaps. He didn't know her; at least not intimately. No restraining order showed up when I checked her out. Nicky is trying to avoid whatever dope involvement there is. Must be a good reason why.

He might think I'm a rival dealer looking to squeeze him. Or Delilah's new man.

He comes out.

"Do you remember Benny in there?"

Gasping. His head tries to nod against my fist bunching his hair.

"All I had to do was stand on his cock and he squealed everything. *Everything.* Stop trying my patience. You want to avoid what I will do next," I say, leaning in close enough to smell that whoever pissed last was very dehydrated.

I crack my neck; tilt my head side-to-side. Eyeball him.

"Talk."

"Please, mister! I don't know what you're talking about—"

Back in the toilet he goes. I don't have all night. When my Rum Coast is ready to be put out I yank his head back into the world.

"Know what I'm talking about yet?" I ask, the final bit of my smoldering cigarette tip staring at his eye. I lean it in enough to singe his frantic, fluttering eyelashes and just as I'm making contact with his cornea he screams: "Alright! Alright! She pawned a shit ton of my dope off on a rival dealer and I'm lookin' at a turf war! A motherfuckin' turf *war*! " He screams. I think he's crying now. I pull the smoke back just enough to encourage his cooperation.

"Why? Is she a street pusher of yours?"

"No! Here's the score, alright? No lies, I swear! I met some broad named Candy Layne at a strip joint, okay? *Bouncers* over on Topping by the old grain wharfs. The bitch was hot and hooked on my shit. I let her fuck me for free dope.

"Well, she was a friend of a friend of Delilah's and one night after blowin' me Candy was goin' go to a party over there and she wanted me to come. Said I could probably deal some small shit on the down-low to some partiers. I was in a good mood. What the hell, right?"

Rivulets of blood are coming out of the wound above his teeth. Every word puffs the droplets out of his mouth and pepper the toilet lid. He's crying. Maybe it's because I threatened to rape him with a toilet plunger. Maybe because my cigarette is burning a half inch from his eyeball.

"It wadden't a gold mine or nothin' but I made an easy wad of cash. So we came back. The Delilah bitch seemed real happy with a houseful of strangers. Like she was winnin' a popularity contest or somethin'.

"People started talkin' hush-hush like and pretty soon I was meetin' folks. Just one or two dudes lookin' to do business. So we made a date and used her party as a cover. I rolled up with ten pounds of Big Fry—"

Unbelievable: "Ten pounds?"

"I swear! No lies, I—"

"Where would some shitbird starving artist like you get that much dope in a single drop?"

"I got an operation! I got people! I got muscle! Now if the people you represent want to do business you know what I can produce and treatin' me like this is just goin' get your families killed you bullheaded piece of shit—"

Bounce.

"I represent no one." I say, looking down at his now out of alignment nose. "Still want to make threats?"

Sobbing.

"I never said stop talking."

"Oh God...oh, someone help me..."

I light a new smoke.

"I...I brought the ten spot. We started talkin', and the cops came. Some neighbor musta...musta bitched. I think she had a new stereo and was showin' it off and...and the cops came."

"So?"

"So I stashed the ten spot in her garage and we rolled out while the cops were breakin' up the party."

"How cut was the drug?"

"It was barely cut at all. Fuck me I lost so much damn money—the fuckin' pigs never roll up when you call them for help but when you're makin' a score it's like them pieces of shit just *smell* it—"

"What turf war are you bitching about?"

"Shit comes and goes here. Man, if you knew the streets you wouldn't be askin' this shit. Elvis the Spic was untouchable five years ago sellin' shit right in front of police HQ and the next thing you know he's found sawed in half by the Jamaicans. Not the ones north of the river but the ones south. Those two cartels off-ed each other until us smaller guys started gettin' footholds. Pushed 'em out."

"And the other small guys?"

"Picked off. Jimmy Cagaloni whacked Mickey the Beef and then some coon with a mohawk whacked Jimmy. That coon went down for rape and his network melted, killin' each other. I just kept pickin' up scraps and then those two twats ruined my shit! Delilah and Candy's stupid ass totally fucked me!"

"How?"

"Candy was driving the night I stashed the ten spot and she always always *always* speeds. *Always.* It's like the bitch can only floor the pedal. She got pulled over and I was never more glad I stashed the dope. 'Cuz she had a warrant so they ran me and I had one too. We both were taken in."

"What about the dudes you were doing business with? Who were they?"

"A guy named Pete and some other dude named Pinky Meyers."

"They go back and get the dope?"

"No. There was a shit storm over that. I swear! They never knew I stashed it and when I sent Candy back for it—she got out before I did—Delilah said she found it and fuckin' freaked. The bitch said she dumped it off on some ex-boyfriend who middle-manned it. Told Candy to kick rocks and never come back 'round again or she'd call the cops."

"And?"

"And that crack whore stripper didn't want no part of drug dealin'. Just wanted to get high. Twat found another dealer. I hear she's dead. Fuck her. Probably bad shit."

"Candy is dead?"

"What I hear. Now get off—"

"You have her killed?"

"I mighta called a favor in from a prison buddy, I dunno."

Bounce.

"Try and *know* for me, please."

A shower of blood from his mouth, tears from his eyes: "The big guy out there! The big guy you elbowed in the fuckin' face! He whacked the bitch! I never asked where he stashed her! I swear!"

"So, after Candy flopped on your request you sent Benny over there to double check?"

"He was goin' muscle her a bit if he needed to, yeah. You know how much she robbed me for? You got any fuckin' idea?"

"I doubt very much you produce high quality drugs. Who else is looking for her?"

"I don't know and I don't care! My boys are sellin'. I'll look that bitch up in due time and roll her ass and *you* motherfucker, *you*, I got people and *you*—"

"You're crashing in a shithole apartment complex in the Burrows. Operation my ass." I take a long drag, feel the burn running down my throat. We're about done here.

Honest, detached intrigue: "Are you really the manager?"

"No! The manager buys from me! I'm staying here for a while!"

"Where is he?"

"Extended vacation! Okay? Extended vacation!"

Dead.

"Get the fuck offa me cocksucker—"

His face goes back in the toilet. A full two cigarettes after he stops struggling I let go.

I get up, walk out of the shitter. The mess in the living room. I put Benny's gun in his dead hand and aim at the unconscious Cyclops thug.

In this complex a gunshot goes unnoticed.

20

Graham Clevenger: born in Wyoming.

I forget where. North end of the state. I remember that much. He said his childhood was spent on a cattle ranch doing the kind of thing real cowboys do. Herd cattle, cook chili, drink and fight. When he was eighteen he enlisted into the Navy. Being a former Marine that is something I never let him live down.

The service took him here. He said he was glad for it; he's got family here. After his tour he decided to stay for a while because his girlfriend at the time, a gal by the name of Molly, lived here. He joined the Saint Ansgar PD after he watched me in action. No joke.

I was actively engaged in a pursuit with a guy by the name of Denton Philips. They called him "Hulk" on the street. He was a huge man who abused his size and used it as the *because I can* reason when it came to bullying folks and beating up women. He had some gang affiliations, a rap sheet for things like assault, battery, domestic violence, resisting, armed this and that and drug charges.

Hulk was wanted for beating a man severely in a bar fight. Hulk pounded him into the tabletop and left, throwing over chairs and smashing beer bottles on his way out. Man-child in a temper tantrum. Apparently once Hulk was spun up everyone had to suffer through his bullshit fits.

The guy Hulk beat died later on in the hospital. Brain bleed. I hear the surgeon opened the guy's skull and drained it, went the whole nine yards but the thing was hosed before he got there. Hulk was looking at some real time for this.

Hulk disapproved.

A few nights after the guy died, some unnamed beat cop did a traffic stop on Hulk. Seven miles away Clevenger was sitting down to dinner on an outside patio with Molly. He was going to be discharged from the Navy in another month.

The beat cop, a veteran guy who was never getting out of patrol, made two mistakes. His first was he called out the plate to Dispatch and then approached the car before he received the return. Sign of complacency. You want to get up on that car before they can stash their dope or pull a gun, but hear your return first.

If he'd waited he would have heard the warning that the registered owner had a homicide warrant. But he didn't. The beat cop approached Hulk's car. Did the whole spiel. *Evening. My name is so-and-so, I work for the Saint Ansgar PD and the reason I stopped you...*Hulk had his license ready and was offering it before the cop asked. A set up. Just a worm on a line.

The second mistake: Hulk held the license inside the window enough to where he'd have leverage over the cop. What the guy should have done is told Hulk to reach out the window.

In a quick flash Hulk dropped the license, grabbed the cop by the wrist and gunned the engine.

Just like that we have what we call in the biz an *oh shit* moment.

He held onto the beat cop just long enough to be trouble. The beat cop was wearing steel-toed shoes and got his left foot run over by the vehicle as it took off. Hulk let go and the beat cop collapsed into the street. The steel toe is actually just a dome of metal over the toe in the boot, which, when the weight of a car is applied to it, fails miserably. The steel toe dome smashed down, severing all five toes on the cop's foot. Later the beat cop said he missed the return because he was speaking with the driver and turned his radio down so he wouldn't have to shout over it.

I heard the return on the radio. A moment later I heard a cop scream *officer down*. Every available unit started speeding that way.

I was close by. *Homicide warrant* and *officer down* is a good way to get me focused. My coffee and sandwich dropped to the ground as I bolted for my car.

I went hunting and in no time I found my prey.

Hulk saw another cop car in his rearview and he went apeshit. Some perps decide that if they're going down, they're going down in a ball of fire. Forget stoplights, other traffic, pedestrians. He was going to escape or he was going to wreck the city on his way out. I really thought about shooting him. Just drawing my iron and firing right through my windshield into the back of his head. I was already under a microscope for pistol-whipping a john who had brutally raped a whore a few months back so I decided to let this one play out in traffic. If Hulk killed someone in that neighborhood it would probably be a drug dealer anyways.

The car chase went as chases do. Hulk drove the wrong way in traffic for a spell until a semi-truck came nose-to-nose with him. He ran every red light. Doubled the speed limit. Went over curbs. This went on for a few minutes and then one of the SAPD guys ahead of us deployed some variation of a spike strip. Hulk hit it with all four tires. Effective. Hulk gunned the engine even harder as the car was struggling more. We were three blocks away from Clevenger.

The precinct captain got on the air and told us to end this thing quick. We were leaving the rough neighborhoods and getting into the classier ones. I guess he just wanted us to wave our magic wands and safely bring all vehicles to a complete stop.

Hulk fought his steering wheel to maintain some semblance of control while traveling fast enough to lose the devil. He couldn't shake me, though. He was heading for the Mannsmith Memorial Bridge.

Clevenger said he looked up when he heard the sirens, faint as old regrets calling in the distance. He said everyone seated at the tables around him were trying to ignore the nightly soundtrack until it became apparent that whatever was going on was coming their way.

Clevenger, nursing a beer, staring at Molly, gorgeous as Aphrodite. A cool, pleasant night eating outside. Forty feet away, a car, battered and near death, shrieking on tire rims, taking the corner too fast and skidding sideways. Rolling onto the roof. Sliding nearer with a cascade of sparks like fireworks. Molly screaming. Jumping up. Everyone around erupting in terror.

Fifteen feet. Cop cars spilling forward like a dam broke. Before the suspect vehicle even came to a complete halt, the huge man inside it punching through the cracked driver's side window. Hits the curb, rocks unsteady for a moment. The driver emerges, sees an older man and woman standing there.

Clevenger said Hulk clapped the older man upside the head and he crumbled like a wet sack of irons. Hulk grabbed the older woman. She screamed so hard her teeth flew out of her mouth. Then I was there, appearing out of nowhere. Clevenger heard Hulk bellow out *this cunt dies if anyone*—and then BOOM. My muzzle to his head, making the older woman safe.

Just like that we have what we call in the biz *a firearm solution.*

Clevenger said he was already making plans to pick up an application the next day at a police station near his apartment. Molly said, "I'm glad you don't have friends like that cop."

Ha.

I toss Nicky's pad.

I find a duffle bag, an overloaded ash tray full of cheap cigarette butts and roaches and a couple of spoons, scorched on the bottom and stained in the bowl. Mainlining. Needles in the trash. Empty Chinese food containers. Beer bottles. Porn.

The door to the single bathroom is hollow-core. Too heavy on top. I leave it open, get a chair; stand on it. The top ledge of the door itself has been pried off. Tool marks along one side. I peel it back.

Hollow-core doors are partitioned inside by slats of cardboard. Users will sometimes remove the top and stash contraband inside them. Nicky has several ounces of weed in one section. About three ounces of cocaine in the next. He's got a .22 caliber with no serial number next to the top hinge.

On the back patio there is a barbeque grill filled with paper ashes. No charcoal ashes. No wood. Paper. Burning his notes and ledgers. The organized distribution folks will have to keep some kind of temporary paperwork. When the shipment is complete they'll destroy the paperwork, so that it does not become evidence against them.

Still, the ashes are cold and there is no smell of fire in the air.

These are old. Maybe Nicky really did have some degree of an operation going on here.

Plot point: assuming Nicky was some kind of network man, it's possible that Delilah, among other problems, hosed the wrong dealer who just happened to be in a turf war. Losing a shipment like that would cost big bucks.

Tweakers kill over a few granules of meth or a single Big Fry pill. Giving the long screw to a dealer over an entire shipment is suicide, whether she knew what she was doing or not.

Sold it to an ex-boyfriend who middle-manned a deal. Pierce White? James Dobbins? Some third player?

I go back to the duffle bag—no doubt Nicky's entire life packed up—and I dig. There are some clothes, a carton of the cheap cigarettes same as the butts that fill the ashtray, some mementos from a previous life where he was apparently a loving boyfriend or husband and father. These must be prior to his Big Fry existence. You see these remnants of ordinary, person-next-door lives with meth addicts, alcoholics, everybody.

You learn to despise addictions in a new way when you see what was sacrificed for them. If I felt sadness I would for the woman and child Nicky left behind.

I wonder what they would think knowing the Nicky they loved is dead, scrawny and weathered beyond his years, floating tits up and face down in a piss-filled toilet.

At the bottom of the bag is a five-subject spiral-bound notebook. The first two subjects have been torn out. Burned, I'm sure. The third subject is missing pages but when I open the cover up there are handwritten notes.

They have to do with the current production schedule. Excellent.

I walk out the door to Jeremiah's car. On the way I flip open my cell phone and dial the best man I know. On the third ring he picks up.

21

Out of that armpit and back up north.

Jeremiah meets me at the corner. I get out, leave it running and light a smoke.

"You smoke in my car?" he asks.

"*You* smoke in your car."

"Yeah, but it's *my* car."

"So?"

"So don't smoke in *my* car."

"Well, I didn't smoke in it."

"I don't believe you," he says and pops the trunk.

"There's no dead bodies back there, Jeremiah."

"So says you." He goes around to the back and makes a grand spectacle of checking the space. Truth be told, I did consider stuffing someone from Nicky's apartment in there as a joke but I didn't want the headache of having to dump it somewhere else. I don't have the time right now.

And I'll probably need to borrow Jeremiah's car in the future. So, as funny as it is, my future plans will not include using a friend's trunk as a meat locker for amusement.

Small talk: "How are things going today?"

"Usual. Frequent flyers pill shopping. Did you fill this thing up?"

"No."

"You're a son of a bitch, you know that? It's riding on empty."

"What's in the bag?" I motion to a plastic sack dangling from his backpack. It's in an opened pocket about ready to fall out.

"What?" He turns to fidget with it and it spills onto the street.

Pill bottles.

"You walking out of there with meds?"

"Naw, man. Ain't my way."

"So you *take* them?"

He looks about for a moment and draws near to me. "I swear, RDB. If you tell—"

"Blah blah blah."

"Every now and then one of the admitting nurses likes to shake it up a bit and get down on one of the meds I hand out to some of the patients. So I hook her up if one of the patients isn't conscious when I deliver the drug."

"What about when they are conscious?"

"I give it to them."

"No, I mean what about *after,* when they come to and don't have any meds?"

"The stuff I got ain't the stuff the junkies come in to trade their dope for, see. This is different shit. The people takin' these pills, they don't want to be taking them. Psychiatric meds. It takes a month, month and a half for the appropriate tolerances to build up. Usually. If the levels ain't right they mess up the patient. Then of course you've got your Benzodiazepines, your Chloral Hydrates. Fun pills. Easy. No one bitches when they weren't force fed their shit. Besides, if they need this stuff they're beyond help. Trust me."

Chloral Hydrate: Mickeys. This guy, I swear.

"You just pretend you gave it to them? Is that what you tell the patient?"

"Yeah. I just say, *You took your pill like a good boy.*" Jeremiah says.

"I'll be dipped in shit and rolled in corn flakes if your patients buy that crock."

"Time to shut your mouth and thank me for the car. Again."

"You're talking about jail time, Jeremiah. Not that I care," I say, laughing.

"The nurse shakes it up with *me*, too. I figure I scratch her back—"

"Yeah, yeah." I wave him off.

"Thanks for your shitbox car," I say. "Now scram. I've got someone else meeting me here and he'd hate to find out you're stealing prescriptions from rehab patients and using them to barter for pussy." I smirk. "Or date rape."

Jeremiah stares at me, incredulous at my joke. I think he knows I'm razzing him. I think. But, then again, he's stolen drugs before and gotten busted so maybe he doesn't think it's so funny.

"Next time, RDB, when you want a favor you show up with cash."

"If it's going to be like that, Jeremiah, I'll show up with cops." I smile. He turns his head to the side and spits because he doesn't dare do it in my direction. He ducks into the car and leaves.

He flips me the bird as he passes out of existence here on this snow-covered avenue. I laugh and blow smoke chasing after him. I don't think it catches up.

I'm not even done with my smoke before the unmarked SAPD car rolls up; its headlights twin beacons cutting through the noir swath of life stretched out all around me.

22

I walk up to my old partner, comfortably seated inside his car, warm as a hotbox.

The window rolls down and Graham Clevenger's elbow dangles out. I lean in.

"This notebook will be quite a find," I say, smiling in earnest to my old friend. The ambient heat washing out from the open window is a welcome blanket covering me in the frigid exterior here. I'd sit in the car but I want to smoke more than I want to be warm.

Clevenger looks at me and readily accepts the spiral-bound ledger, begins to leaf through it.

"Did you take this off a doctor or something?"

"Big Fry dealer. *Former* dealer."

"This guy could have written prescriptions, alright. Oh—" His eyes widen at the text. "Where'd you get this again?"

"Nowhere in particular."

"I gotta tell the captain it's from somewhere."

"That depends on the captain. Is it Captain Reichland or Captain Moody now?"

"Jesus, Buckner. I told you back in August that Moody died."

"Really?"

"Yes."

"Hmmm...Oh that's right." I smile. "Moody died?"

"Yes, Buckner. How many times—"

"Moody's dead?" I ask, finding this to be hilarious.

"Bastard," Clevenger says. "I know how you felt about the guy but let his body rest."

"Probably not." I didn't care for Moody at all. Hearing he's dead over and over again is my idea of fun.

Clevenger clears his throat and says, "And not Reichland either."

"No? You're shitting me. The Nazi holdover is gone also? Who then?"

"You'll love this. Flemming's the new captain."

"When?" Sour. Sour memories.

"Maybe two months ago, now. It's still fresh."

"How does an incompetent shitbird like her get commander? Seriously?"

"I know. We all asked that. She'll be chief one day. You wait and see." Clevenger leafs through the notebook some more, and then, "It was her that crucified Burns, Smole and Philips, right? When she was IA?"

I nod, blow smoke through my nose. "Indeed, friend. Indeed. She spent the majority of her formidable years hunting cops. Burns, Smole and Philips weren't the only ones she strung up. You know that."

"I do."

I have to force the next words out of my mouth. "*Captain* Flemming. Unbelievable." It leaves a bitter taste with me. Flemming and I butted heads enough to leave scars. I owe her something fierce.

"And the word really is that she might be Chief of Police later in life," Clevenger says. "Travesty, I tell you. A blood sucker like that calling the shots."

"If she becomes chief I hope Sheriff McDonald is still around. That guy is too old school to put up with her shit. Who'd she blow to earn those stripes anyways?"

"Always the sweet gentleman, you are." Clevenger keeps reading the ledger, flipping back and forth as if Nicky's chicken-scratched ignorant script will vanish like the details of nightmares upon waking.

"I gave Flemming her fair chance and she showed her true colors."

"That's true, Buckner. Despite your abrasiveness—

which Molly and I both love—you *do* give fair chances. And if they don't impress you, well, you shoot them."

"But seriously, how did Flemming get commander?"

"The major passed it around through his drinking buddies that the chief thought she did a bang-up job during all those years in IA. Asked her what she wanted."

"*What she wanted?* Is she a detective?"

"No. Administrator. You don't need the qualification to get the desk in the detective's shop anymore."

"Incredible. I wish things happened like that before they tossed me," I say.

"Yeah. But ten years ago it was a different PD."

"True. Ten years ago you looked up to me," I say.

"I wouldn't call it that," he says, shutting the notebook. "But ten years ago I was green, you had a real job and Molly was dating a loser. Two out of three of those things improved."

"I have to run to Three Mile High for a day or two. How'd it go digging for what I was asking?" I say, suddenly feeling the weight of the day.

"No problems." I love Clevenger. No hesitation, no excuses. He's the guy you want in a foxhole when a grenade comes flying in. Both of you will jump on it to save the other, but he'll instigate a fistfight to get you off. "Here you go."

He hands me a sheaf of papers. I leaf through them. Reports about the Bellview house and Boothe's disappearance. There's some arrest reports about Benny.

"So, again, where'd you get this notebook?" Clevenger asks.

"That Benny guy told me a line of complete bullshit but he laid the tracks back to this dealer named Nicky."

"And I've got Nicky's ledger in my hands?"

"That you do."

"Sweet. Thank you by the way."

"I roughed up Benny and followed him to Nicky. You'll find them in the manager's office."

"And the labs written in the ledger?"

"All in the complex," I say. "I assume. I didn't go to the doors and knock. But if the ledger is accurate Nicky has his budding operation spread throughout the complex. He told me the manager was a client who was letting him crash. He said the manager was on 'extended vacation.'"

"Where do you think he dumped him?"

"I don't know."

"I bet this punk has a rap sheet a mile long."

"I'm sure he went down for distribution somewhere before now. His book keeping and operation, clients, all that, it's too experienced for this to be his first start."

"I'll look into it. So, what do I tell Captain Flemming?"

"Tell her to go fuck herself."

"That sounds like a great idea."

"Tell her some tweaked out Big Fry addict who was pissed at Nicky for a raw deal decided to be a real bitch and stole the ledger and gave it to the first cop he saw."

"*I'm* the first cop a pissed off junkie sees?"

"Yup. Sounds solid enough."

"We have done busts on less."

"Oh, and I should tell you, you'll find some dead bodies."

"Naturally." Clevenger eyeballs the ledger and I can see the gears turning behind his eyes. He'll adjust the story a little bit before he tells Flemming. He knows she won't buy it because she's never been a real cop. Real cops know that sort of thing happens here and there. Maybe not to every cop, but it does happen. "Where you going now?"

"Back to my office."

"Want a lift?"

"No, thanks. I'm going to think."

"You get some sleep. Tell Molly I said hello."

I slug his elbow and walk off into the snow, shadows trailing a thin line of smoke behind me.

23

Clevenger was his academy class president.

He did well in patrol and was qualified as an FTO for two years before Molly got pregnant. A detective's test coincided with their pregnancy so Clevenger put in for it and was selected. The raise was nice but two weeks later they lost the baby.

"Your new partner will be late reporting," the captain said. Up to this point I had heard Clevenger's name a time or two but that was it.

"Why?" I ask. "His pussy hurt?"

"Took some time off. His wife miscarried or something so he wants to be with her. I guess it's bad."

Those were the first and last ill words I put out into the world against Graham Clevenger.

"Coffee first," I said to Clevenger when he finally did arrive at the homicide bureau.

We stewed in silence for a moment. Clevenger knew me by reputation and said later while he was glad to be partnered with SAPD's most brilliant, handsome, cultured and successful detective he would be lying if he didn't admit he was also intimidated. I do that to people.

"There's a place called Gina's Kitchen on the 8600 block of West Fulsom Boulevard that makes it the best," Clevenger said.

"Gina's been arrested for opiates before, you know," I said. "But you're right. Her coffee is the best."

We left the detective's bureau to the elevator. Inside the car was the most gangsta-looking female I had seen in a long time. She reeked of weed and I knew her face from somewhere. And, of course, in her hand was an application for the PD.

"Sweet, the poh-poh," she said, her mouth full of gold. "I'm gonna apply. I can't wait to be the poh-poh."

In the world of Richard Dean Buckner, the word poh-poh is on equal footing with nigger, spic, peckerwood and all the other glorious epithets used to instill hate and resentment. The mere fact this broad called me the poh-poh raised fury in my veins.

"Applying, huh?" I asked. Clevenger hit the G button. The doors closed. It was just the three of us.

"Yeah. Never thought I'd do this," she beamed.

"Well, we wish you the best of luck," Clevenger said with a smile I soon learned was his phony one. "I'm sure you're well-qualified."

"Thanks. I got my GED last month."

"Congratulations. What made you want to apply?"

"My momma's house been shot up twice now this year. Ain't no poh-poh helpin', neither. We call, they just show up and ask if we know the people who done it. Then they leave. If we was white it'd be different. No offense. But I guess I got to do it myself. So I'm gonna do it myself."

"That's terrible. What's your mom's address?"

Some house over on 10th and Watson. Now I know where I've seen her. I recognize the address. I've been there. Bad neighborhood. Our city, like the rest of the country, has huge difficulties getting inner-city folks to cooperate with investigations. It's the whole *snitches wind up in ditches* bullshit. They won't inform on the bad guys.

This gal's mom was a bigger bitch than most. Half the time we'd show up we'd wind up arresting her for battery or drugs.

Mom has this daughter and three sons. One son is dead. Gang violence. I knew both the others have spent time in prison. Gang violence. Mom knows who has shot at her house, and they were probably trying to do it to kill one of her kids. She'll just turn her boys loose on them and then whine that the poh-poh aren't doing enough.

"Maybe we can help," Clevenger said. "Got any military experience?"

"Nah."

"What about college?"

"Nah."

"Clean driving record?"

"Sure. I got tickets before, but I take care of my business."

"Good," I say.

"Ever been in trouble?" Clevenger said. "The reason why I ask now is because they'll ask after the testing. I figure you'd want to be front-loaded with the process. It makes applying easier."

"When I was a kid. But what kid hasn't been?" she said, smiling.

"Okay," Clevenger nodded and looked away. He walked her right into it.

"You think they care if I got some warrants?" she asked. "Just traffic and shit, but still."

"I thought you took care of your business?" I asked.

"I *do*. It's just that I wanted to work for a few months to get the money before I turn myself in. That's all."

My real grin stretched ear-to-ear. "Well, we *should* find out." My handcuffs were on her before she knew what was happening.

"What the fuck? WHAT THE FUCK!"

"Calm down, honey. The poh-poh's just checking on your warrants."

The elevator doors opened to the ground floor, which contains three things: the lobby, reception and the jail.

Traffic warrant? Maybe, buried under all the other ones. She had an NCIC hit for an armed robbery two states over. The stupidity of humanity is unparalleled. She actually confessed that she didn't think she was a suspect because they hadn't found her *yet*. *Yet*. I love arresting felons, but I'd rather do it after my coffee.

And that was Clevenger and I's first bust together.

The walk back to my office is bitterly cold, but still and quiet as a graveyard.

The snow dances in swirls as it falls, a ballet of flittering ice, distorting the sallow luminescence from the street lamps lining the avenue.

Eventually I get on my building's street and I shake off the frost's arresting grip. Two blocks later and I can see the office building loom over the skyline.

I fix my eyes to the building itself and its surroundings well before I get within its sights. As I walk calmly, hands in pockets, cigarette hanging from my mouth, my eyes inspect every shadow, every pool of darkness, every car parked along the street, every window that could be open to take a shot at me.

All this and I don't see a thing. The street seems dead. But the best predators act deceased when their prey is expecting it to be alive.

I climb the steps to the front door and go inside. I shed a mantle of snow from my coat as if it were a sheath of dead reptile scales. My footprints follow me written in dirty puddles of melt. The elevator is slow as usual. The doors open with a creak. The button for my floor sticks. The two bulbs that should be dripping light into the elevator car flicker like they always do.

My floor greets me. As second nature, I examine the lock on my door. Look for scratch marks, chiseling. I look at the door jamb. The glass. Watch for black shadows moving through blacker shadows. Once, many years ago a guy I put in prison was waiting for me inside this very office. When it was over, we both left the building. I was on foot, he was not.

The door opens now, .44 Magnum sweeping the room. This is routine. I thump on the light switch. All the shadows evaporate. A quick look behind my desk tells me I am alone, and I sit down in the familiar old leather chair.

I open the bottom drawer and remove my whiskey bottle. A quick pull on it and I exhale with the satisfaction of a good whiskey burn.

Another long pull on the whiskey and I lean back. I draw my .44 and keep it resting on my chest as I shut my eyes to sleep for a few hours.

In an hour buried deep below midnight, the darkness is sliced in half. My phone rings as shrill and unwelcome as a mother-in-law. Clevenger. He never calls at this hour. Not unless someone is dead.

I answer.

Someone is.

24

I get out of the cab and walk up to my old partner.

Sleep still husks my voice. I light a smoke. I'm sure he can smell the whiskey on my breath. He eyeballs me, looking for my night cap. Flutter. I hand him the flask I keep in my jacket. He swigs. Swigs again. Clevenger doesn't drink all that much. But he is tonight. A tell.

The lawn is all muddy, trampled snow and soaking wet from the fire engine. The rich smell of burnt everything clings to the air like souls of the damned; the burning, the char, the thick bulk of stench.

The roar of the blaze killed off an hour ago by water. The steam and the frigid air fight each other for dominance. Everything painted the colors of emergency flashers. Walkie-talkies squelching. My head hurts.

The ambulance crew puts the body in the back, shuts the doors. Any amount of solemnity that would accompany the duty of transporting the dead is washed out in flashing strobes of blue and red.

Neighbors still perch on their doorsteps. Cop cars in the driveway. Fire engine #3 alongside the road. Three ambulances; one a tomb. The smoke in the air burns my eyes. My shoulders collect small flakes of ash as they swirl about.

Clevenger points. Useless, but he fidgets at times like these.

"Arson," he says. The sleep in his voice cracks under the weight of the word.

"How'd you pull the squawk on this one?"

"Not mine officially. If it were I'm pretty sure I wouldn't be drinking at the scene. Remember Riggens from Narcotics?"

"Yup."

"His kid brother is a rookie over at Arson. Fresh meat like three weeks ago. His last beat as a street cop took him here for that call you asked me to dig up. The intruder, Benny whatever. I spoke to Riggens' kid brother about it earlier; he filled me in and sent the file my way."

Clevenger looks into the heap the home has been reduced to. Went fast.

"So when the neighbors called nine-one-one on this...the kid brother caught wind of it and called me."

"What do they figure?" I ask, crushing out my Rum Coast. "It's the kid brother's case?"

"Yeah. I think it's his first one."

I rub my eyes. I look at the wife, who is only half lucid, sobbing. She holds her head like an axe is buried in it. Abigail Bellview, her life obliterated.

"Ugly shit. Very ugly shit tonight." Clevenger takes the pack of smokes from my shirt pocket.

"Molly is going to be pissed at you."

"Let her."

He lights up. Coughs. Drags again. "Be a pal and make this my only one, will ya?"

"Sure," I say. Light my own. "So, what's he got so far?"

"He says the arsonist broke in. Damage to the structure now...probably never know where. Wife's story is the bad guy came into the bedroom and clubbed the family while asleep. Dad first; eliminates the biggest threat. Mom next. The kid was sleeping in their bed also."

"He whack the kid?"

"Yup."

"With what?"

"Judging by the wound, something blunt. Just one strike to the head, keep 'em docile. Baseball bat maybe. Not hard enough to kill; too much of a coward for that."

"Let the fire kill?"

"Yeah. That way the arsonist doesn't have to see the fruits of his labor."

"Like carpet bombing."

"Yup."

"What does the mom remember about the intruder?" Give me a description so I can set a fire inside his mouth.

"Nothing besides he was male. It was dark. It all happened so fast. You know."

"Where'd he set the fire?"

"All over. Must have soaked the home. In the hallway there's a pool of melted red plastic. Probably a standard can of gasoline."

"And this?" I nod towards the ambulances.

"Dad came to first. Saw the flames. Probably eating the house by then. A lot. Jimmy figured he had his wits enough to know he had one trip out the door; no time to come back in for round two."

Exhaling smoke through his nostrils, Clevenger says: "So he carried both Mom and daughter out the front fucking door."

"No other exit?"

"Who knows what he tried or figured. Conked pretty hard on the head, flames everywhere, smoke, any infrastructure damage he might have come across, losing seconds with every thought. He went out the front."

I nod.

"The neighbor over there said he was engulfed by the time he dropped the family on the front lawn."

An old woman is shuddering next door, a cop and an EMT at her side. A down coat over a bathrobe. Coffee mug in her hands. Looking like she aged a decade with one sight.

"She said it was all he could do to not collapse on them."

I stare into the wreckage. Husk. The heat is still oppressing.

"How'd he catch fire like that? Not the other two?"

"If he slept at the edge of the bed and got splashed, maybe. The mom and kid weren't soaked...so either he was wet with fuel or somehow it got on him exiting."

"It doesn't fit the MO," I say. "The whole family bopped just hard enough to keep them unconscious while the fire was set. Left alive at that point. If the arsonist was there to directly murder as well, why the dad? And why risk *just* soaking him and leaving the wife and kid a chance for survival? Why not shoot or stab? Slit his throat?"

"Beef with the dad alone? Couldn't bear the thought of hurting a woman? A child?"

"Maybe. But if so he had to of known they'd just die in the fire."

"You're right."

"Maybe he intended to let them die, but the dad fought back first."

"Struggle. DNA."

"The arsonist just wanted a slick night: in, set the fire, get out—but Dad woke up and threw down."

"Arsonist gains the upper hand. Which isn't hard, considering he's fighting a guy just waking up, transitioning from lying down to on his feet in a hurry, probably in his underwear."

"But Dad makes him hurt anyways. Maybe gets some DNA under his fingernails. Spills blood."

"Arsonist gets one good whack on Dad, knocks him out. Clocks Mom and the kid, who are of course awake. Soaks Dad along with every floor inside the place. Lights the house."

"We should be telling Riggen's kid brother all this."

"I will."

"Were his fingers left after the fire?" I ask.

Clevenger shrugs and looks off in the distance.

Almost an afterthought: "Paramedic pronounced him at the scene. Obvious mortal injury. I got a peek at him. No argument."

"A good man."

"To the end."

"Any motive?" Abigail's agony begins to siren higher than the cacophony of the scene. Another paramedic stands beside her, talking in that detached-but-trying-to-be-compassionate way the ones do who have a hard time faking they care.

"None so far. What do you think?"

"Looks amateur. Leaving the gas can. Attacking but not killing the family. Cowardly. New to the game. I wonder if he tossed the place."

"Can't tell. The burn job was thorough."

"Yeah. A blaze like this, I'll bet there was more than one gasoline can."

"Probably. Jimmy thought as much. He's checking around."

"It's either melted or taken from the scene after he emptied it."

"Got five black and whites canvassing now. None of the neighbors recalls a vehicle parked in the driveway or on the street nearby," Clevenger says, puts out the cigarette. "And I agree on the amateur angle; some losers this green to the whole murder/arson thing *would* park in the driveway."

"Yeah. I doubt they brought this on themselves, but who knew what kind of enemies they might have had. Not to mention that dirtball Benny."

Looking off into the distance, avoiding what I'm thinking: "If this was a dope beef with Benny and Nicky...they're not going to spill it now."

"It's not your fault, RDB."

"We'll see when it shakes out if it's my fault or not. Keep that angle in the back of your head."

"I will. If you get anything let me know; I'll filter it to Riggens' kid brother."

"And if it's connected...I'll tie the loose ends."

"That's the RDB I know." He claps me on the back.

We're done here. I rub my scalp; kick at some snow the inferno didn't melt. Look around. A bad scene. Poor Abigail.

"I'll drive you home," Clevenger says. "Give me another cigarette, would ya?"

"The other one was your only one, right?"

"It *was*. I heard the mom crying, looked at her. She was looking over there at the other ambulance, so I looked too."

"And?"

"And I forgot. Right before you showed up, the EMTs said the little girl took her knock like Mom and Dad...but her skull didn't work as well as theirs."

"Jesus Christ," I say.

I hand him another cigarette. We drain the flask.

25

The next day I wake up and call Elam Derne.

Let him know about the blaze. He can't come to the phone.

His house burnt down as well.

26

Elam Derne survived his fire.

His terminally ill wife did not. A different investigator caught this one: a guy named Volksman. I know Volksman. I can't stand that guy. I wouldn't piss in his ass if his shit was on fire.

Thomas Volksman: shitbird. Saying he was a poor street cop is like saying Clay Aiken was hiding his homosexuality well. Volksman would get dispatched to calls and deliberately drag his feet until his back up arrived first. Then he'd show up, radio that he was on-scene, get credit for the call and not be the responsible officer.

Volksman is the guy who would take felony drugs off of a suspect and flush them. Throw away paraphernalia. A lot of cops will empty a small baggie of weed rather than do all the paperwork and evidence processing. But Volksman would toss heroin.

Volksman pulled a guy over one night who was so drunk he drug his car's passenger side along a forty-foot stretch of retaining wall. Even back then DUI's were a lot of paperwork. Volksman has an allergy to paperwork. He let the guy go with a warning.

The next county over, deputies spent hours processing the wreck Volksman's drunk got into. The investigator theorized the drunk got off on the wrong exit, wandered off into the country. He hit a cow who was fortunate enough to find a break in the pasture fence. Cow died. Drunk died. Volksman slipped by.

There are always reliable sources entrenched in the rumor mill. Nameless, faceless cops, janitors, dispatchers and others who make it their business to know the business of others. Faint rumors, as quiet as a mouse-fart, popped up one day saying that Volksman, who wouldn't investigate his own mother's murder, who wouldn't do the paperwork necessary to claim a million dollar cash prize, got promoted.

It was fast. It was without fanfare. It was odd. It was kept hush-hush. But it *was*. Volksman was promoted to an arson investigator's position.

The mouse-fart quiet rumor mill also stated the baffling reason for Volksman's promotion: he has some Grade-A dirt on an arson captain. Something that greased the path into his promotion. I don't know what it is; the arson captain might have been boning a TV evangelist while Rome was burning. I don't know. But it was powerful stuff.

Stuff that needs to be kept buried to the point where Volksman could use it to buy himself a cozy gig sifting through ashes and turning over charred timbers, getting fatter and more useless with each passing day. Something cozy where he can pontificate and play with his molester 'stache while directing his subordinates to do everything he should be doing.

The arson captain probably hopes Volksman winds up meandering around some burnt building and steps on a fire-weakened floorboard and takes the Grade-A dirt with him on his fall down.

Three obvious arsons last night. Three different MO's. Derne's place had an attached garage whose back door was unlocked. It was opened and left that way. Neither Derne nor his wife was assaulted. Their possessions were rifled through. It's hard to tell what is missing and what was incinerated now.

While three in one night is a rarity in these parts, the different MO's will be the monkey wrench in the works. Clevenger told Riggens about the Delilah Boothe connection. Riggens is a lightweight at Bomb and Arson,

Volksman is an egomaniacal cocksucker. The third investigator, Jennifer Rudd, I don't know.

Elam Derne suffered smoke inhalation while trying to pull his wife from the blaze. He also did a number on his back. I guess his wife was heavy. Cancer hadn't had time to whittle her down yet. He's in traction, on muscle relaxers and pain meds.

In the hospital he cradles his head. Nurses said if he keeps sobbing the way he is, they might just medicate him. "Just a little something to calm him down so he can sleep." I asked if there was anything you couldn't get doped up for nowadays. One mumbled, *Being an asshole.* The others didn't answer.

Derne's not much help. What he does say is all sobs; the vowels losing their identities in his anguish. Crying and consonants, when that's all you speak, are not good storytellers. My patience more than anything drives me from his room. He says something. I turn around.

He holds a faded picture of his wife, looks like it was removed from his wallet. He clears his throat and whispers, "Darla's house burnt down."

I already know; called Clevenger when I found about Derne. Clevenger checked in on it. Fire number three.

Busy night for the demons that feed off of lives burning. I leave the hospital. I need to be in Three Mile High.

27

A note on me: cops, like firemen and EMS, are always looking for good calls.

What might be the best call of your life might be the worst headache of your supervisor's life. That just might be that kind of outlook that got me in trouble so much. I handled things old school while the rest of the law enforcement community steered away from that playground of fists and intimidation and headed towards the nicer, gentler new school.

There was a day when tuning up some asshole was the correct way to fix the problem. Nowadays cops fear scrutiny just a tad less than they fear death. Actual death. They fear scrutiny with good cause, to be sure, but still. The best way to teach a child abuser to stop abusing is not counseling. It is not therapy. It is a mouth full of broken teeth, and arms that when the bones heal cannot produce the force necessary to hit or burn another child. The gift that keeps on giving. That is how I sleep at night.

So, the good calls, they just pop up. They pop up five minutes 'til the shift is over. They pop up while you're taking a simple burglary report and you do everything you can to rush the report without making the burglary victim feel like he is what he is: the lowest priority ever.

I had a good call one night. Maybe it was the last good call for me. Because it was also my supervisor's worst nightmare, and she, in turn, made it mine. That nightmare had resounding effects. Made little ripples in the water of my life. Those ripples still lap at the shores today.

Jefferson Stoke and his boy Thomas popped up while Clevenger and I were two blocks away, interviewing a witness about a completely separate case. The mom called in, said her soon-to-be ex-husband Jefferson was rough-handling his boy and she wanted it stopped. I never pass up an opportunity to become a fearful memory in the mind of a man big enough to hurt a child.

Even though we were homicide detectives, we snatched up the call.

Any real cop will say this matter-of-factly: what is reported to dispatch and what you actually find can sometimes be two hugely different things. Case in point: Jefferson Stoke.

Two months prior to that night, Jennifer Stoke found her bank account drained into two separate funds: her husband's private alcohol reserve, and her husband's private erotic dancing reserve. When she confronted him about it she found out two interesting facts about her husband: he had lost his job five months previously for threatening to kill his boss with a shotgun, and he had been lying to her about going to work while actually going to strip clubs and spending their savings, their investments and her inheritance from her recently deceased mother.

Don't ask me how these shenanigans go on for almost half a year undetected. But when she did find out, Mrs. Stoke decided to go back to her maiden name. Jennifer screamed divorce, took their son Thomas, moved in with her sister. Jefferson got to see the boy here and there while squatting in their almost-foreclosed on home.

Fast forward to the *good call* night. The *worst headache of my supervisor's life* night. Jennifer and Thomas go to their former home and visit Jefferson. Clevenger and I are a few blocks away, Jennifer calls 911 and says Jefferson is being aggressive with his six-year-old. We take it.

Jennifer meets us on the lawn, disheveled, hair a mess, her face the kind of red that comes with a good backhand, crying. Something about Jefferson inside beating up the boy. Something about him drinking, hating his life, blah blah blah.

I mount the steps. The screen door has been torn from its hinges. Hole in the drywall. The room at dusk is lit only by the cockeyed light from an overturned table lamp; the conical shade now on its side and pressing an oval of light against the wall horizontally.

The place smells of a broken home, torn in two by lies. Even now, I can still fill my nostrils with the acrid, stale air of that house. It makes me snarl and grit my teeth. I can hear the whimperings. Even before I see Jefferson Stoke I can hear him adjust his one-handed grip on the shotgun. The weight is getting to him; he has to support the pump action weapon with his strong arm only because in his off-hand he holds his boy still.

Better to keep the muzzle pointed at his head that way.

"One more step and I'll fucking do it, I swear," he says, the voice of a man who is desperately searching inside for the balls to end this thing with bloodshed. Suicides come in two categories: the ones who think they want it but are stilling working up to do it, and the ones who have already found their peace with it.

"I can rack rounds in this gun faster than you can regret showing up here," he says, looking me in the eye. "This doesn't involve you; it's my damn family, and I will do what's best. *To all of us.*"

Not *for* all of us. *To* all of us.

The hippies got it wrong: peace does not solve things. It clears the path to do what apprehension was formerly holding at bay. Reference the suicide typologies. Stoke was not really ready to kill his boy yet, but he was running down that road faster than I could keep up.

"Don't kill the boy," I say. Use the word "kill" rather than "hurt" or "injure." It brings the situation home. It makes it real. Clevenger behind me, staying back far enough to give Stoke a sense of security. Best not to have him get rash until the boy is clear.

"Don't tell me what to do!" Stoke says, readjusts his grip. Somewhere, a million miles behind me, Clevenger backs up further and gets on his radio. We need more cops.

"Fine," I say. "Kill yourself. But let your son come over here. He's got no business with your final solution. Stop scaring the child and let him go outside."

"None of this is my fault. I was forced into this. Do you hear me? You think I picked getting shitcanned? You think I wanted Jen's mother to get fat and diabetic and get her feet cut off and drop dead and make my wife all cold and withdrawn? You think I wanted to start fucking chicks out at the damn strip club? Where they give mercy jerks for a twenty spot?"

People will say the darndest things in situations like this. They deflect blame and culpability like they were oil and water. Let them talk; it takes energy to be spastic, crazy and angry. They wear down. Drop their guard. Then come in with the haymaker.

"That bitch stole everything from me! Everything! I can't afford food! I can't afford this house! She won't even let me keep the kid overnight! I get all the problems and all the bullshit, and she just packs up and leaves when it gets tough! Well she ain't fucking getting my boy! SHE AIN'T!"

Ten minutes ago Clevenger and I were interviewing witnesses. That might as well have been in the 1950s it feels so long ago. I look at Stoke.

"Listen to me. My name is Richard. I'm a policeman and *I want to help you.* Okay?" My first name. Rapport building. He doesn't really acknowledge me beyond simply shutting up, and that's fine. It's a start.

"Sure. The woman backed you into this. They all did.

Let me make sure I've got this right. Let me start with her mother, okay? Gets sick because she doesn't take care of herself, right? Doesn't take care of herself even after she's sick. Her body speaks up when she needs her feet amputated. That's what you said, right? Good. She still doesn't take care of herself even after *all that* and in the end she just dies.

"Then your wife, she gets all upset about her mother. Now, this is the same woman who had all the signs in front of her and didn't notice. You all could see that coming a mile away and yet your wife still gets bent out of shape? How? Why would your wife be upset about that?"

Stoke has no answer. I fix a knowing eyeball on him and say: "Because she *can be*, and she can take it out on you. So she does. She steals the little man here—the only other man like you in this sea of women—and goes and lives with yet *another* woman. Who is, by the way, probably feeding your wife more lies about you.

"So you go and find a titty club. Perfectly reasonable. Your wife ain't taking care of it, so you have to spend her mom's money to get it taken care of. Makes sense, right? Mother-in-law caused all the problems, might as well be her dime that fixes those problems."

Paraphrase and summarize. Rapport building. He nods.

"Now, tell me what happened at work, Jefferson." His first name. Rapport building.

"I was drunk," Jefferson says. "Not a lot, not any more than Todd is every damn day. But the boss loves Todd and hates me so I get caught with a beer on my breath and get fired, *boom,* just like that. What was I supposed to do? Fucking cunt. What was I supposed to do?"

"Okay. Tell me something else, Stoke: was your boss a *woman?*"

"YES! Yes, damnit, I fucking said that! Why would I call a man a *cunt?*"

131

"Just checking. Like I said earlier, I want to make sure I understand you completely." People will never listen harder than when they hear their own words coming out of someone else's mouth. By asking questions and repeating things people know you are really listening rather than just waiting for a chance to interrupt.

Rapport building.

"See your problem pattern here?" I ask.

"Yes, I do." He says this matter-of-factly, shoots a glance at the boy. The boy is small. Brown hair trimmed into a bowl cut. Slicks of bright red blood from both nostrils. He's shuddering like a man who has just been stabbed clear through in the eye.

He is cradling his left arm. I see the purple discoloration just below the elbow. Not good. He turns another tint lighter towards pale. His eyes have cried so hard they are bloodshot and sandpaper dry. He has run out of tears.

Pitiful. Thomas looks pitiful. No child should have to be exposed to this kind of raw-nerve horror. Kids have two things in early life: Mom and Dad. People fail their children in ways that should never be. People expect their children to endure things they would never put themselves through. Just look around.

Jefferson has decided to make his boy sit in a front row seat while he puts on the failure show of his lifetime.

I continue: "You see your problem pattern? Yes? Then why are you making it your boy's?"

"What?"

"Your boy stands by you, Jefferson. Even now he is respectful, obedient. With your gun to his head he's in his dad's arms. What do you think about that?"

"He's my boy," Jefferson says. "I raised him to be this way."

"Right. And now you're going to kill him because you and pussy mix about as well as a pissed off bull and an anal probe."

"What?"

"Yeah. You know I'm right. Think about it. In the end there's just a huge fight and shit everywhere."

Jefferson looks at me. His grip on the kid has let up some. *Some.* In these situations infinitesimally small concessions like that are to be counted as blessings. They wear down. Drop their guard. Then come in with the haymaker. I can see the calculations going on in those drained, beady eyes.

"I want to help you here, Jefferson. That's why I came," I say, taking a minute step forward. This has to work just so. "The kid? The kid is scared and hurt and he's on autopilot. Believe me, I've been a cop a long time and I know how kids are in bad situations. Would you agree this is a bad situation for the boy?"

He slowly nods yes. Slowly.

"Yes, women fuck up everything. Yes, women are all around us. Yes, women are the reason why any man will do anything. Women are the fuel in our engines. But let the boy get old enough to make his own problems with women. Don't shove your burden on him." Twist that rapport knife. This is what crisis-intervention folks will tell people *not* to do.

Build it; don't use it to agitate. But I'm old school. The old school guys say I have enough of the war in me to not be *their* type of old school. Maybe I'm just something else altogether. So be it.

Jefferson's face scrunches and fights crying. His eyes redden and squint, his lips purse and then—just nothing. Blank. The calculations stop. Here we go. Suicides come in two categories: the ones who think they want it but are still working up to do it, and the ones who have already found their peace with it.

Stoke looks down to his scared, battered child and says: "Hey, kiddo. Want to go see your mom outside?" He says this with a bit of a smile, fawning eyes and he sniffs back a tear. Too late I realize Jefferson Stoke asks this question because he wants to hear his boy say no, he wants to stay with his daddy.

But instead Thomas does not hesitate to say, "Yes, Daddy. I want to go outside with Mommy."

In the blink of an eye. These things take the blink of an eye. Fawning smile to roaring, contorted mask of contempt and bitter jealousy. Thomas is thrown, shotgun leveled. Why he didn't pull the trigger with it next to his head God only knows. I think Jefferson wanted one last expression of fury before he cleaved his boy in two with buckshot. I jump, snatch the shotgun, turn it. The blast is deafening. The drywall reduces to a cloud of shards and choking dust. I move, lose my footing. A single hot shotgun shell ejects from the port and hits me in the face. Jesus Christ, this fucker can re-rack a shell before I can regret showing up. One hand shoves the firearm somewhere else besides the boy's general direction. The other hand finds the boy and I shove him towards Clevenger, towards the door. "GO!" I shout. I slip. Jefferson slips. Knee to my gut. Drywall dust in my eyes. Aggression pulses and I throw my body at him. The second shot sprays across the living room and I hear the boy scream. I see Clevenger cover the child with his own body and nosedive out the front door. One hand to the shotgun barrel. The other to the pistol grip. Jefferson's drained beady eyes an inch from my own. I slam my head into his like we are rams competing for a mate and I intend to win. Blood. Stars behind my eyelids. Another knee. Another head-butt. He screams. Sirens outside.

Clevenger shouting. We collapse in a heap. Stoke on bottom. One solid heave and the barrel stabs him in the mouth. Blood made watery with his saliva cuts a river path down the steel. In an instant he has slobber-coated his peace of mind; a tube filled with violence to end his suffering. I wrangle one of my feet up to my chest and step on the gun, all my weight holding the shotgun to his head. Blood drizzles from my face down to him. My suit is ruined.

There was a day when tuning up some asshole was the correct way to fix the problem. The best way to teach a child abuser to stop abusing is not counseling.

It is not therapy.

It is a mouth full of broken teeth.

And worse.

Bold. Bold now because that is what is required. I free one hand and rack a round. Business time. I grab his hand, put it to the pistol grip.

I never pass up an opportunity to become a fearful memory in the mind of a man big enough to hurt a child. His guardian angel with razored feathers for wings, ready to aid him to the Promised Land the only way I know how.

I look him in the eye, calm: "Here is your Number One Problem Solver, Jefferson Stoke. Take care of business."

He knows the fight is over. Time to be a man. I stand up as he makes his call.

The blast goes off just as the SRT fellas breech the front door. Everyone saw something different; it's how I got to keep my job.

It is also how I was ruined.

Now, after all the fires and Derne's sobbing, I leave before the sun breaks over the world.

No new snow yet but it's coming. Thick stretches of pregnant, angry clouds are amassing on the eastern horizon. A tide of frost. The Rail station isn't far. I walk. Enjoy the bitter breeze. Bitter as I am becoming.

A word on the Rail: the Rail, as it is commonly referred to, is actually the Dual Community Rail Transit System. It was a pet project back in the '80s between Saint Ansgar and Three Mile High and their mayors. In the '70s Saint Ansgar was trying as hard as it could be to be the most ultra-liberal city in America. In some respects it succeeded. Any of those triumphs took very little time to become curses on the city.

One such success was the city's stance on criminal rights. The '70s were very gentle towards criminals. That's why movies like *Dirty Harry* were created back in that decade. That's also why guys like Dirty Harry were so popular. Citizens and safety took a back seat to the every imaginable right of a criminal.

Eventually in the early '80s Saint Ansgar became swamped with lawsuits placed against them by the families of all the victims who, because of a slight, minute, worthless technicality, received no justice. The city did what it could to swim under these lawsuits but in the end they were effectively ruined.

New political blood began pumping up from everywhere, and the mayor's office, the sheriff's office, the city council and beyond were swept away and replaced by folks who spoke highly of reinventing the city. Ideas were vast and as different as any ideas could be, but there were a lot to choose from.

One thing everyone wanted to do was install a rail system. During the '70s the criminal friendliness became such a plague that a good amount of Saint Ansgar's taxpayer income got up and moved. No one—especially those people who made higher salaries and therefore paid more taxes—were going to sit through nearly a decade of the city government making it less and less safe to live within its walls.

So they moved out. And the people who were left were light on cash. No cash equals no cars. They wanted some incentive to stay before they pulled up chalks and left also. So a rail system it was.

Meanwhile, all those years ago Three Mile High was struggling burg nestled up to the mountain range on Saint Ansgar's east side. Theirs was a nice place to visit but as far as being a fulltime, growing community Three Mile High was a failure. A lot of Saint Ansgar's upper crust relocated there because they could still conduct business in Saint Ansgar without the pain of residing in a city overrun with scum.

When they heard the ruined Saint Ansgar was looking to finance a public transportation system, ideas sprang up there as well. Three Mile High jumped right in and they got things worked out in such a way to connect the rails to each city, thereby creating a lifeline between to the two. Each city knew the other had less than selfless reasons but who cares? Politics might have been founded on the idea of noble prosperity but it runs off of selfish interests and the backs of others.

The rail opened the doors to Three Mile High for Saint Ansgar's commerce, travel, vacation and business. It was no longer a three-hour drive through winding roads and tunnels excavated during The Great Depression to transverse between cities. It was a one-hour train ride. People can live in one town and work in the other if they want. Feasibility had a new face.

There is only one rail line going each way, to and from each, and with very good reason.

Three Mile High was clean then and still mostly clean now; Saint Ansgar has never been clean. Three Mile's city government knew they would be installing a revolving door for their neighboring town's trash to commute back and forth, committing crimes and scumming up the place as they went. But they did it smartly.

Three Mile High put the incoming rail station platform inside a newly constructed complex that just happened to have a police station inside it. The whole thing resembles the vast underground subway stations of New York City and wherever else. Vaulted ceilings, arches, everything tiled and decorated, newsstands and small food vendors. And cops right there, walking a beat and eyeballing everybody. They'd put plain-clothes officers on board the Rail who would ferret out potential jail candidates and radio ahead. Some days I heard it was like shooting fish in a barrel.

Drug mules and common thugs learned very quickly that when they got off the Rail the first thing they encountered were the hungriest, cockiest motherfuckers in law enforcement.

To this day Three Mile High has done a remarkably good job keeping themselves connected to us while not contracting Saint Ansgar's prevalent and vicious diseases. Of course the Big Fry made it there; it made it everywhere. But, overall, it's a better place to be.

The rail station I wait at is empty save for the homeless guy passed out in the corner. The platform smells like stale beer and urine, and the housekeeping crew hasn't been here to tidy up since the Clinton administration.

Standing on the platform tasting the Siberian tinge to the coming morning, I go over the facts again: Abigail can't recall anything about their attacker. Said it was a frenzy; pitch black. Fear scrambled her brains. She was trying to protect the little girl. Her husband got a few good punches in, put the guy through the drywall. Football tackle. Said the attacker took that one pretty hard but in the end he clubbed Tyler. Then went right for her. She said she took the blow cradling the baby; shielding the girl with her body.

Darla Boothe was at work. Came home and her place was already being tended to by the FD. Investigator Rudd filled her in on the sketchy details. The front door was kicked in. Various misogynistic phrases were spray painted on the walls. It seemed the intruder graffitied the place and then used rubbing alcohol to soak a pile of bed sheets. Only half the place had been eaten alive by the time the FD started fighting. So far, Clevenger said no prints. Rudd is checking ex-boyfriends, guys Darla thinks she might have given the wrong impression to.

Apparently Benjamin Boothe just got out of stir. He took a beef for rape. Date rape. Drunk and on drugs, he said she was cool with it and she said she wasn't. The sentencing judge was compassionate with him.

Maybe Ben Boothe is tearing through his old hit list. Wife, daughter, Derne: man who took his place. I wonder who the rape complainant was. If it is Ben Boothe doing this, she's got to have it coming. If she hasn't bitten it already. Clevenger said he heard from Investigator Rudd that Boothe's old cellmate was a firebug.

I need to talk to Ben Boothe. I'd like to talk to the rape victim.

Finally the train comes rolling along, its metal-on-metal screeching a mating call in the ice-crusted night. It stops and the doors open but no one steps off. No one wants to come here. I step on in the first car and the doors shut me inside.

A homeless woman sits propped up in a corner snoring so loud I have to get three cars away from her before the sound ceases. Two punks are huddled together a few cars back but neither takes notice of me as I pass by. The population is sparse and bleak. I ease myself into a seat and shift the weight of my revolver.

The snow has been falling heavier in the last few hours. I settle in for the ride. The cocooning white-out dances about, a ravenously hungry thing opening its mouth for us at the final train whistle.

28

With a ghostly hum of metal on metal, the Rail meets Three Mile High and stops.

I've spent the ride drawing lines along the case, which is quickly becoming something much bigger than Derne hiring me to find one little lost lamb.

The brakes squeal as we slow. I start to get up and notice a runner of color streak down my vision. I sit back down. Easy. Another runner drips across the world. My heart gallops. I hate it when this happens and I'm in public. You never know the intentions of those walking past you. One might get an idea. Hand on my iron and then the world floods with the numbing effects of the Big Fry.

Blooms of cancerous color explode before me. My damaged brain fires off in flourishes of hot pigments before they transubstantiate into gentler, colder hues. Drizzles of that sickly vividness paint my internal everything and then, one by one, slowly erase as if all my mind needed to do was misfire for a moment before it simply reset.

I think one woman was startled by me. As I come back around she's staring at me and nearly trips as she exits the train. I clear my throat, check to make sure I haven't pissed myself, get up, get off the train.

The usual: throngs of morning commuters bustling this way and that. I break the underground's threshold and the crisp mountain air tastes positively delicious.

Three Mile High in all its glory. A clean landscape of an ice blue metropolis. Tones of cobalt, azure, glacial sapphires and diamonds fill my world. This town is the ski resort polar opposite of Saint Ansgar. About the only thing they have in common is Three Mile High got the snow also. Blankets on the city.

My phone starts rattling. Clevenger.

"Hey, buddy."

Clevenger snorts. Then, "Just thought you'd want to know that Pierce White's wife said he went missing."

"When?"

"This morning."

"Hmmm..."

"Not a missing persons report or anything, just he's left and not returned. Nothing special to report other than I know you've had an eye on him."

"Yeah. He was an old boyfriend of Delilah Boothe's. Got shit-canned over their affair. Divorced, too. Admitted that a few months back right before she disappeared he was sleeping with her again. He seemed to think she gave him an STD."

"You think he took off looking for her?"

"Don't know. He already railroaded himself once over her. His entire life went tits up. Maybe I shouldn't have teased him with Delilah."

"Yeah. But it could just be that his new wife is a huge bitch or he's tired of the ghosts he's got in this town. I'll keep you posted."

"Thanks. I'm in Three Mile High. Looking up the other boyfriend Boothe got fired. This one should be more fun. He's a hophead."

"You and drug addicts. This should end poorly."

"One can only hope," I say.

"Be careful up there in that quiet mountain vacation spot. Word is the Freaky Frigid Flasher is back at the ski resort. He struck again last night. I also hear they raised their court fees so don't get pulled over. And some thief is vandalizing ATMs. Hit a string of them in the past two months."

"If only the most horrible crime we came up with in Saint Ansgar was ATM robbers," I say, looking around. "If the Freaky Frigid Flasher runs up to me, opens his coat and shows me his cold, shrunken package, I'll throw a hot cup of coffee on his nude pieces."

"And that's why you're my favorite guy, Richard," Clevenger says. "Because I know you'll do it."

He knows I'll do it because I've done it before. He and I were canvassing a bayside shopping strip for a crime we caught the week before. It was getting pretty cold so the homeless were starting to do things that would get them arrested.

Any given homeless guy carried a warrant or two with him wherever he went. They were like an insurance policy. Homeless would dodge the cops in all the seasons except winter. Then they'd do some stupid shit right in front of someone, get arrested and the warrant would be revealed on a records check. The bum was essentially cashing in that insurance policy.

It paid off. A warm bed, three meals a day. A sentence that would last them until spring.

Anyways, Clevenger and I were canvassing. It was cold out. I had my large, black coffee. The lid was off to cool it down enough to drink instead of sip. I hate sipping. Sipping is for fags. Some homeless guy pops up, yells "Hey fuzz!" and exposes his entire chest and groin to us. A white belly like a dead fish. Large, ungainly nipples separated by a patch of wiry hair. Ribs protruding like they were the most important detail in the picture.

He just wanted to get arrested. What he got instead was my whole cup of steaming coffee flung at his gut. The dead fish white belly went angry red as it splashed up and down him. He screamed, threw his jacket back in place and ran. Clevenger kept saying "No one saw, no one saw, no one saw, no one saw..." as we continued on canvassing like nothing happened.

So he knows I'll do it.

I say goodbye and I take a look around. Across the street is a breakfast joint. I make my way over.

The double doors open and the warmth hits me like a wall. Stainless steel and vinyl everywhere. Bright lights. I can smell butter, bacon and coffee as overwhelming as the scent of blood in a slaughterhouse. I walk up to the counter. The help is sandy blonde, early twenties, ripe. Her neck is all slender curves and creamy skin. Her breasts would fit nicely in my hand. She smacks her gum and looks at me. Her disinterest couldn't be more apparent. No desire in being awake this early.

"Tall black coffee and the phone book," I say.

"I don't know if we have one of those."

"A big cup of coffee? Or the phone book?"

"Phone book." Annoyed.

"Check."

"Just call 411."

"No."

"Fine." Huff.

"Oh, and leave room for cream."

A cup of coffee appears on the counter and I take it. She digs for a minute in the back and comes out with their battered copy of the city directory.

"Leave it on the counter. My boss doesn't want you walking off with it."

"Sure."

She either doesn't notice or care as I uncap the coffee and produce a flask from my jacket. If she watches me take it out she's got to see my iron also. I top off the coffee with booze. She sets a half and half creamer carafe before me and I drop a single white tear into the cup, as milky as the skin running down from her jaw and disappearing into her blouse.

I take an envelope out from my jacket and open up a printed copy of my notes for the case. James Dobbins. Arrested two months ago on possession with intent to distribute. Released on bail. Arrested two years back for public intoxication. Three DUI's. Criminal use of weapons. Resisting. Obstruction. Assault. I look at the address I found for him; look in the phone book. Bingo. Got him. Maybe four miles away. Too early for a convicted junkie to be awake.

I look at the girl. She's still standing there, watching me. She has her own cup now, a tall one with very little coffee lurking at the bottom. She smacks her gum. I make eye contact. Hazel. Her left ear is pierced twice; her right once.

I look at her breasts. She taps her cup on the rim. Must be the fee for staring.

I shrug. I top her off with the rest of my whiskey. Tear out the page with Dobbins' address just to be safe. I don't pay. She doesn't say anything.

The door closes behind me and the mountain-side air washes over me. This place feels so clean and pure, as if it were a pocket of Heaven cradled into the planet.

And I am going to look for the devils that nest here.

29

Three crisp cigarettes later and I hail a cab, maybe half a mile away from the breakfast joint.

The cab disgorges me a few blocks east of Dobbins' place. I walk the rest of the way. Scouting.

Dobbins' house: a shitty bungalow in a shitty neighborhood. Fifty feet by one hundred feet of land, all bland, flat and featureless. No bushes. One tree, struggling to be anything more than an oversized twig. Dead brown grass exposed through the snow by rings of dog piss. The siding is old. The windows are old. The roof is peeling like scales on a diseased reptile. The front door looks cheap. Easy to kick in. No car in the splintered, uneven driveway. No garage at all. One story. A stoop held up by two rotting wooden beams with the house numbers nailed into it.

He must have inherited this place from his folks. They probably paid it off back in the late '70s, died in the late '90s and now he crashes here and lets it rot. A junkie's dream: having a safe pad to bump and virtually no responsibility for it.

Derne said this cat walked the straight and narrow for the time he was in and out of Delilah's life. Married to a gal for a year or so before he started dating Delilah. Able to land a semi-respectable job with the skills he learned in some trade college before he doped out. Met Delilah, ruined it all. Got back on the poison. Leads him here.

You see them around; you went to school with them. They were all in elementary. All but one or two were in middle. Less made it to high school. A few held their brain cells together long enough to graduate.

The rest: folks who have talent, smarts and a good

beginning to their lives. Clean-cut people who have a jagged edge to their decision making process. Sometimes the important choices fall into the crack underneath that jagged edge. They just up and try drugs one day. Then you see those same folks two, three, five years later and they've aged eighty years. They're skeletons with no teeth, lines running through their patch-colored skin so deep you can't imagine the things they've seen over dope. The things they've *done* over dope. Open sores are little more than a nuisance to be nervously picked at.

I go around back. A few lawn chairs on a patio. Mounds of cigarette butts and beer bottles strewn about. I smell ordure and vomit. Party place. Opium den.

I draw my iron and nudge the backdoor. Quiet.

The rank scent inside hits me: a wet ashtray mixed with alcohol mixed with emesis mixed with the metallic odors of burning drugs. The hardwood floors are so chewed up and marred they might as well be firewood. The kitchen is filthy; the sink is spilling garbage and food like a dumpster after an animal picks through it.

I smell dog shit. I don't see a dog. The curtains in the living room are drawn but the morning sun fights through. It creates an ashen, smoggy haze; a dungeon gloom. The bathroom is grimy. One bedroom is empty. Used and dirty drug paraphernalia litter the next bedroom. Inside it a TV is still turned on with some tripped-out Japanimation porno running in the background.

Cartoon sex and needles. A burnt spoon.

The third bedroom has a male, maybe thirty, scrawny, passed out face down on a mattress. No box springs. No frame. Just a mattress sitting on the floor. There is an indent where his head lays. There is one brown stain on top of the next where his crotch lays. I get the feeling he's had this mattress for a long time and he's been abusing it since day one. A single dresser with one drawer missing.

A wallet sits on the dresser. I open it. James Dobbins. Non-driver state-issued ID. He's got two twenties. I take both.

I don't see any weapons. I don't see anything that could be used as one. No one asleep anywhere else. He snores like he hasn't slept in days. Might not have. I kick him.

"James." My voice carries through the still house like a titan's demand rattling out of a cave.

He barely stirs. I kick again. Harder. Ribs.

"*James.*"

"Huhhh...what?"

His eyes burst open when they recognize the barrel of a gun pointed at him.

"Where is Delilah Boothe?"

"Oh my God, dude, Jesus fucking Christ, I—what the fuck is going on here man! Who are—"

"Tell me where Boothe is."

I cock back the hammer. His bloodshot, watery eyes glisten with all the moisture he has left in his body. His teeth are varying shades of yellow and black. His track marks are ten shades darker than his light complexion. Black hair mussed and matted by days of indifference. His lips so parched they crack. New blood spots dried next to old blood spots. Sores. Hard lines. Sunken cheeks. Waste.

"Delilah Boothe," I say. His eyes search for recognition of the English language.

People who are poor liars will show it. Their eyes dart everywhere looking for a convincing answer. I've had illegal Mexicans mumble and speak gibberish—not Spanish, gibberish—when I ask for ID. I've had drug dealers make up a new story with every breath when I ask for details. I've had warrant arrests that lie about what the warrant is for. They accuse police of making shit up. *I took care of that last month, Officer. I swear. There must be some mistake.* I've arrested a DUI who told me the reason he doesn't have a license is because he was recently robbed at gunpoint. He gave me a fake case number. He never mentioned how his driving privileges were permanently revoked. And later on, I found one license in his front seat. I found another one in his glove box. Then he couldn't figure out how in the world him having those was possible. Liars lie.

Drug abusers are disconnected from reality. Obviously. Their brains sometimes have to legitimately search for facts, details and chains of events. That makes things more difficult. Their minds are scattered and awkwardly jump from one important focus to the next. And the universal rule about that is: whatever is an important focus to a drug user during questioning is never what is important to the officer during questioning. Berating hopheads to keep them on topic is one technique I'm good at. Coming down hard on anybody for anything is one technique I'm good at.

And of course, most times the drug abusers are also poor liars.

"Dude, I got no fucking clue! Dude! I don't even know a Deborah!"

"Delilah. You ruined your marriage for her. Remember her now?"

"My marriage? To Autumn? Hey, that was years back, man. I got—"

"Try harder. Delilah Boothe. She fenced some dope through you not too long ago."

"I, uhhh..." The first sweat bead runs down his face. Bingo. I press my heater against his forehead. "Oh shit...you're the five-oh, ain't ya?"

"No."

"You gotta be. With that hair cut? You gotta be. I think I uhhh...I think that—oh! Delilah! Yes. Yes she came over for dinner. It was just tacos and shit. I think she left a pair of panties here somewhere...just let me dig around—"

I lean in. "Where is she?"

Two ideas suddenly make a connection with James. A new look of horror now: "You...you with the dealer she took from? Oh Christ, say you ain't—"

Let him believe it. New angle: "I'm willing to work with you on this."

He tries to cry. I'm not sure if he's trying to drum up sympathy in me or if he's really this distraught. Either way, I don't care.

"Tears don't mean shit, James. Answers do."

"Dude, I swear the last time I seen her was about three months ago. Okay?"

Me, staring.

Brink of hyperventilation: "Yeah, so it was like four— no! Five months ago and I, uhh...I—"

Me, still staring. The timeline is bullshit but asking a junkie for solid, unwavering numbers is like asking Nancy Pelosi to wipe that insane plastic surgery surprise off her face.

"She rolled in all scared, had a load of shit with her. Said she didn't know where to turn. Knew I dabbled in the shit, thought I could help. She got all at ease with me when she realized I knew enough to score for us both. She'd been evicted, bro. Her old man or whatever tossed her ass from the house we used to party in and everything. I guess he got out of prison and came home and just threw her shit out. What a dick. But she needed cash. She didn't have shit. Hell, she coasted into my driveway on fumes. I had to take a gas can like two miles down the road just to—"

"I don't care about her fuel situation. I want to know about the dope and her."

"Right, right. Give me a minute to remember. I'm not Einstein or anything. Well, I told her I knew some dudes

150

who sold to me here and there. I woulda sold it myself but my PO, she's a cunt. She doesn't piss test me so often anymore but if word got 'round that I was dealin'...damn I'd be in stir for fuckin' life."

"What are you on probation for?"

"I was set up. Cops actin' like I killed somebody but I just went for a drive and they're sayin' I was high or some shit—"

"What's your PO's name?"

"Officer Something. Bro, put your gun down."

"Forget that," I say. "Delilah Boothe. Talk."

He's sweating now. Nothing like waking up to a gun and the end of your life.

"Yeah, okay. Okay." He wipes his face, then one armpit. He wipes the other, drags his hands down his flannel sleeping pants. I can smell the BO. "So anyways...I took some off the top of the shit—had to pay myself first, right? —and I brokered a deal with these guys. A cool ten grand for the shit. I got no idea where they scored the money, honest. The shit was easily worth fifteen or twenty on the streets but she jumped at it. I think she wanted to be rid of it, is all. They coulda offered her twenty bucks and she woulda took it. She'd take anythin'."

"How'd she get it?"

"Said some friends left it in her house and then went to jail. Found it while she was packin' to move out. Didn't want the jail birds to squeal and her go down for it also."

"Why not just dump it then? Or turn it over to the police?"

"How the fuck would I know, huh? Scared, I guess. No, no nono. It was more than that, I bet. Money, bro. The root of all evil. The reason why Nixon went into Vietnam, bro. Cash money."

"Sure. Then what?"

"We sold it and she took her cut—supposed to be

five—and stole most of mine. Bitch breezed right out the fuckin' door while I was asleep."

I raise an eyebrow.

"Alright, I was passed out. But the meds my doc has me on right now are really bad for my skin and I'm just so fuckin' tired all the time—"

"Then what?"

"Uhhh...then, then...then I called around for her a little bit, down at Roscoe's and shit, but nobody seen her. Bitch fuckin' rammed one up in me."

"What is Roscoe's? Why call there?"

"Bar. Watering hole, you know. I know people there. I introduced her to people there. People go there. Make sense?"

"No. Is that the place where you introduced her to the buyers?"

"I introduced her to everybody there, man. It's fuckin' *Roscoe's.*"

"*Is that the place where you introduced her to the buyers?*"

"Yeah. I think so."

"No one has seen her?"

"No. No. If they had, I'd get my money back. But like I said, bitch rammed one up in me."

"That's it? You just lose all that money and blow it off?"

"Look, bro, I been to prison and I'm on thin ice now. I dig too deep or cast a net too wide and my PO hears about. I go back on the inside. Officer Something ain't got no tolerance for anything. I thought I'd seen the last of Delilah fuckin' Boothe when she broke up with me after we were fired. She showed back up. She'll show up again. It's her way."

I reach over to his wallet. His PO's business card is one of the few things left inside now that I've taken his cash.

There's an extra-large condom which I take out, giggle and toss to the side. Some delusions are funnier than others. I keep the card. I'll probably not do anything with it, but there are never enough small details.

"What about your ex-wife?"

"What about her?"

"She hunting for Boothe?"

"She was pissed as hell, sure. But she's gettin' alimony from my folks while I'm jobless so she can go fuck herself."

"Your mommy and daddy pay your alimony?"

"Fuck you. It's my trust fund. My mom and dad died. After the divorce Autumn took everything but this house. Everything. I shoulda never married the bitch in the first place. As soon as we tied the knot she was going on and on about kids. Fuck that. No kids. Not ever."

"Really?"

"Never. If she got pregnant I had made up my mind to drive her ass right to the abortion clinic. Right to it. If she said no, there's always a stair case."

"That a fact?"

"Fact."

"Get fixed? Take care of the problem on your end?"

"Fuck no. My spunk is all man. I ain't trimmin' my shit just because."

"You sleep with Boothe while she was here with the dope?"

"Yeah. Until we sold the shit."

"You pretty heavy-handed on the meth?" I ask. This guy is not the father. That much is obvious.

"None of your business."

"I just don't get meth. When was the last time you actually blew a load?"

"Fuck you. Ain't none of your business," he says, fuming under his sore-riddled skin.

"Meth increases the sex drive but severely lowers the ability to climax. But you already know that, don't you?"

He just looks away. He hasn't gotten up off his heroin mattress. Finally, eyes still examining the stains on his bed, he says, "Get out of my house, bro. I hooked you up already."

"First things first before I leave. Name the buyers."

"Dude, I don't want—"

"Boothe isn't around to take the hit, you won't name names. You're all I've got. You want to pay the price for it? Be my guest."

He turns whiter than he was before. His sores and track marks glow like Christmas tree lights against his skin. He was getting comfortable there for a minute.

"Dude, if I tell you this then what's gonna happen—"

"Worry about what's going to happen if you *don't*."

"Danny, Blimpie's older brother and some buddy of his. We call him Cherry but he hates it. That's all."

"Who is Blimpie?"

"Some fat retard over at Roscoe's."

"Last name. Address."

"I don't know the street. They both live with their mom. She makes lemonade and spikes it like you've never tasted—"

"Last name and address."

"Gibbens, I think. Gibbens or Gibson or something. I don't know. Danny, man. *Danny.* Lives on Holland. I know that. Holland, like where the drugs are. Get it?"

"How do I find them?"

"Blimpie. That's how *I* find them. Only been to his mom's a few times."

"You better pack your shit and wind up somewhere on the east coast, my friend. I'll be knocking on your door again."

I start to walk out the door.

"Tell Cherry you're looking for her. He might back off," he says.

"Back off what?"

"Her. Delilah. He wants her too, you know."

"Why is that?"

"You can't score that shit once and let it go. And with his temper...if he finds her first and she says she ain't got the juice to get some more...Cherry's been in stir for what he's done to women."

"What good does having that much dope do? If he's a user he'll be set for quite some time. Or he OD's and the problem is solved."

"Naw, bro. Danny and Cherry got a racket goin' on. Word on the street is they've been knockin' over ATMs for capital. Trying to buy into the game. And Delilah, she showed up and dropped the mother-load in their laps. No production costs, high quality shit. Just *bam!* And they sell it. He ain't gonna let it go. No way."

"You don't care one bit, huh?"

"Like I said. The bitch fucked me over and over. There's some voodoo magic about her pussy. It makes you feel invincible and ten-foot-tall. But when it's gone...it's like withdrawal. What it leaves behind destroys a man. Believe me?"

"Your place is a shithole." I walk out, forty bucks richer.

"I keep this place as clean as you keep your shave," he calls after me. I'm at the door when he comes out of the room, excited. Anxious.

"Hey, make sure and tell your people I'm clean of this whole thing and...and I did a lot to help you guys out."

"No," I say and leave.

Let him sweat for it.

30

After the whole Jefferson Stoke thing, the brass decided to transfer me out of homicide.

There were some questions about the incident. Like I said, the SRT boys who made it into the house when the shot went off gave conflicting stories. I passed a polygraph on Stoke's death. I'm that good.

But so did every SRT member who "saw" what happened. Each was little different. It's the inherent problem with the bullshit polygraph. George Constanza announced it to his best buddy and all of America one night on prime time television: "Remember, Jerry, it's not a lie if *you* believe it."

The SRT boys had nothing to lose. They were honest. Belief.

If you can focus on a single dot on the wall, you can pass it. If you can keep yourself from sweating bullets, you can pass it. If you take some blood pressure meds beforehand, you can pass it. Nothing is certain anywhere, and I'll bet my annual take-home that any polygraph examiner will be throwing the bullshit flag on me for stating that, but trust me and the countless number of other folks in jobs where they had to pass a polygraph.

You can pass it and lie your ass off.

Back to Stoke: there were five different polygraphs, five different stories, five truthful read-outs. In the end it was ruled as a suicide. That's good; Jefferson Stoke pulled his own trigger. So it *was* suicide. I just focused on that. I also tiptoed around any kind of allegation that had the word "assistance" in it. It was a careful dance; but I'm a damned six-foot-two ballerina when it comes to such things.

The air cleared. Took a while, but it blew over. There

were lingering crosshairs aimed at me. This wasn't the first time IA and I ran into each other. Seems no one notices you while you're setting records in homicide for closing cases with convictions. But as soon as a questionable death by violent means pops up—literally—in your lap all of a sudden you might not be a great cop.

A woman by the name of Cassandra Flemming worked in IA. Headhunter. Internal Affairs is a necessary branch of police departments; they keep the cops in line who take dope off of pushers and then sell it on the street themselves. They take care of the cops who help themselves to the evidence locker when no one is looking.

Flemming made it her business to sink good cops. Our breed deals with three things: tension, uncertainty and rapidly evolving circumstances. Cops make decisions in deep shit all the time. Some are better than others. Some are more costly than others. Some you can't let get away. Some just need a slap on the wrist or further training.

Flemming didn't slap wrists; she slit throats. Or she lodged knives in peoples' backs. That's not IA. That's a wolf in sheep's clothing. And she didn't like me. The situation with Stoke opened the door and she shouldered her way in.

Any transfers in the department that do not occur on a payday Sunday are disciplinary. I was transferred on a Wednesday afternoon.

That told me something.

I was sent to the stolen vehicles unit, where rookies who barely passed the detectives' exam went to cut their teeth. There is an ancient legend that has been passed down in whispers from investigator to investigator about the stolen cars unit: it was created as a reservoir of those the PD wishes to forget, or push out.

The PD wasn't going to forget me. Not after Stoke. Not after a lot of things, really.

They wanted me out. Cassandra Flemming wanted me out. She got stolen vehicles instead. Same thing, longer period of suffering.

Good detectives will have good cases wherever they work. I tried. My time there was unremarkable save one thing. One thing that, in the end, cost me everything. Jared Garrett came knocking.

Narcotics will pull in fresh faces now and then to do controlled buys. Cops are easier to trust than CI's. Garrett asked me to do some controlled buys against a Big Fry dealer. Seems his case was hinged on some crackhead CI who was so-so to begin with and had turned up dead. OD. I wanted anything I could get to pull me away from my punishment desk in stolen vehicles. So I said yes. I should not have.

Doing the buys weren't hard. It was the hit afterwards that cooked my goose.

Roscoe's.

Somewhere around 9 a.m. a fat bald guy unlocks the door to the bar. Two guys have been waiting outside the place longer than me. Both go right to the counter. The fat guy walks around the place and grabs two mugs. Fills them up. Serves. No orders, no talk. All habit.

My kind of bartender.

I watch the door for a moment, see if the off-coming police shift walks in. Sometimes that happens. Midnights get off work as the sun rises but to them, it's their evening. And who doesn't want a beer or two before bed? Lord knows I do. But no cops show up.

I sit down away from the customers and I light up a smoke. The fat guy comes over.

"City says you can't do that."

"I say I can. What do you say?"

He reaches under the bar a little ways down and produces an ashtray. "I don't tell customers what they can't do." He holds the ashtray in his hand. "You a customer?"

"I am today."

"What'll it be then?"

"So eager to get booze in a man at this hour?"

"The way I see it, you're sitting at bar, maybe *I* ain't the one so eager to get booze in you. If you ash on the floor instead of in this here tray you'll be fucking up my mop job. I don't take kindly to that. So you want to smoke, you need an ashtray. You need an ashtray; so you need to be a customer. What'll it be?"

I smile. My kind of bartender. "Stout on tap?"

"Yup. Local brew."

"Like it?"

"Yup."

"I'll take one."

He sets down the ashtray. Mozies off. Returns with the beer.

"Anything else?"

"Yeah. Blimpie." I sit my smoke down in the ashtray and eyeball him. The bartender gives me a distrusting look.

"Blimpie don't work today," he says.

"What'll it cost to whip up a shift for him that started ten minutes ago?"

"Five hundred. Cash." No hesitation. None.

I drop the bills on the counter. Derne, it goes on your tab.

The bartender walks off and picks up a phone. Dials, no answer. Hangs up. Does it again. And again. The fourth time he speaks to someone. Shouts. Hangs up. Walks back over to me.

"Give him a half hour or so. And no blood in the bar."

"No problem," I say. "One more beer."

I'll try to hold good to the no blood in the bar part. I'll try.

31

Blimpie looks inbred.

Fat retard. Close enough description coming from a junkie. Blimpie comes shuffling through the door, and the bartender shoots me a weary glance. I snap my fingers. Blimpie looks my way, and I point at him. Point to the stool next to me. He hesitates. I will not snap again.

He slinks over as much as his rotund shuffle will allow. Stares at my neck, my collar. My jaw. Over my shoulder. Not my eyes. Too submissive.

"Sit."

He does.

"I want to see your brother. Now."

"Why?"

"The dope they bought off that dame a while back, the one who knows Dobbins."

"I don't—?"

"It wasn't her dope."

"Wait? Dobbins sent you here? Looking for *me*?"

"You, Danny and Cherry."

"Dobbins? Everybody knows that guy as the dude caught sucking dick in the shitter for blow."

"So?"

"So you gonna listen to fags?"

"Yes. Where is Danny?"

"I don't keep tabs."

I lean in. This is pissing me off. "Blimpie, you better *start* keeping tabs. Danny isn't here but *you* are. Get it?"

"I thought I had to work—"

He looks to the bartender and he flicks his eyes at me. Blimpie looks back and I fluff my jacket, showing him the firepower.

"I thought I had to work—"

I grab him by the scruff. One dude at the bar has his wallet open, drops a bill and gets up to leave.

"*I'm* the job today. Where?"

"Okay! Okay!" he trails off, looks away. I blow smoke on him. He coughs, hacks wet.

"Got his number? I'll call him myself." Say it so close my skin burns with the fearful heat radiating off of him.

"No. He'd kill me if—"

"Set it up then. Tell him I represent the folks who rightfully own that shit. Tell him *now*."

At the mention he becomes as uneasy as a rodent in the claws of a bird of prey. They must have talked about what would happen if one day a guy saying what I am saying showed up. There's no way some chick from Saint Ansgar would just roll into town with a load of dope needing to pawn it off who didn't come with some baggage. She had to get it from somewhere. That somewhere is looking for it.

Now Blimpie is sitting across from that guy.

"Now look, mister...*I* had nothing to do with all that, okay? See, I just drop a baggie here and there and I don't think—"

"You better run that mouth of yours into your cell phone before I fucking kill you right here, or I'll take it from your pocket and call your brother while I'm driving to your mother's house over on Holland to blast her. Got it?"

Wide-eyed stare. Any perp thinks you don't know shit. They think they're smarter than they really are. So when you start dropping real life facts about them, stuff like where their mom lives, it helps. They start to sum up the situation in a more realistic way. He looks like he just shit his pants as he says, "Okay, okay."

He dials the number. Fidgets like a heroin addict a few

hours past when they should have bumped but didn't.

"No answer," he says, like that is a final answer to everything and I have to let him go.

"Call Cherry then."

He acts like he didn't think of that before he spoke up. Maybe he didn't. The brains of any operation this kid ain't.

He dials a new number. Bingo.

"Cherry?" he says, nervous as hell calling this guy so early in the morning. A tell about Cherry. "It's Blimpie. Listen...uhhh, you know that thing you and Danny talked about? The thing with the dope...yeah I know, it's just that, well, their guy is *here. He found me and you guys.*"

Interesting how he phrases it *me and you guys.* Not *us.*

He leans away from me, whispers: "He's got a gun."

His eyes crawl to me. I can hear the voice on the other line but the words are nothing.

"Give me the phone."

He shakes his head. No.

No one tells me no.

I take the phone in one swift snatch and my other hand lands in his solar plexus. His dumpy form melts and rolls off the stool in one weighted glob. Slaps the floor.

"You tell that fucking guy he can cut you up all he wants he ain't getting his shit back no way no how! Blimpie? Blimpie! Your fat ass better be repeating me word for fucking word or I swear—"

"Mr. Cherry?" I say.

The other end of the line sobers up.

"Who am I speaking with?" The voice on the other end tries to be firm. I can hear the caged fury eeking out between his teeth. Mad that I show up, derail his perfect plan.

I clear my throat. "My name is Mr. Honey Bunny."

"And what have you done with Blimpie, Honey Bunny."

"*Mr.* Honey Bunny. Blimpie is on the floor, hoping I do not shoot him in the face. First off, Mr. Cherry, I want to assure you and Mr. Danny that the people I represent are not angry with you. They are angry with the woman, but that is another matter which does not concern you. I have it on good authority that you are seeking her out to obtain more of the product you received earlier. Am I correct on that?"

Hesitates. Worried I'm a cop: "I don't know anything about a 'product.'"

"Let her go, Mr. Cherry. I hear James Dobbins turned her dyke. And anyways, she ran off. *Let her go.*" I need to turn him off of the idea of looking for Delilah Boothe. The drug deal will be my angle to refocus him.

"I, uhhh...what?"

"Now, down to business. If you have a market here for our product, we would like to move it. Ideally we would ship twice a month through mules and drop off at a mutually agreeable third party location where you and your associates would distribute. You would be allowed to keep thirty percent. How amenable are you to such a proposition?"

A pause. The silent air of confusion becomes the stinging air of seething anger on Cherry's end. He doesn't buy a word of it and neither would I. Read on Cherry: dumb, impetuous and steers his life wherever his rage problem wants to go.

Finally he says, "I don't know what you're talking about and tell you what, bub, go fuck yourself."

Click. Silence.

I look down to Blimpie. I look at the phone and finger through his buttons to the REDIAL command. Press it. Voice mail.

"Mr. Cherry, this is Mr. Honey Bunny. Have it your way then. The offer has been retracted. Within twenty-four hours you, your families and your friends will be red smears. No one tells us to fuck ourselves."

I hang up. Pocket the phone.

"Alright. We're done."

Blimpie recoils into his lard. A jelly turtle, scared and alone.

I crush out the smoke, drain my beer. Stand up. Blimpie crawls like a bug cut in half but still trying to move.

I drop one of Dobbins' twenties and head out. I hear Blimpie use the bar top to lift himself and the bartender says, "Where're you goin'?"

Blimpie says, "I thought *he* was the job today?"

The bartender says, "He *was*. Now sweep the parlor and do a better job than you did last night."

32

Hail a cab.

Got to make this quick. I ask the cabbie to take me to a liquor store where the clerk speaks English. Takes him several minutes to think of one, and of course he drives around the whole time. Takes him close to fifteen to get there. I go in, come out with two packages and tell him where to go next.

The breakfast joint is the same way I left it. I walk in, the waitress notices me. We meet at the counter.

I set the bottle down on the counter. Brown paper bag. She eyeballs it, looks to me.

"You wanna fuck me or somethin'?"

"Would the bottle do it?"

"Seriously?"

"I need your phone book again."

"You wanna know my age?"

"No."

"Probably the right answer, mister."

She snatches the bottle off the counter and comes back with the directory. I look up Danny Gibbens-something. Bingo. Daniel Gibson, address on Holland. Tear the page out.

I walk out and hear the waitress say, "The bottle *would* do it. In case you're curious."

"Yes, I was curious," I mutter and leave.

33

The cabbie drops me a block away from Roscoe's.

I walk the distance. Smoke. Hide the bottle in my jacket. It keeps me warm. I make it to the bar and both Danny and Cherry are already there. I can see them through the front window. Danny looks like Blimpie only thinner and with less hair. Cherry must be the third guy. They're berating Blimpie.

The bartender mans up and kicks them out. They storm off to a delivery van, peel out. I note the license plate.

Blimpie wanders out onto the sidewalk and stares down the road as the two others streak off. He looks like the word *distraught* doesn't begin to suffice right now. I used to see the same look on dudes who had gotten out of prison and immediately get arrested for another felony. They knew they were going back and this time it'd be worse. That's Blimpie right now.

I walk up behind him. Take him by the arm and keep walking. He startles at my touch. Darts his head my way and his face scrunches up into a little baby's cry-face.

"Just walk. If you cry this will get out of hand," I say, lift up on his arm. He walks. Chokes back the tears.

"Let me get this straight," I say, light a smoke with one hand. "Dobbins sold you guys a pretty good score of Big Fry."

"Y-yes," he squeaks out. "Well, Danny and Cherry really. Not me. I just work at the bar—"

"Why those two?"

"They used to deal small stuff. Little bit of weed and whatnot."

"So Dobbins picks the first dealer he can think of and drops the score of a lifetime in their lap?"

"Well, I-ughhh...I guess. Well, Cherry had been spreading the word they were trying to bust into the game, you know? Make it work—"

"They were trying to become full-time dealers?"

"Yeah, that's it. I'm not really involved—"

"Knock off your horseshit. You're involved." I hate that. Anyone who's afraid of the consequences will dime out their own mother if that's what it takes. Every second of everyday a cop hears a chicken shit downplay his role in crime and shift all the blame onto someone else.

"Have they broken in?" I ask. We round the corner.

"They uhhh...they sold the stuff Dobbin's got 'em and now they're uhhh...popular. They needed more dope is all. Dobbins couldn't turn up anymore, especially for the price he took for the first batch. So they want the girl. Well, Cherry does more than Danny. The folks they sold to are starting to go to other dealers already. Their street cred is drying up. They found another supplier who wants a shitload of cash. And...uhhh..."

Blimpie trails off. Of course their street credit is drying up. Junkies don't wait for a hit. They move on to whoever has their fix.

Blimpie doesn't start back up and I grip him by the neck. We round the next corner. One more right hand turn and we'll be heading back to the bar.

"Finish the story, turd," I say as I squeeze his neck until his eyes close and his teeth grit. "You were doing so well."

"Okay!" he says and I let up. Encouragement. "They stole those ATM's that have turned up missing...you know, the three that were on the evening news? They went to a hotel and stole a truck. They used that to hit three ATM's and drag them to a storage shed outside of town. Just *bam bam bam.* Cherry said it would be like the movie *Gone in 60 Seconds.* You know, by the time they notice the first one missing all three will be hidden. That was like two days ago."

"Have they gotten inside them yet?"

"They don't tell me that kind of stuff, man. I just work at the bar. Okay? I didn't steal your drugs or nothin'. I just—"

"So why do they still want the girl?"

"She's got the fuckin' hook-ups, bro! Cherry was pissed he needed to steal an ATM to get the same amount that girl sold 'em for next to nothin'. Cherry said it cut into the bottom line."

We round the corner and stop two storefronts down from the bar.

"So those two douchebags sell some pot to high school friends, then decide it's time to become full-time dealers and the girl comes along and gives them the score of a lifetime. That's not enough so they look for her again, can't find her, steal ATMs and now are hunting for her because the bottom line isn't what Cherry thinks it should be. Do I have the story?"

"Yeah. I guess. I'm not really in their deals or nothin', man. I'm on the outside of it all."

"Get back in the bar," I say. "If you tell Danny and Cherry about this I'll fucking kill you. Got it?"

He shakes his head. Turns white. I let go and he numbly walks into the bar. Obedient.

I pull out Blimpie's phone. Dial Danny's number from the address book.

"What?" Danny screams. Blimpie must have forgotten to mention I took his phone.

"Back at the bar, Danny. You forgot something."

"What?"

"*You forgot something at the bar, Danny.*"

Dawning realization now: "Who—who is this?"

"Better pick him up before I do." I hang up.

I finish another cigarette before they make it back. Park the van, leave it running. Doors unlocked. Rush inside. I'm in the back of the van before they get back out.

34

They make Blimpie drive his own car.

I'm lying down in the back of the van, .44 Magnum out, the gun panting. Asking impatiently to shoot someone. All in due time.

We're on the street, Cherry driving. We're breaking the speed limit, that's for sure.

The conversation is not good.

Cherry: "Dude, I know he's your brother but who cares? I mean, first of all he's only your *half*-brother. Even your mom says she doesn't know who his father is—"

Danny: "Dude. She knows, she's just embarrassed or something about it because, quite frankly, she dates a lot of guys. But who even cares? Seriously, we're in over our heads here—"

Cherry: "*No*, we are *not*. These are growing pains. I told you shit is going to happen. Just does. This game pays, Danny. But, sometimes it fucks with you, that's all. You fuck back. This is top-dog shit right here. We're gonna be top-dog."

Danny: "Dude, watch where you're going and slow down. Blimpie can barely keep up. Now, listen. I know *growing pains* and all but this—"

Cherry: "Whoever these guys are looking for their dope, and whoever this bull is muscling Blimpie, they've got nothing. Understand me? What, a fiend cocksucker like Dobbins diming us out? I'm still not sure that wasn't a sting. The bull is probably a Three Mile High cop and—"

Danny: "I don't care. We get out of this. We're already in deep shit if they figure out how we got the cash to buy into the market in the first place. Dude, what if they *are* cops?"

Cherry: "We lay low. I got a real job; you got a real job—"

"Dude, you're a night attendant at a gas station and I clean—"

"Shut the fuck up. Bottom line, Danny: Blimpie and Dobbins are the weak links here. Simple. You and I would be avoiding this mess completely if it weren't for them. Think about it. Simple, bro. Simple."

Danny: "I'm not going to do anything to Blimpie just because he's dumb and scared—"

"Then fuck yourself. You listen to me, Danny. *You fucking listen good.* I *owe* your stupid retard brother one for squealing to the cops about me and Loren—"

"Dude, drop that shit! Seriously! He never—"

"I got convicted of domestic violence for that! You know I can't legally even go hunting now! I can't own a damn rifle!"

"You really think the cops needed Blimpie's story? You really think that? 'Cuz I think Loren, with a broken nose, fractured arm and contusion—I think that little tune-up spelled it out for you! So stop calling my brother a fat retard! I ain't going down with you on this dope shit!"

"You think *you* got troubles with this, Danny? Do ya? If we get convicted on distribution that'll be my third strike! Get me? I ain't talkin' about no baseball! *Third strike! You're out!* Gone for life!"

Danny mumbles. I'm sure he's quite tired of being lectured and yelled at. Cherry takes some deep breaths. Rolls down a window. I hear the spark of flint, smell tobacco.

Cherry: "Fuck that. I'll do whatever it takes. I ain't goin' back. No way. This is my time, Danny. *Our* time. We've got a plan and we've stuck to it. This shit ain't more than a hiccup."

Danny: "Are you saying Blimpie and Dobbins are only

'hiccups'? What're you gonna do, Cherry? What are you gonna do?"

"I said *I'll do whatever it takes.*" Cherry goes cold. I've heard that tone from an interview room a few times. When an animal masquerading as a man finds itself cornered and at the end of the line, sometimes they'll turn like this. This situation just grew thorns. "Keep that in mind, Danny."

"You're talking about murder and that ain't no hiccups—"

The scenery changes. The ride becomes rough. Sliding. Off road.

Danny: "What the fu—Where are you goin'?"

Cherry: "Short cut. Trust me."

Danny: "Jesus, Cherry. I can't believe Blimpie is following us. You are out of—"

Cherry: "Don't forget that your half-brother knows about the ATMs. And the drugs. And everything."

No response from Danny.

"What if that bull shows back up at Dobbins' place and offers him immunity to testify that he set up the deal between us and the bitch?"

Danny: "No one said for sure the bull was a cop. He might just be muscle—"

"Pig or muscle; who cares? Either way, Dobbins and Blimpie will squeal. Both those lousy fucks. If the bull is a Three Mile High cop he's going to be squeezing Blimpie. He probably already did. Put the fear of God in him about going to prison over this horseshit. Retards don't last in the pen. Trust me."

"For the last time, he ain't retarded! He's just stupid. Besides, I thought you were looking for the girl."

Cherry: "Yeah, I was. And that piece of shit Dobbins told me she was shackin' up with her daddy."

Well, Mr. Dobbins. Funny that didn't come up earlier.

Cherry some more: "But it don't matter now 'cuz that muscle found us!"

Danny: "He said he represented who—"

Cherry: "And it's bullshit, Danny! He's a cop and he's wired, tryin' to get us to admit sellin' dope! Somebody squealed!"

"I cannot believe you want me to consider...*Blimpie. Blimpie, man.* Fuck you."

"Then you're a bigger retard than that lardass brother of yours. I'm telling you."

"I swear, Cherry, you listen to me. *Now.* You try and hurt Blimpie and I will take the whole thing to the cops myself! Got me? *I'll* squeal and then you won't have to blame my little brother—"

Cherry: "Fuck you then!"

"Fuck *me*? No, fuck *you*! I'm out!"

"You're damn right you're out, Danny. *You and your fat retard brother both.*" Cold.

Go time.

Gunshot. Just like that. Loud as cannon fire in this enclosed space. Danny slumps. Still breathing. Not flailing or moaning. Just taking his time to blink out.

I hear something pouring. Quick and consistent at first, then a drizzle. Then individual splashes. The carpet beneath him is red.

35

A blur.

The van yanks to a stuttering halt and banks off to the left. We hit something. Another car. Gunfire. Blimpie screaming; even through the two vehicles and all the glass and metal and the smell of gunfire and the shots resonating, I can hear Roscoe's whipping boy in his death throes.

Cherry screaming to no one left alive: "I ain't goin' back to the fuckin' pen on a third strike! I'll play the game on my own! Fuck you guys!"

A screeching halt. Engine killed. I look around the bases of the seats. See his leg sticking through. I shoot it. There goes his entire knee.

Screams. He empties his weapon. Half in the ceiling; shock, surprise, agony. The other half back my direction; way too high. He doesn't know what he's shooting at. He's just shooting.

I count fifteen empty clicks from the weapon. I hear the glove box fumble Then nothing. I stand up. Claim my prize.

36

Danny's facial expression is that telltale mix of blank, relaxed and peaceful that only the dead wear.

Blimpie is slumped over his steering wheel, forehead resting on it. His brains painted along the inside driver's window. A mess. Cherry has lost so much blood his skin as white as the innocence of a newborn.

We're at least a half-mile off the road. This part of Three Mile High is desolate, near the foothills of the mountains. Bizarrely flat. No wandering cars or police will be moseying by unless they see the snow tracks running off the road back a ways. I figure I have a little time, which is more than Cherry does.

In my back pocket I keep a pair of good latex gloves. Slap them on.

I take a bottle of water rolling around the inside of the van and flip the cap off. Splash Cherry. Must be freezing.

"Uhhh—" is all he can manage.

"What is this girl's name?"

Delirious. Pain-racked and mostly dead: "I just—I..."

I shake him. Think about splashing more water. "Her name. What did Dobbins say her name was?"

"Start with...a 'B.' No...'D.' As is...I can't think now. My leg..."

"Dobbins said she was living with her father?"

"Yeah..."

"Did he say when?"

"Now...I guess...he—"

I wait. Nothing. Splash some more water. His eyes jut open. Shock of it. Frigid shock.

"What did Dobbins do?"

"He had an...address..."

"Hers?"

"Don't- don't know. It—she lived...Dobbins gave—"

"Gave it to you?"

His head nods *yes.* So Dobbins actually *knows* Ben Boothe's address and sold Delilah out to Cherry. Cherry, the winner convicted of DV and whatever other felonies who is perfectly willing and able to kill his own friends.

"Where is the address now?"

Fading: "Dresser...right on top..."

He looks off in the distance. Smiles. I'm sure he sees the long line of his ancestors coming to greet him into their family in the afterlife. I'm sure right now they are beautiful and forgiving and just want him to be with them where it is safe and warm and far from knowing pain.

He can't help me anymore. But thanks to this asshole I'm going to have to walk back to the road. I cover his mouth and nose with my glove. He doesn't struggle. Off, go on your way, Cherry.

I wonder if his ancestors could see that.

37

Takes three hours total.

Cherry was digging in his glove box for a spare magazine. I found it. Siphon gas from the car tanks, soak the insides of the cars. The inferno sends smoke into a good wind which carries it towards the mountains and not the city. Gives me time to beat feet before EMS arrives.

The sun is high and still the world is frozen when I get to Dobbins' house. He's alone. In through the back door; he hasn't done much about it from when I entered this morning.

There is he is, the accoutrement of a dirt bag surrounding him: pipe laying on the carpet, crumpled wrapper from a Twinkie, a skin mag dedicated to publishing amateur photos taken in poorly-lit basements with girls who might or might not be legally sound mind enough for consent.

Both thumbs slapping away on a joystick to a video game system. He looks up. He's shirtless, has on sweat pants. The crotch darkens with urine.

"Hey, buddy," I say. The controller falls from his hands. Limp now. "I thought you hadn't seen Delilah Boothe for a while now."

"Yeah—well, no—I just—see, this is the thing—"

"But you knew she was crashing with her dad, huh?"

"Now that was like last week, man. Who knows where she is—"

"How did you find this out?"

"I took her there," he says. Small. Very small. His eyes turn red. Wet. "Look, mister, I—"

"Anything else you left out?"

"No. I swear. I—"

"Why'd she go to her dad's?"

"I dunno but she's there. She's *there.* Please understand that whatever Danny and Cherry said—"

I say goodbye with six rounds from Cherry's gun.

38

Cab picks me up four blocks over.

Drops me off a few blocks from Cherry's house. I tear a twenty in half, drop one piece in the front seat and say, "Meet me here in half an hour." He nods, pockets the piece where his boss won't be checking.

I smoke, walk. Find it, go right up the front steps. I knock on the front door. No answer. I know where two out of the possible three occupants are.

A guy I know—and maybe he's somebody I shouldn't be seen with—sells me bump keys by the shitload. They're a lock-picking device used to circumvent pin tumbler locks, which are generally inside cylinder locks. They work and they don't damage the system. No one will know.

I slide a bump key into the front door lock; give it three solid taps with the butt of my .44 Magnum, turn. Open. Inside.

Cherry's room: sparse furniture, messy in the way a hotel room is when the occupant is in town for a lot of business and not very organized. I go to the dresser.

Folded paper. Address written on it. The name "Delilah" scribbled across the top like a marquee banner spray-painted by a junkie. In my pocket.

I leave. Pick the cab back up four blocks away. I drop the other half along with another twenty and say, "For being timely."

The cabbie nods, asks, "Where to?"

"Rail station." Time to go back home.

On the ride home I find my eyelids heavy. The seat is too firm. My left suspender is too loose, and no matter how many times I tuck the tail of my shirt in it pulls out. My socks and pant cuffs are soaked through. My knees have wet spots on them. My ears buzz from the gunshots. Headache that's moved down into my teeth.

My cell rings. Derne. I almost let it go to voice mail.

"Hello, Mr. Derne."

"Hello, Mr. Buckner," he says, almost numb.

"What can I do for you?"

"Find her fast, Mr. Buckner—"

"I assure you I'm working as quickly as possible with—"

"Life is like this, Mr. Buckner," he says this, not like before. I despise being interrupted but I've spoken with enough folks who have something to say to know to let this play out.

"Losing my wife like this...with her cancer we both knew she'd be...well, *called home* I guess. The fire...I hope it was painless."

I can hear the void in him. Inside him. As barren as the soul of a mother who has lost her child. That same void filled me with its vast emptiness the day I laid my own wife to rest. She and I weren't married an iota of the length of time Derne and his wife were. I'm glad I lost her so soon so I don't have to sound the way Derne does now. No one would take me seriously.

"In the hospital, the doctors did a lot of tests," he says. "Blood tests revealed a problem with my liver. I forget the fancy doctor terms they used. All I paid attention to was *terminal.*"

I see now.

"Find Delilah fast, Mr. Buckner. Seems my clock is winding down."

39

The next day, bright and early: Elam Derne calls.

Tells me if I want I may attend his wife's funeral. I can't. Pierce White has been found.

In pieces.

40

Pierce White's current wife is nowhere to be found.

Janet Richley, the former Mrs. White, had the kids this week. Lucky for Pierce Jr., age seven, and Felicity, age five. They should have been with their father and the new Mrs. White but Ms. Richley had a family reunion out of town and worked out a deal where she could bring her children along.

Clevenger has been in contact with Ms. Richley. She told him she traded Pierce a holiday for the reunion. Looks like she got the holiday back free of charge.

He leans against the doorway outside. Techs walk back and forth. Police tape and the lingering miasma of old blood and fingerprinting dust. We enter.

The crime scene: family room. A flat screen LCD HD TV set so large it requires its own stadium seating and concession stand. Carpet thick and lush enough to make a bald man green with envy. Tasteful original art hanging on the walls. Looks like oil to me. But anything outside of a comic book looks like oil to me.

"How is Molly?" I ask, rubbing my five o'clock shadow.

"Good. Taking a pottery class this season at the community college."

"Is she going to make me anything?"

"An ash tray, I'm sure."

The blood was well-contained. Pierce was jumped. An axe sunk into the back of his skull deep enough for him to taste the keen, acuminous edge. The murderer looked like he put all his fury into that one swing. The mess of his bone and brains left at the entry wound means the killer tried for a while to un-jimmy the axe from Pierce's head. Pried out; rocked back and forth. Yanked.

"Have you eaten at that new Japanese place near the water? Sixteenth and Bayline?" Clevenger asks as he crouches and studies the skull.

"The only thing I eat raw comes from the ass of a cow," I say. "Anything else was intended by God to be cooked first."

"Sushi is very good. And healthy. I'd recommend you trying something easy first like a California roll or salmon nigiri or—"

"Put a sock in it, Clevenger. You know you ain't gonna convince me to eat that shit. I ever tell you about the cuisine during the war?"

"I know, I know. Dog and monkey. They'd dice up a cat and tell you it was chicken."

"Right."

The body was left lying on a tarp. Standard blue. M.E. thinks a serious hunting knife took the limbs off. Both arms and legs were severed and stacked on one end of the tarp, firewood style. His torso was exposed and carved with the knife tip. The word *Betrayer* carved over and over. Good for handwriting analysis.

"How is your car coming along?"

"Ordering parts. Mechanics."

"I told you not to go there. They're cheap for a reason. I know a guy named Eric, and he's the one you want—"

"Tell me about him next time, then."

Pierce White has his genitals in his mouth, like a roasting pig biting an apple. Good thing he had an axe buried in his noggin before his cock was sawed off and fed to him. Arrogant jack-off or not, that's no way to be found dead.

"Came in through the back," Clevenger says, kneeling by the body. Absently picks at something. Stands.

"With a backdoor like that, I would too." The backdoor was paneled with glass. There is more breakable surface on that door than wood. It was for looks, not security.

"Pretty straight forward," Clevenger says, points out back. "Footprints."

There's a hefty, disheveled trail running through the backyard. It looks like the killer intentionally drug his or her feet through the snow to destroy any easy footprints. I assume the killer followed the same path back out in similar fashion.

"The killer opened the wooden privacy fence gate— unlocked, of course—and meandered up into the backyard. One pane of glass is right next to the backdoor handle. Broken out. Unlocked from the inside. There's even tape residue around the glass where our murderer must have patched the hole."

Didn't want ol' Pierce here to come home from a long day at the office and feel his house twenty degrees cooler. That tells me the killer showed up much earlier than White did. Means the killer didn't know White's schedule so he made allowances for time or he needed time in advance to set something up.

"Then, just wait. Jump. Mutilate," Clevenger says.

"Any chance at all this was a burglary he walked in on?" I ask, knowing the answer.

Clevenger looks at me and raises an eyebrow.

"All right. Never mind," I say. "Your killer knew Pierce."

"I'd put money on it."

"I'd hope he did anyways," I say. I want a cigarette. The kind of wounds Pierce sustained says intimate knowledge. No one just cuts someone's family jewels off and stuffs them into a mouth without reason. Barring complete insanity, there is motive behind it.

We look at each other for a moment. Like the old days.

"This done by your girl?" Clevenger asks.

"Maybe. I don't know her style."

"The question is, why?"

"If Delilah Boothe did this it could be because she was seriously delusional and madly in love," I say, collecting plot points. "And she somehow found out he considered her...what'd he call it? A *sport fuck*. She loses her job over it, he blows her off, divorces the woman she wanted him to divorce, marries some other gal instead of her."

"It would jive with the *Betrayer* carving."

"And the dick in his mouth."

"A woman scorned."

"Yup," I say, stepping outside for a smoke. "A woman scorned."

41

The buy: Jared Garrett's informant was a weasel he dug up who had a laundry list of charges and bench warrants pending and we squeezed in all the right places.

His name was Alfonso, but everyone knew him as Rodent. It fit him. Your informant is only as trustworthy as the gun you have to his head, and we held enough iron to his to ensure compliance.

Rodent introduced Garrett and I to the seller. We bought for a while and built a case. The seller went down, along with six other guys. The bust was huge. The D.A. looked like he was made out of twenty-four karat gold. I thought it was my ticket back to homicide.

I'd call Graham just about every day, feeling like an excited little school girl. Tell him to dump his partner and make sure I had a big desk to return to.

Rodent got hooked up for the bust, but even with that he got fifteen to life when it was all said and done. A few months after he went in he was found dead, stuffed in a crevice somewhere in the prison's laundry facility. We didn't think anything of it; he was arrogant and annoying; an ankle-biter of a man with an obnoxious voice and a penchant for stirring the pot just to see the fireworks.

Then Garrett didn't come into work one day. I didn't care a bit; Flemming had just sent me an official notice I was getting an extension at stolen autos. I was planning on how I was going to ruin Flemming's life while Garrett was being beaten by some associates of the dealer we hit. And Garrett sang. Told them everything.

They dropped him off on a street four blocks from the Saint Ansgar riverfront about the same time I was finishing a hamburger and fries at the local cop-friendly joint.

Garrett didn't call the unit, didn't call me. Instead, battered and half-dead he wandered around in a daze until EMS picked him up. He even managed to wet himself. His lips were bloody and swollen. His chest was knifed up pretty bad. Both hands broken. One foot as well. His face was one solid mass of purple swelling. His right ear cauliflowered.

His wife and kids were untouched, and I think *that* threat, the threat to kill Monica and the twins, that was what got my name out of his lips.

As mad as I get for how my life was ruined, when I see the mental picture of Monica, her dark hair swaying in the wind as she coddled both those infants that Garrett was so proud of, I forgive him. Then her image washes from my mind like sparkles in a heavy breeze, floating away to pepper some other area with their glitter. And then, I hate him all over again.

I never saw it coming. Someone clocked me good and it was all I could do to not piss my pants as I went down. Whatever happened next the doctors and I speculated. All I can think about was the blackness that swam over me in that one split second where I knew I was hit because I was still feeling it connect, but there was nothing I could do.

An indiscernible amount of time later and the veil of shadows stretched across my life began to slowly, unsteadily lift. I came to and my head was poisoned. My stomach was turning over and over. My body was alive with an electricity that frightened me with its power. Shapes and colors were dancing in my skull and I vomited. It was red with blood. And black with a coffee ground-like substance. Half-digested blood looks like that.

Ditched in an alley. Like trash. I walked out of that tight brick corridor onto a major street I would have recognized if I were in my own mind and body. A woman in a business suit walked past me. I think I asked her something along the lines of *where am I* and she refused to answer.

Instead, she screamed. She screamed bloody murder.

Her eyes were drawn to my neck, which burned molten and infected. I ignored her, feeling various shades of that pain up and down my body. I threw up again. Reeling from the fit of nausea I blacked out in the street. I guess EMS got me also. I came and went for an hour or so and eventually the scenery changed from the street to a trauma room.

Inside, all the words in my head, all the questions, pleas for help, outrages at my condition, they were cotton in my mouth. Useless and jumbled like a handful of marbles without a jack.

Two nurses and a tech took possession of me. They extracted a syringe from my neck, the source of all that blistering hot pain and misery. Left there by my assailants as a message, they shot me so full of the Big Fry that even without a gray matter detonation I should have been poisoned to death. Whacked. Eighty-sixed.

My head was split open, my face gashed. Maybe it was cut. Maybe it ripped open from the fall I took after being knocked unconscious. Or being thrown out of a vehicle into an alley.

The hospital did their best for me, and in the end the only resounding effect I have is the damage to my mind. The smearing. The lost time.

After surgery, after the drug overdose treatment, I got to share a room with another man whose luck had run out that day. Every now and then his family would leave his side to check on me. I would look up through bleary and unsure eyes, not trusting their information anymore, but I would see Monica looming over me, telling me that Garrett says he's sorry and everything will be all right.

But it was not, and the police decided I could not serve them anymore.

As the detective sergeant for his squad, Pierce White's murder is Clevenger's squawk if he wants it.

After the murder scene. Coffee. Clevenger with pancakes, me with Tabasco and hash.

"You *are* going to catch this one, right?"

"Why?"

"Because I need you to. How else am I going to get the resources of SAPD to find this chick?"

Sarcastic: "Sure, buddy. Anything I can do to stall official police work into a murder to help you earn a paycheck."

Honest: "Oh good. For a second I thought you were going to fuck me on this one."

Interested: "How do you want to play it?"

"Okay, this is how I see it—"

"I'm just entertaining you, by the way. I'll see what parts of your idea Captain Flemming will let me get away with."

"Right, right," I say. "Here's the plan..."

42

Riggens, Rudd and Volksman all in the same room at the same time.

SAPD headquarters. Detective's bureau. One of the three conference rooms. The other two rooms have their own projector screens; they were booked.

No one has smoked in this building in twenty years but the stale grit of long-gone tobacco holds firmly in the brick and mortar. The floors are wood and in desperate need of refinishing. As it is the bottom-of-the-barrel, the house cleaning crew just runs a buffer over it once a week and calls it good.

The incandescent light bulbs cast a harsh patina across the bureau. One socket buzzes no matter what maintenance does. The socket hangs over a desk we all called the FNG Desk. Every new detective spends time under the buzzing light, waiting for the next rookie to get promoted.

Rudd looks fairly severe and all business. That's too bad because I like the shape of her. If she were in a school girl's outfit, snapping a ruler against one palm, I think I'd stick around for detention. Riggens looks young, naïve and a little too blockheaded to be in this job so early. Volksman looks like he should be hung over the side of a bridge and made to cry a little bit before he's dropped.

Clevenger walks in, papers in hand. Copied, collated and bound. Drops them on the table, sits. Slides a packet across to everybody.

"Pamela Rudd, Art Riggens, Richard Dean Buckner."

They nod. So do I. I look to the egomaniac seated to my right. He smirks and I'm not sure if it's a greeting or an acknowledgment of his feelings towards me. Either way I don't like it.

"Okay," Clevenger says, sipping coffee. "We're all here because I think our separate cases tie in. I want to put our pieces together as best we can and—"

"What the fuck is this burnt out piece of shit doing here?" Volkman asks.

"Oh, Thomas..." I say, rubbing my knuckles. Clevenger grunts and I see him shaking his head. I guess my old partner would look bad if I cleaned this fat turd's clock right here, right now. I might do it anyways. I wonder what it would take to get Clevenger to forgive me for it.

"Mr. Buckner is here because he is working a related case and his information will tie in. And watch your mouth, *Detective*."

Volksman's eyes light with a fury and I love it. *Detective*. That's got to sting. I know the story but I hate this worthless fuck so much it'll be worth the delay in real police work to see what I can stir up.

"Detective, huh?" I look at Volksman, smile, interlace my fingers and place my arms on the table. Lean his way. Shit-eating grin written all over me. "Last I heard, you were on the list for Detective Sergeant."

"RDB," Clevenger says.

One more: "What could possibly knock you down?"

"*Richard*."

One more again: "You noodle a school girl?"

"Damn it, Richard."

One more again for the last time: "Your wife find out about that Filipino chick you were keeping south of the river?"

"Jesus, RDB, don't make me throw you out," Clevenger is getting honestly pissed.

With a laugh: "Okay. My fun is over," I say to Clevenger.

Without a laugh, as cold as I can make it: "Watch who you call a piece of shit, Volksman. Ears around here still listen to me."

"I doubt that, RDB," Volksman says, picking under his fingernails.

"Then answer two questions for me. Why haven't I been tossed from this room yet?"

He pauses, looks around, but not at me. Finally: "What's the second question?"

"Why won't you look me in the eye?"

"What does that have to do with people on the PD still listening to you?"

"Nothing." I lean in. Whisper, challenge: "But you're a pussy."

Volksman says nothing. Does nothing. I whisper, truth: "Why some sack of shit like you gets to stay on and I am labeled *unserviceable* is beyond me. Because we both know who was of any worth to this PD."

Clevenger groans. Head in hands, rubbing the bridge of his nose. I love that kind of thing. Because, I used to own this department. And I'll say the truth: I can take stabs at some worthless disgraced piece of shit like Thomas Volksman all day and no one is going to eject me from the department.

No one. *No one* has the balls. Not the Chief, not Captain Flemming. No one.

Rudd and Riggens just fiddle with their paper packets and whistle Dixie. Rudd has smoothed her pant skirt several times. Riggens has run his index fingers along his eyebrows. His own brand of smoothing.

I look to Clevenger.

"Would you like to begin?"

43

The dry erase board says "Delilah Boothe" in Clevenger's trim, efficient script.

He circles her name. Looks to me. Holds out the marker and says, "You do it."

"Sure thing," I say. Take the marker. "Delilah Boothe is the sun in our collective universe. Her old address is your case, Riggens. Her mom is your case, Rudd. Her surrogate father is your case, Volksman. Three arsons in one night all drawing lines to one woman are too coincidental to ignore. Not to mention Clevenger's murder victim, Pierce White, is Delilah Boothe's ex-boyfriend."

"Three MO's for three fires and one murder," Volksman says dryly. As if those two words shatter reality.

"So what?" I say.

"Three MO's points to three different firebugs. Like the one Delilah Boothe's father bunked with in prison. You telling me he did all three?"

"I'm telling you one firebug—whoever he is—used three different MO's," I say. Look to Clevenger. "And the murder was just icing."

"Ex-boyfriend?" Rudd asks.

"Yeah. They had an office romance that got them both canned and him divorced," Clevenger says.

"There's your firebug," Rudd says.

"No. He's got no history," I say.

"Did he have a history of cheating on his wife before he did it?" she asks, eyebrow raised.

"I didn't ask before he got his dick cut off and shoved down his throat."

"There's your murderer," she says flatly.

"I'm not ruling out Delilah at all for the murder. We

concentrate on the arsons," I say. Rudd is lucky she has a neck I'd like to put my mouth on. Her personality is starting to come through. But like my old friend Howard Michigan always says: *You're not getting off with their personality.*

I continue: "*One* firebug torched the three homes. Killed three people. We're all in this together."

"Pierce White," she says. Volksman scoffs at me because he's an asshole and Riggens is just taking notes.

"That guy has no reason to burn down three homes," I say.

"Hitler had no previous history of starting wars until he did, Dahmer had no history of eating his lovers until he started one day and Darth Vader had no history of throwing his boss down a shaft until the mood struck him. Everybody starts somewhere, Mr. Buckner."

"So Mr. White is *your* prime suspect?" I ask.

"I'm looking into Darla Boothe's ex-husband," Rudd says, turning a pencil over in her hands. "His record shows he has beef with women, he and his ex-wife have a long-smoldering feud over their life together and he shared a cell with a firebug before he got out. Less than a month later the last known address of his ex-, his daughter and his daughter's new daddy burn down."

"The last known address for his daughter *was* her mother's place."

"Tomato, to*ma*to, Mr. Buckner. It all burns the same."

"No," I say, "Ben Boothe's record says different. He's too impulsive. He's got nothing on there saying he thinks before he acts. He just flips out. Did it when he abandoned his family, did it whenever he'd get drunk and call his ex-wife, threatening. Hell, he let his anger get the best of him in the divorce proceedings. They hauled his ass out of court when Darla Boothe started getting everything. And the rape? Just one more example. No plans. No forethought whatsoever, let alone the brains to plan three different arsons using three distinctly different MO's on the same night and get away with it."

"He hasn't gotten away with it, Mr. Buckner."

Okay. She's getting old now.

"Find him?" I ask.

"Yes."

"Where?"

"He is renting a small home over on the east side. Off of 142nd and Regal."

"Alibi?"

"A girl vouches for him. Picked her up at a bar. Spent the night."

"Her name?"

"Not your concern."

"So Mr. White is your prime suspect?"

"I didn't say that. I have serious doubts Ben Boothe was with the girl," she says, removing her stylish frames and rubbing one lens with a cloth. "She spoke in vague terms, acted like she was reading from a script. Their stories lined up but they weren't very complicated either."

The best lies are simple and formed from kernels of truth. I bet Boothe met her at the bar, maybe bought her a drink. Got a blowjob in the shitter. Patted her on the head and left here there as he went to the next bar. It's not hard to buy her some drugs as a bribe and tell her *if anyone comes sniffing around, showing a badge, you and me went back to my place for the whole night. Got it?*

"Is she dirty?" I ask.

"Long history of petty things."

"Obstruction? Resisting? Dope? Disorderly conduct?"

"All of it. Why?"

"Obstruction, resisting and disorderly all point to someone willing to lie and make life harder for the police. Respect issues. No cooperation, lying, misleading, avoiding, all disrespect. It equals obstruction. Escalating a situation, throwing a fit when the police try to control that situation, resisting. Fit throwing equals disorderly."

"And the dope?"

"Junkies, as a species, are liars as well. Comes with the territory."

"So what? How does it add up?"

"She is...a *liar*." Am I the last investigator left on the planet? "If you think she lied to you as an alibi and she has a history of lying to police, then squeeze her. She'll talk."

"I'm not *like you*, Mr. Buckner," she says with a tone that tells me she very clearly differentiates her breed and my own.

"That's obvious," I say and openly stare at her breasts.

She groans and adjusts her shirt over her business cleavage. "That's *not* what I meant and you know it."

"I guess I don't."

"Ponder it for a while, then," she says and closes her notebook. She's finished. Simple as that. Body language says done. I pity the poor schmuck in her life.

We're quiet for a beat and then I turn to my favorite turd in the world.

"Volksman, what'd you think?" I ask.

"I'm wondering why you're here at all, RDB."

"I'm here on Mr. Derne's behalf." True but skewed. Doesn't matter.

"He hired you to do the real police's job and investigate his tragedy? Didn't tell me that."

"Doesn't have to. Consider me saying what I have so far a favor to you. Face it, Volksman, without me working this case it'll never get solved."

"Fuck you," he says

"Any other thoughts? Case-related?"

Huffs, plays along. "He's an older man. Sweet but

197

grumpy. Friends and neighbors say he's warm-hearted, generous. They also says he's a dude who has a penchant for popping off here and there. Blows his lid, then gets all great again. You know the type."

"Booze?"

"Asshole."

"You think he did it?"

"Hardly. Owns a small business in rock masonry and has been in litigation with various other businesses for years. Hell, the job he and his crew did at the new General Bank of America over on Tillson last year is being scrutinized for shoddy work. Five years ago he did some landscaping for a new business office over off of 38 West and he got sued for it."

"Small businesses catch grief sometimes."

"He also crossed Erminio Andretti."

"Mob?" Erminio Andretti is the latest in a line of Andrettis who have run a semi-functional mob family in Saint Ansgar. I've personally dealt with a few of their people both as a cop and as a PI.

My dealings as a PI were more fun. Their main torch man was a goof named Paulie Torreno. I make a note to look him up. He has an ear in the fire; he might have heard some buzz. Or, he might have done them.

"Yes, mob," Volksman says, annoyed. "Six years ago he was redoing the stone front to Andretti's Italian restaurant over in the hills and they had some dispute. Some bullshit over the price of Arkansas River rock versus Missouri limestone. I dunno. Anyways, they wound up in court and Derne won."

"Why wait six years?" I ask. "Andretti's dad and older brother both were as impulsive as a two coked-out dudes starring in their first porno. They wouldn't wait six minutes to sweep the trash from their front porch, let alone six whole years."

"Maybe Erminio learned from their mistakes."

"No. If he had he'd have rebuilt their family by now. If anything the family has a weaker hold on things than they did before he was the head."

"Point is Derne's got enemies with deep pockets. Nothing pisses off a businessman more than being cost money. Derne's company—innocently or not—has done it."

"Recently?"

"Here and there over the past thirty years."

"So a patient businessman is unhappy with his rock masonry and waits thirty years before he burns down three houses just to try and get Derne?"

"Mob. They'd do it."

"The mob would drag him out to the Bay and drown him or take him over the airport and execute him while a plane flies over. How do you connect the fires then?"

"Don't have to."

"Seriously, Volksman?"

"Rudd needs to investigate her case, Riggens needs to investigate his, and I need to investigate mine."

"Can't you see the obvious connection here?"

"Again, RDB: *I don't have to.*"

"Oh, I see," I rub my face. "The standards for investigator have been lowered that much, eh?"

"Say what you want, RDB. Don't think I don't know it was you who leaked the Filipino girl thing around here."

"It wasn't me," I say. "I wouldn't have to. It was a running joke in the department that your wife would follow you around town. What kind of cop doesn't know he's being tailed by his own lady?"

Volksman is that kind of cop. It's true: his ex-old lady suspected him of cheating and followed him for weeks until he led her right to his other woman.

Volksman's left eye twitches: tell. Big time. He shoots

up out of his chair. I rear back to swing. Clevenger catches my fist. He's one of only a few people who can do that and actually stop my punch. He's had practice for years now.

Standoff. Clevenger knows just how bad I'll fuck up Volksman. Volksman knows it too; he's just too big a cocksucker to care about his hospital stay right now.

Clevenger's got both his hands gripping my right fist. I think about throwing a left cross and drilling Volksman into next spring but I don't. This is Clevenger's show and even if I don't have to face the music—Volksman will never press charges—I don't want to put my old buddy's ass in a sling.

I ease up. My eyes still on Volksman's. Clevenger lets go, presses me backwards. Same to Volksman. He backs away easily; he doesn't need to be told he'll lose the fight and welcomes Clevenger making distance. Although Volksman still plays the gangster theatrics—tough talk, throwing his arms up, acting like he's not going to get his ass handed to him—so he can look good. In reality he looks like a retard doing a chicken dance.

His neck and face flush red. His thin chest puffed out as far as it will go. His arms out to his sides in that *come on* posture. All done so he can look like he didn't need Clevenger to stop me from demolishing him.

"Scram, Volksman," Clevenger says. "If Reichman were still alive you could bitch at him for laughing about the Filipino girl."

"Sure. Blame the dead guy to protect your fucking butt buddy," Volksman nearly shouts. He grabs the packet of paper Clevenger gave him and throws it. Clevenger's neatly organized case rains down in a thousand white squares. The gentle way they flutter through the tension in the room, the quiet paper snap each sheet makes is an explosion.

I smile, say, "Even your fits of rage are girly-weak, Volksman. But thanks for playing with the big boys."

"Fuck the both of you," he says, wasting no time heading for the door. "You're the kind of cop nobody likes to be around, Clevenger."

Clevenger makes an act of looking to both sides before acting shocked that Volksman would say such a thing. "Who? This guy?" Clevenger asks, pointing at himself.

"Yes, *you.*"

"Why on earth are you being so downright hateful?"

"Because you're *his* little protégé and everybody hates *that* piece of shit." Volksman points to me. "Don't think there's a person on this force who knew RDB that doesn't see his ugly fucking face when they look at *you*. Not *one*."

Volksman storms out like a child. Nobody says anything for a moment. Rudd starts gathering her things and Riggens looks like a sixth grader who just had front row tickets to the big fight between jocks. I can tell he's fighting showing his giddiness.

"Rudd," I say. She stops and looks at me. "Do *you* like being around Clevenger here?"

Her smile is shallow and all-business. "Detective Sergeant Clevenger is fine with me, Mr. Buckner."

"Do you like being around me?"

"I don't know you so I can't comment with any authority."

"Well...we can fix that." I wink. She gets my drift immediately. I get her return drift immediately. I don't like it.

"Thanks, Mr. Buckner, but the only thing that upsets my stomach more than a man covered in tattoos and scars is pure, unadulterated, testosterone-induced arrogance. That takes you out of the running to even hold the door open for me. My dead corpse wouldn't spread its legs for you."

"Holy shit," I say.

"Good day, Detectives."

Rudd leaves. I watch her go and decide her ass is too big for me. Clevenger gives me that look he always has when I get shot down like that. He's had practice for years now. Riggens looks positively giddy. Waiting to see if I bat a thousand for clearing the room.

I look to him. Bright-eyed, bushy-tailed. "Riggens, would your corpse spread its legs for me?"

44

Riggens doesn't answer the question but he doesn't leave either.

The three of us are at the dry erase board. "Delilah Boothe" still circled in the middle. I reach up to start writing something brilliant and the white barrel of the marker turns to water in my hand. Spills down, mixing with the black print on it. The names and lines on the board drizzle into blurry streaks. My brain is shattered with a freeze I can taste. My eyes explode with needles of burning everything and I think the marker falls from my hand. I stand very still. Light is blinding me and I close my eyes against it. But the light is coming from behind my eyes and sealed lids do no good.

I stumble back on step and roll my foot on the marker. I almost fall and then the bubble pops. Clevenger is up on his feet. I feel the palm of his hand between my shoulder blades as he holds me upright. We've been at this for some time now. The color washes away and the world rights itself. I'm still cleaved in half but I reach down and snatch up the marker from the floor. Uncap it.

Clevenger doesn't ask. He knows when he's done. He sits. I huff out with a long exhale and steady myself on my feet. Then, it's ops normal. I tap her name with the marker and start writing.

"Okay, so she loses the house and Derne sells it to the couple. Tyler and Abigail Bellview," I say. "It burns down and you catch it. Have you looked into their background at all?"

Riggens nods. "Pretty clean, actually. Both have a few traffic tickets from over the years but nothing else. He was an MP in the Army in Tulsa for one tour. Did the usual stuff there, no huge busts or anything."

"Just blah? No nothing?"

"Not really. Unless he busted someone on base and they came back for revenge now. But really, on paper anyways it seems like that was a quiet four years."

"No crazy friends?"

"No."

"Crazy work associates?"

"No."

"Family?"

"Run-of-the-mill. Boring. Law abiding, tax-paying belong-to-the-neighborhood-watch family."

"Okay," I say, needing a smoke. "Abigail?"

"Her? She's a stay-at-home mom; last job was three years ago before the kid."

We all see the little girl in our minds and push her memory away. No one likes thinking of dead children.

"The jobs were mostly retail and cash register stuff. No titty dancing or prostitution. No former bosses who showed up on radar as bad people. I interviewed the last three of 'em and they don't recall her having any enemies at work nor do they recall any other employees with records of arson."

"What about personal life? Family, friends?"

"You got me thinking Delilah Boothe now. It fits."

"Like anybody before now?" I ask.

"Little bit. My eyes have been creeping towards an ex-boyfriend of hers from high school. A guy by the name of Blane Tapolski. Right after they graduated he went into the pen for setting fire to another kid's car. Unoccupied, if you're wondering. I guess the victim dated Tapolski's older sister and the relationship went sour. The kid smacked her a time or two and Blane decided to even the score."

"Did Abigail break up with Shitski to date Tyler?"

"Shitski? You mean Tapolski?" Riggens asks.

"RDB calls anybody with a Polish last name 'Shitski,'" Clevenger says. "He's that kind of asshole."

"Oh. Well, kind of. Abigail was dating Tapolski their senior year, they graduate, Tapolski sets the fire, she breaks up with him, gets subpoenaed to testify against him in court, offers nothing relevant—they'd already broken up so it's not like he told her about it—he goes off to the clink, she dates and marries Bellview."

"Shit," I say. I draw it out on the board.

I step back and think to myself. The word MOTIVE screams. What is it? I tap it with the marker and tap it again. Riggens and Clevenger stand there, pondering also.

taptaptaptaptaptaptaptaptaptaptaptaptaptaptapt aptaptaptaptaptaptaptaptaptaptaptap

"One person," I say.

Clevenger: "On the surface. Yes. One person."

"Who?" Riggens asks.

"It's pretty obvious," I say. I write "Delilah Boothe" under the word MOTIVE.

45

"So you think your missing person is our arsonist?" Riggens asks.

"Not entirely, no. But looking at these three fires, yes."

"That doesn't make sense."

"There's still motive. I can see revenge against Derne for evicting her and the Bellviews for buying what she thought was her place—"

"And killing Pierce White," Clevenger says.

"Yeah, but why now? Why not burn his shit to the ground also?"

"Three different arsons, three different MO's. Maybe she's more clever than we give her credit for," Clevenger says.

"Maybe."

"Her mom?"

"Not her own mother," I say. "She took her in. She was doing what Derne was not. I'll have to talk to her again and see if there is something she's not telling me that would make me think Delilah would do this."

We stare. Clevenger takes the dry erase marker and writes "Pierce White" under the three arsons and draws a box around it. BODY COUNT: 1.

Under all that: TOTAL BODY COUNT (SO FAR): 4

"We should look into her other boyfriends," Clevenger says.

"Yeah," Riggens says. "Maybe she's on a cock-slaughter fest."

"It makes sense tying White to Delilah because she lost her good job with him, and it began the domino effect that lost her the house," I say.

"So the next boyfriend—the one she lost her *second* job

206

with—he might be next."

"Weird coincidence," I say, wondering how to put this in front of Riggens. I wouldn't say anything at all about Dobbins but I see Riggens picking up a trail. "I was looking him up. He lives in Three Mile High. A buddy of mine up at the PD there said her second boyfriend was found shot to death in his pad—"

"I *knew* it!" Riggens shouts. "Cock-slaughter fest! I knew it. *I knew it.*"

"No," I say, trying to get him off this one. It looks good, I know that. It would make sense if we were pinning this whole thing on Delilah but I don't like it. Also, I know why Dobbins is dead.

"The Three Mile High cops found the murder weapon left at the scene. Some other guy he was selling drugs to."

"Did they find the shooter?"

"Yeah. Dead."

"So maybe she killed *him*," Riggens looks me in the eye, his youth betraying him. "Like I said. *Cock. Slaughter. Fest.*"

"No," I say, hand on his shoulder. "Drug deal gone bad."

"I dunno, Mr. Buckner."

"I do. My buddy said so."

"Well, I should at least give him a call. What's your buddy's name?"

"Smith," I look at Clevenger who knows exactly what happened even though I never told him. He knows me.

"Smith? Okay. What—"

"No. Jones," I say.

"What? Smith or Jones? Which is it?"

"What?"

"You said Smith and then Jones. Which—"

"You mean Johnson?" Clevenger rolls his eyes. Riggens can't see it.

"Who?"

"Up in Three Mile High."

"Yeah. What was your friend's name that—"

"What are you talking about?"

"No, what are *you* talking about?"

I turn the kid away from the dry erase board. "Tell you what. This doesn't sit right to me. I need you to keep working the Shitski angle until he's alibied out of it."

"Here are all the pieces," Riggens says, trying to motion to the board. "Fit 'em together. How can this not sit right with you?"

"I've been solving crimes since you were practicing undoing a bra with your mother's dirty laundry. Trust my gut when it says something doesn't sit right in it. Understand me?"

"Yeah. Sure." Riggens looks away. Looks back. Disappointed.

I slap his shoulder and turn him towards the door. "Dig around for Shitski. Keep your ears out for those other two flame-dicks in your department. Let me know what they turn up. I'm pretty sure they won't get back with me."

"Okay." He takes my card and heads for the door. I look to Clevenger, he looks to me.

"Oh, and, Mr. Buckner?" Riggens says.

"Yeah?"

"I *have* heard of you. I know you been gone a long time but people still speak your name. And no matter what anybody's opinion of you is they all say one thing."

"Really? What?"

"You're the baddest motherfucker to ever wear this uniform."

"I could have told you that."

I think he smiles and leaves. Clevenger closes the blinds and comes back to the board.

"Alright. Catch me up," he says, hands me the marker.

46

I tell Clevenger about the dope angle. Cherry and Danny. The other buyer, this Pinky Meyers.

"Might be Delilah killed everybody. Burned everything down," Clevenger says.

"Sure. Maybe," I say, thinking.

Clevenger looks at me and says: "What now?"

"I start talking to more people."

He snickers. Then: "Think you might kill one of 'em?"

I look him in the eye and start erasing the board. Ben Boothe's name disappears. Finally I say: "Yeah. Probably before it's over."

47

What I remember is Clevenger beside me at my hospital bed.

I think Molly was with him sometimes. The constant beep of the monitors. The way my arms were restricted by medical tape and IV needles. Having to lay flat on my back. No amount of pain killer took away the dull, pervasive throb of my head wound. The catheter pinched. It was foreign; the sensation of something sneaky trying to invade my body through alternate routes. Slithering.

I never had a lucid head while in the hospital. My memories of that place are as vivid as a strong dream: scenes cut from one moment to the next. No connections or clarity as to why the movie reel of my mind was running the way it did. Dialogue stood out clearly, but for the life of me I couldn't tell who said what. I might have imagined the whole thing. It was a thousand piece puzzle broken up and scattered just enough to where the picture could be made out even without the pieces fitting together. But the light in the room kept changing colors and the brain never made sense of the puzzle. The function wasn't there.

So many things fragmented. My mind smearing was so much worse then. The boiling frustration at the onset. The realization that a human brain is eons more complex than any traffic scheme, any computer program simultaneously solving multiple algorithms, more complex than the movement of the winds and the tides and the interplay between all life and nonlife.

The realization that my brain had been derailed. Permanently. The sickening feeling of it. I had arrested guys like me. The smeared. I hated dealing with them. Now I was one.

But one night I know Molly was there. Her voice was a song from out of an old Disney movie. Through the beeps of the monitors she asked: "So, Richard, why did you want to be a cop?"

Anything that came in through my eyes was a blur. The light was too much, the shadows made me afraid. Her hair had a glow; a blonde aura that gently hung about her. An angel's halo. But the question, it was small talk. I think my answer didn't make sense. She never brought it up again.

"My mother took one beautiful picture," I said. "It was on the mantle."

It wasn't a real mantle, my folks just called the central shelf a *mantle* the way they also called Miracle Whip *mayonnaise*, the way the called Spam *dinner* and oil-stained scraps of cloth diapers were *Kleenex*.

The smell of my childhood home greeted me with the memory of a place I have painted black. Home. Parked on three wheels and a jack. Utilities being constantly cut off and switched back on. I never liked it when it came back on—even in winter—because that meant that dad had spent his beer money on the utilities. Ergo, he'd become a real motherfucker.

My mother fought her instincts and tried to be domestic, planted flowers once in the community garden. Mrs. Beckman had to tend them, the same way she wound up tending to me as I grew up.

The smell of wet ash rising out of the throw rug mom laid down still filled my nostrils all those years forward. The lights illuminating the highway billboard outside the park we called a neighborhood would drown out the starlight and the moon. Billboard light would rain down through my bedroom window, which was a screen with a tear through it and a towel for a curtain. There was no glass at all. Ever. Got kind of shitty during the winter. I got good at taping up trash bags as patches. They would breathe with the night breeze and *whoosh* in and out. I'd fall asleep to that constant sound. Like the tide.

"I was seven when she killed herself. My one-picture mother."

I say killed herself because that's what it amounts to. What I call suicide Dad called adultery and come-upins. He died in a bar fight long before I ever had the balls to ask how he got away with it. Mom's suicide.

"Dad stopped in every now and again to make sure the fridge was stocked with beer. It was for the next time he stopped by. Realizing he had some milligram of responsibility for me, he would go to the bulk store and buy a cardboard palette of Spam and some canned vegetable. It changed every time. Lima beans, carrots, stewed tomatoes. Once he bought an entire palette of mixed peppers. Jalapenos were the mildest in the bunch. Left the palettes on the kitchen table with a can opener. It was my breakfast, lunch and dinner."

I remember sneezing then in the hospital and how much it hurt. "Whenever his bar tab would come due I knew I had to make the palettes last. New ones wouldn't be forthcoming."

My throat was dry all the time in the hospital. Not having a cigarette killed me. It was the longest five weeks of my life.

"My first job was at the age of eight. I used it to buy a hot plate. I hate cold Spam, and when they shut off the gas the next time Dad left it alone. *He* would shower at a girlfriend's house. But having *our* gas off, it would ease the financial burden on his drinking. Everything seemed to revolve around that."

After he died the bar came after me to settle his debt. I gave them the lousy seventeen dollars I had. At age thirteen that's not bad. The bouncers asked for the other six hundred or so and when I quipped that I couldn't believe they let him drink that much on credit they didn't find it funny.

Dad always hit me in the ribs and kidneys. I assume it was to avoid visible marks. Maybe it was because he just got used to never hitting Mom in the face because he wanted her to always be pretty and those were muscle-memory habits he would then use on me.

The bouncers, they hit me in the face.

In the hospital bed, my head swam. I remember that. Molly just sat there, her hand, a loving oasis in the sea of my pure misery, it rested inside mine. Here and there she would squeeze harder. I was worried Clevenger didn't like it. He never said anything. Looking back on it I'm sure he knew it was for comfort.

"Dad would stare at Mom's one beautiful picture on the mantle and say: 'Dick, two other greaser hounds was drooling over your mother, same time I was. Sniffing her skirt. The things men do, you know. And your mother, she picked me. Sometimes I'd think about if she ever wondered what her life woulda been if she'd picked differently.'

"He'd look at me and I'd be afraid to look away, but too mortified to look him directly in his eye. He called that respect. 'And when I think about her picking somebody else, it'd fill me with rage, Dick. *It'd fill me with rage.*'"

We had that one-sided conversation several times up to the point my useless old man fucked with the wrong biker and took a face-full of buckshot from twin barrels. Never talk shit when you're so hammered you've pissed yourself unless you know for a fact you are bulletproof.

"I remember one time after he said *it'd fill me with rage*, me being thirteen and him being within five months of a pine box, us standing in the doorway, he just nodded his head and opened the front door. Then he said: 'I would think about it all the damn time.'

"Then he left."

I turned my head towards Molly and my neck scorched from the injection site. "I guess I became a cop because I really liked *Dragnet*."

And that was true.

Little Italy in Saint Ansgar's north end.

I walk into the old barber shop on the corner of 77th and Roma. It's been a staple in this community for decades. Francis "Temples" Forelli is gently shaving the neck of some greased wop who's tilted back in an old-fashioned barber's chair. Five fat guys, all relics of a bygone age where the film *The Godfather* was a contemporary statement, they're all lined against one wall and smoking, chattering back and forth. Half their conversations are in their home language. They're not here for haircuts; this will be the entire day.

I don't like coming here. They know my face and they don't like it.

The place is redolent with stale cigarette smoke and stark aftershave. Black and white photographs adorn the walls. Snapshots of the shop just after World War II. Guys long dead standing outside the front door on summer days with a bullet-nosed Studebaker in the background. Big Italian dinner table stuffed full of people. The floor is checkered. There is a candy striper pole outside. Sinatra is crooning from the grave on a record loop somewhere.

Temples has got to be pushing sixty-five but the full head of hair he has is jet black and lustrous with oil, save his brilliant, snow white temples. I guess that's the nickname's origin. I brush the snow off my shoes at the welcome mat. The bell jingling above my entrance draws

Temples' eye. He gives a slight acknowledgement and I step off to the side. Leave my coat on. Don't bother with a seat. I'm not here for a cut.

Temples finishes and cleans up the patron. He snaps the towel off in a crisp, efficient manner, and the old man stands, makes his way back to the other men mumbling back and forth. Temples lights a smoke and walks over to me.

"You know the city banned smoking indoors?" I say, lighting my own.

"To hell with them crooks," Temples says. Exhales. "Let 'em cite me for it. I know a guy. He'll make it go away."

"I bet you do." I smile. Temples *does* know guys. That's why I'm here. "Well, what's new?"

"Hey, Temples," one of the old fat guys shouts in a tone meant for the entire block to hear, "get that fucking pig outta here."

Temples give a side-long look over his shoulder. "Yeah, yeah."

"Razor sends his regards, ya damn mook," another chimes in.

"You know they don't like me talkin' to you. Not after Razor got hard time," Temples says.

"I know." I look at the men. They'll remember me until the end of time. It's why I don't like coming here. It's not that they're anything of a threat; even if one pulled out a sidearm I doubt he could hit the sky if he emptied the magazine.

But, each man is a phone call away from every greaser in town who thinks he's Joe Pesci in *Good Fellas*. No one left in this city is that kind of guido badass but they think they are. That's almost worse. All I need is a bunch of mostly inept wannabe gangsters trying to fill me with lead while they eat cannoli. They won't hit me but they'll more than likely shoot up everyone around me. It's better to play this in a reserved manner.

I say, "Let's talk outside. It'll only be a minute."

"Yeah," Temples says, "let's."

"Razor was a good barber. You had no right—" one of the old men shouts.

"Being a barber has nothing to do with killing his wife," I say.

"She was a cheatin' whore!"

"So was he. Is he still in prison?" I ask as Temples put a hand to my shoulder and eases me out the door.

"Whaddya think, ya fuckin' pig?"

"Oh, that's right," I say, smirking. "Later, fellas."

"Okay. Okay," Temples says. He shuts the door behind us and the bell jingles inside.

Razor worked here for almost a decade. This was a long time ago now. Razor was known for two things: being a quality barber and cheating on his wife. Notorious for both. Razor was cool with his own infidelities; he was not cool when he discovered his wife had an affair of her own. Razor unceremoniously opened his wife's neck with his best shaving blade. I guess that's the nickname's origin.

Clevenger and I caught the case when her body was found on a trash heap in the city dump. It led here. Razor very proudly admitted what he did. He declared he would not be cuckolded. He declared things were square now.

So Razor is cutting hair in prison. Which is where he will die.

Outside Temples says, "They're still sore about him. I never cared for the adultery, myself."

"Thanks for talking to me anyways," I say.

"Sure." Temples looks around and says to the world around us, "He was a good barber, I guess."

Oh well. "I need Paulie Torreno," I say.

"Now that's one rat bastard you should put in the slammer."

"I'm not a cop anymore. I don't have access to the slammer."

"Well, then. Off the mook."

"We'll get there when we get there. Can you get word to him?"

"I can whisper in ears. Yes."

"Spread the word for tonight at the old Navy pier. I'll be there at one a.m."

"Sure. Sure."

"I'll wait until one-fifteen."

"Sure. Sure."

"This stays between us, right?"

"You need to ask?"

"I guess not," I say. "Thanks, Temples. Good to see you again."

"Sure. Sure. Now get outta here before those pissy sons-a-bitches inside hold this against me."

Navy pier.

1:12 a.m. I rented a car for this occasion. Some four-door sedan job: silver, tinted, nothing fancy. Looks like every other car on the road, which is why I picked it. I'm sure they'll be pissed I'm chain-smoking inside of it but oh well. I've smoked half a pack waiting for this jack off.

My hand lifts to the gear shift. I'm leaving and then in my rearview Paulie Torreno comes walking towards me from some shadow. He pauses ten feet back and huddles his face in front of his hands. A few orange flickers and he's dragging off his own cigarette. He starts walking again.

He comes to the driver side window and my .44 Magnum is in my lap, pointed his direction. He gets to the window, looks in and sees the iron.

"I been set up?" he says, blowing smoke in my face.

"No. I just don't trust you."

"Well, you wanted to see *me*, Dick. What's on your mind?"

"Sit down inside."

"I like the cold."

"See, that's strange. I hear you like heat."

"People say things. I like the cold."

"I didn't ask what you like. I said sit down. We need to talk business."

Torreno drags deep off the smoke and his aging eyes turn to slits. He lowers the cigarette and gives me a hard stare before suddenly smiling bright.

"Oh, what the hell," he says, cheery. "I ain't got nothing to worry about from old Dick Buckner anymore. You can't even write me a parking ticket these days."

He walks around the hood and comes to the door. Swings it open. Plops down into the seat.

Paulie Torreno is one of the main firebugs who had his heyday working for the mob years back. In the '70s, if a building burnt down, Paulie did it. The mob liked Paulie because he had a knack for being thorough and for getting away with it. He's too old for constant work now. He spends his days doing whatever retired mob guys do. How he ever came into my sights is forever lost but his name used to get circulated a lot in the PD. Somehow he never went down for a torch job. Not even the jobs where there were people inside.

Seemed to be a lot of those by the end.

Whoever did the houses connected to Delilah Boothe, if it was a pro, Torreno will know something. Torreno is an animal. He's a serial killer with a Bic lighter. This is a long shot but I cover my bases.

"What's so important, Dick?" Torreno says. His

arrogance fills the car like a bad stink. He's old now. Older than me. He moves slow. Slower than me. He might be five-foot-eight, one-fifty. His snug wool hat with its slight brim makes him look Irish. He smells like fire and brimstone.

"Did you see the torch jobs on the news?"

"I mighta, yeah."

"Somebody pass that gig around? Looking for a man to do them?"

"Why would you ask me?"

"You know why."

"I sold shoes, hats and coats my whole life. Swear on Mother Mary. You know this."

"I know you set fires. Personally I think that job is past you now. But all three of those jobs were done by one man. And if someone was looking for a pro, you would have heard. So spill it."

"I don't know what you're talking about, Dick."

"I told you a long time ago, don't call me Dick."

"Sure, sure. Anything else you wanna waste my time with?"

"You came all this way just to blow me off?" I ask.

"Temples got word to me so I came. I like Temples," Paulie says. "I don't like you. But like I says, you're a pussy cat now, *Dick.* I figure, what's the hurt?"

"I know the folks in those houses that burnt down. I'm looking for answers."

"So? Keep looking."

"I will get answers, Paulie."

"I'm sure your tough guy shtick will work on somebody. Not me."

"Maybe if I just told you the MOs you could think about who might've been able to pull this off."

"Sure. I got a couple of more smokes. Tell me about the burn."

"First house was an invasion. The guy attacked—"

"Nope. No idea. Next one, please," Paulie says.

"Second house had personal messages written on the un-burnt portion of a wall—"

"Sounds terrible but doesn't ring a bell," Paulie says, smiling big and wonderful. "Let me guess, the third house—"

My turn to interrupt. "The third house you don't know about either, right?"

He snubs his smoke out on the dashboard. "Nope. Sorry, Dick. Tell Temples I said hello."

Paulie opens the car door to step out and I grab him by the back of the head and bounce his face off the dashboard. The car bounces. Paulie slumps over and I open the door before he can bleed on the upholstery. He slides out like a wet noodle.

I get out, find him limp and face down on the pier. "How many times do I have to tell you, Paulie. *Do not call me Dick.*" I put my foot just below the base of Paulie's spine, grab his head firmly and yank it back so hard his neck breaks in two. Drag him to the water and throw him in.

Paulie Torreno, the man the mob used to hire to burn down the homes of their enemies, complete with women and children inside as it lit, floats face down on the incoming current next to the ice sheets and other garbage of the city.

Waste of time. I look around for a little while for anyone who might have come with him. No one stirs. No bullet to my chest. Paulie was old and he had outlasted his usefulness, but I'm sure someone besides Temples knew he was here with me. It might not mean shit, but it becomes just another thing I file away. Another reason to check the shadows.

I wish Paulie would have talked if he knew something but this, this was a long time coming.

This was a long time coming.

48

My place: third floor, the smell of the smokehouse next door filing the air with hickory and applewood throughout the night. It competes with the comforting linger of tobacco.

Wood floors, chewed up. Unimaginative trim and baseboards. Simple lines. Front door opens to the first room, occupied with a couch, TV, lamp and bookshelf. Door to the east leads to the toilet and shower. Door to the west leads to the closet I stuffed my bed into. Little else.

In one corner is a kitchen sink, a set of cabinets and an incompetent refrigerator. Toaster oven takes up most of the counter space. Two stove burners set by the sink. I only need one. No microwave, no oven, no dishwasher, no butcher block island with hooks to hang skillets from.

For a time I had a four-legged barstool to make drinking at home alone seem more casual. A guy by the name of Tony Francis Stalwein stopped by my place one night and I had to break that barstool over his head. Long story. I never replaced it.

Curtains cover the one window in the first room. The shower has a window right in it. I have no idea why.

I come in, toss my coat over the couch arm that serves as a coat hanger. Kick my shoes off next to the floorboard heater. Light a smoke off of the left stove burner. It's better for lighting cigarettes than the right. Pour a whiskey and dig through the refrigerator. Half a chicken parm sandwich from yesterday. Good enough. A few minutes in the toaster oven and I'm on the couch, swishing bourbon around in my mouth to numb the taste of ash long enough to detect how little basil is in this marinara on the sandwich.

I keep looking at the other door, the third door in the place. The coat closet door.

The memories I have of her are stored inside that space. Every year I have Father Bentley from Saint Erasmus's come over and bless the coat closet. Not the apartment; just that space.

I finish the sandwich and wish I hadn't started it. Drain the booze. Smoke two cigarettes just sitting there; snub them out slowly. I twist the last Rum Coast butt in a deliberate manner; the kind of motion that brings contemplation to mind. I want to go in the closet, I want her back. I've been shot at, I've been shot, people have looked me in the eye before they've tried to kill me. I've wrecked cars six times as a policeman. A man held a knife to my throat once that still had blood on it from the last person he'd killed. The blood was warm against my skin.

And here I am. The same cannot be said of most of the folks I speak of now.

I received a gift, a divine application. It just seems like I can't be broken. But when she died, when I collected her things and still to this day with each touch, with each whiff of her lingering perfume, with each sight of an item she may only have had fleeting contact with, I am...

Destroyed.

But I stand up anyways. Deliberation is over. Just a moment tonight. I miss her. Warm in the gut from whiskey, feeling that chicken parm roiling in my stomach minutes after choking it down, the last of my tobacco smoke floating out from my lips and nostrils. I walk to the closet. I open the door with a reverence she deserves.

Inside are my deceased wife's belongings that I could not part from. Her folks had come over not too long afterward. After she passed. I let them take of hers what they wanted. They'd had her longer than I did. Her mother cried as she delicately lifted every article of clothing out of its drawer. My mother-in-law pressed her face into every shirt and sobbed harder. My father-in-law took the earrings he got her for her sweet sixteen. The ballerina shoes she had since she was six and kept to her death. I almost hid those shoes before they came over because I knew he would take them and I wanted them for myself. But she was still his little girl. Her sister came and asked for the clothes. Her best friend asked for the half a locket my wife had that they shared. People who were, in reality, mourning the loss of their angel became to me, mere vultures.

By the end I had two cardboard boxes to fill and a fury at God that would not abate. He had given me so little, but He gave me her. And then He snatched her right back. The cardboard boxes found a place for their belongings inside this shrine hidden within my apartment. The fury at God, well, it has found a place hidden within me.

I refinished the wood inside here. The light is sunlight quality. Pictures adorn the walls. Her wedding dress. A shelf chest high with a scattering of the elephant trinkets and miniatures she collected. Here is a detailed miniature of an African elephant cast in resin and hand-painted. Here is a wooden elephant painted in bright colors and abstract designs. Here is one wearing a tunic from the circus. All with their trunks up; a sign of good luck.

Here is a bedside lamp she had as a child with Tinkerbell on the shade. Two pencil sketches she drew in high school. One of a toddler playing with a beach ball, the surf breaking in the background and the other of me sitting in tenth grade science class. I was reading and didn't know she was feverishly copying my image. Ignoring our assignment due by the end of class. She didn't finish the class work, but she was so proud of the drawing. I can smell her perfume. Gardenias. The scent enters me and I can smell her hair, her breath, her skin. My fingertips can trace ghost images of the palm of her hand, the texture of her knuckles, the angle of her jaw. I back out and shut the door before I fall to my knees.

Under my bed I have a suitcase. Inside it I have two changes of clothes, ammo, a carton of cigarettes and almost a quarter million dollars. The threads, bullets and smokes are mine. The cash came off a mob currier I bumped into one night and made dead. If this whole fucking block caught on fire, I'd take that suitcase and dump it out on the bed just so I could fill it with my wife's things.

Father Bentley blesses this shrine. He knows if I ever get caught with my pants down and get the hard goodbye, she needs to be cared for. He has a shelf in the rectory set aside with enough space for two cardboard boxes of some other man's wife's possessions.

I grab the bottle, put my back to the coat closet door, slide down the floor and wake up with whiskey still in my mouth the next day.

Darla Boothe again.

Even through her wrinkles, her dark features inherited by Delilah are pretty. Smoking has aged her the same way it has me. But my tattoos cover up my wrinkles. Weariness and uncompromising sadness have aged in her in a way I haven't known since the war.

"Ms. Boothe—"

"Please call me Darla. That last name is diseased."

"Sure."

She stares off, drags from her smoke. She brought her own this time. Then: "I don't know how long since he walked out the door that I've wanted to get rid of that terrible name and just never did."

"You were busy raising a family."

"Yes. That's true."

We're at a diner. I like this place; the pot roast is cut thick and the beer is ice cold. The scent of bacon is always in the air no matter what meal they are cooking. There's nothing special about the place, which makes it special.

Since Delilah's one horrible phone call and the arsons, Darla's doctor has prescribed her pills to keep her calm. Darla then: fraying at the seams, nervous wreck, almost incoherent. Darla now: mellow. High mellow. Contemplative.

"Tell me about Ben."

"What about him?"

"Was he always a rapist?"

"Ben was...oh God, how can I say this without looking dirty or perverted myself?" Darla studies her coffee like it could provide an answer.

"I don't lump you two together," I say, drag on my cigarette. "If that's what you're worried about."

"Well..." she looks away, embarrassed. "Ben was insatiable. And impulsive. As much as I don't want to compare my sweet baby girl to her dad the date rapist she's kind of the same way."

"Okay."

"It was natural for him to stray from the marriage. Nothing was ever enough. Guys like him could be sleeping with their wives at all hours of the day and night and after a little while it'll just get *old*." She crushes her smoke out, hard. Like it were Ben instead.

"*I got old.*" Bitter. Rightfully so. The betrayal and hostility in those three words speak volumes. The small corner of her soul she has allowed to rot because of her ex-husband has just come out, spoke those words and receded back into the darkness.

Checking her out I don't think she would get old. But I also hear the word "no" to mean "no," so it's difficult to put myself in Ben Boothe's shoes. I wonder if it were Darla's literal age or if he had explored her until he became bored. I don't ask for clarification.

"Dozens of things pushed him out of our house, I'm sure. None the least of which was the way I would not tolerate him looking at our daughters."

Hold the phone.

"Do you think he molested them?" I ask.

A long pause. The world around us revolves through a century before she draws breath to speak. Then: "I think that to Ben...female genitalia are separate entities from anything else in the world. When he walks around viewing God's green earth I think he sees everything we do, but in place of women's faces and personalities and clothes and relation to him he just sees...*something to have sex with.*"

"You mean like women aren't real or they're just objects..."

"I guess so. There's a total disconnect. In the same way I suppose a serial killer will not connect that other people are living entities just like him, I think Ben cannot make the connection that when it comes to having sex there are certain rules to abide by. Morals."

"So you're saying that even if he did molest your girls to him it was simply fulfilling a need."

"Yes."

"Family relation, age, nothing mattered."

"Yes. Any detail, *any* detail would be irrelevant."

"Just sex?"

"Yes."

"He's still a damn child molester," I say. "Did either girl ever tell you he touched them?"

"No. Neither girl likes to talk about him. We just moved on."

"Do you think it's plausible that Delilah went to see her dad?"

"For what?"

"For anything."

"Like what?"

"Some people can just up and leave. It happens. They re-establish themselves somewhere else as somebody else. They have transferrable skills, they have cash on hand, they have some defining moment where they eradicate who and what they are. Look up the Flitcraft Parable from the book *The Maltese Falcon*. But Delilah is not going to disappear without help. Not from how she's been described. I've called anywhere her college degree would take her. No one has a Delilah Boothe working for them. I checked other names, like Delilah White. I checked for her under your maiden name. Nothing.

"Scared people either run for their life or they orbit their familiar locations. Look for the all-clear. So she's programming computers in Fishkill, New York or she's here. In Saint Ansgar. Somewhere."

"But where?"

"That's it. If she's employed I would have found the address her taxes go to. Or the bank account that gets her paycheck. Let's assume she's not. She's getting money from somewhere. She had none herself. She's either found a new cash source—and it's not the government; I checked—or she's stealing. Or bumming."

I have not told Darla about the drug deal that Dobbins arranged. No sense in it really.

"So?"

"So would Ben give her money? A place to crash?"

"He could do anything," Darla says, getting worked up. "I never thought he was a rapist until he was one."

"What about Belinda?"

"No. She wouldn't give her money without telling me everything. She's as worried as I am."

"Have you spoken to her?"

"Yes. She's in the Navy, you know. An officer. Her boat is in a port in Australia right now."

"You can reach her?"

"Yes."

"Give me the number."

49

Belinda Boothe: voice mail. Jeremiah Cross: car keys. Ben Boothe: I'm at his front door.

50

"I'm looking for Delilah. She around?"

Standing at the door, half a cigarette hanging from his mouth. Middle-aged, weary from a lifetime of hard living.

Ben Boothe: wiry guy. It's not so much that he is muscular but rather he has absolutely no body fat. The minimum required muscle it takes to operate the human body is accentuated on him because there is nothing between it and the sandpapered skin stretched taut over it. That illusion makes him appear ripped. Every vein running across him is thick and revealed.

His black hair is heavily salted with an unflattering tone of dirty white. Even at his age his stubble is patchy and thin, but long enough to look scummy. The whites of his eyes are yellow. Small scars from things that look like knife tips are stippled across his body. His nails belong on a rodent. I can see where, back in his early twenties, he might have been handsome. But those years have been pillaged by a lifetime of unbridled self-destruction.

Ben Boothe: human weasel.

He stares right back at me. You can always tell a person who has been hardened by prison. There are lots of things that will harden anyone but prison has its own feel. It chisels with its own style. It makes all the features sharper, detached. Cold the way a serpent is. Somewhere in there are fangs.

I used to ask myself if the fangs were there before the individual went to prison. If they were the *reason* the individual went to stir, or if they appeared after. On the inside. Chicken or egg.

I never found a suitable answer. Not one. Now I don't care. Haven't for a long time.

"No," Ben Boothe says back to me. "She ain't anywheres to be found."

"May I come inside for a moment?"

"No."

"Well, then..." I look around for a moment. It's fucking freezing outside here. But oh well. We do it here then. "When was the last time you'd seen her?" I light a smoke.

"Go ask that twat cop who came sniffin' around here." Rudd's been by.

"I'm asking different questions than she did," I say. "The answers she has won't help me."

"All pork speak the same language. Ask the same shit. It's all you know."

"These are mistakes, friend," I say. Heat is rising. Not so cold anymore.

"Who the fuck are you, pretty boy?" he asks, standing taller.

"*Pretty boy*? Do I look like the cover of a magazine to you? Or is that the pen coming out?"

"You look *pretty*," he says.

I exhale and do my best impersonation of a man who would let a comment like that pass by. I say again: "When was the last time you have seen your youngest daughter?"

"Please, bro. I want to see her as much as I want to see her mother. Fuck off."

"Speaking of her mother, you pick up any tricks from that firebug you bunked with?"

"Goodbye, sweetheart," he says and starts to shut the door. My fist square into his mouth stops it. Ben Boothe crumbles to the floor spitting teeth. I step in, shut the door. We do it here then.

I'm not the kind of guy who minds beating up shitbags. Really, it's not a problem. Hard to believe, but I'll go months of back-to-back cases where I keep my hands to myself the whole time. *Months.*

And then a doozy like Delilah Boothe's case crosses my desk and I am throwing down on fools left and right.

From the welcome mat inside his place, Boothe tries to explode up at me; prison brawl. Unfortunately for him, my right cross—exactly like my left cross—is just short of a freight train.

My knuckles connect just above his eyebrows. There's something very satisfying about punching a man in his forehead. I can't quite put my finger on it but I like it. I punch him hard. Wrecking ball hard.

Boothe's neck freezes as I slug him. The combo of trying to explode up at me and hitting a brick wall with his face might have done a number on his spine. I think he pooped his drawers. He might have whiplash I hit him so fucking hard.

Boothe plops back down into a sitting position. Lays back. Moans so weakly he might be nine-tenths dead. Hands to his face. Stirs ever so slightly. Rolls to and from on his curved back.

"Where is your fucking daughter, Ben?"

His weak moan becomes a pained, forced groan. Hands to face he says: "I ain't seen her in two weeks."

That's a start. Two weeks. Post disappearance. "Give me the rundown."

Bloody hands move from his broken mouth to start rubbing his stiff neck: "She stopped by here. Wanted to live with me. I say *no*. If a broad is staying with me I'm fucking her. Period."

Flashback. Ben's pussy disconnect. File it away for later.

"Gives me the big *you were never there for us as kids and now here's your chance to make up for it.* I told her to hit the road. I finally get outta prison for boning some lying bitch and now this? Gimme a break. Give me a fucking break."

Ben rubs his face, fingers the new holes in his smile.

Spits more blood, safely away from me. Good for him; he's learning how it works.

"Keep talking."

Hate-filled look: "Grubby little bitch says she'll settle for money," Ben snarls. Leans up on an elbow.

"You have cash? Just out of prison?"

"Of course I got money, pig."

"You make her work for it?"

"What's that supposed to mean?"

"That means did you make her *earn* whatever measly cash you gave her?" I squat down beside him; make sure he can see the iron under my jacket. "Grape vine says you didn't discriminate what you have sex with, Ben."

He smirks, the kind that says *hammer on the head of the nail*. Through a blood-smile, holes in the tooth line, fattening lip, he leans away from me and says: "Fucking Darla."

I stand. "Go ahead and answer my question."

"That bore of a wife I used to let follow me around will say anything to demonize me." He gets up. Shaky. Could be trembles from the punch; could be trying to get my guard down. Prison might have taught him that act. I reposition myself and keep an eye on his torso, hands.

"Truth?"

"Who knows? She said a lot of things. Some were true. Sure, I fuck whatever comes along 'cause I *like pussy*."

This guy talks like a thread sewing. Weaves in and out; dodges everything.

"Who was this girl you were convicted of raping?"

"Get her name from the cops." He's becoming less hospitable by the minute. I go for it.

"Did you molest your girls?"

He looks at me, smoldering eyes that say the next time he runs into me on the streets he's going to try and be armed. This guy here was hardened by stir.

"I had forty bucks in my wallet and she took it." Scrawny. All rib bones and sandblasted skin. Wife beater stained by spilt beer, falling cigarette ash and fresh blood. The knuckles in his clenched fists bulge and protrude; the tendons in the backs on his hands flex and become taut like piano strings.

Some humans were birthed as barely tame animals. Later they might become feral. Whatever was decent in Ben Boothe, caused him to fall in love, court, marry, produce children, buy a house, make an attempt at a decent life, it was raped and tossed off to the side by whatever lives behind his eyes now.

And whatever that is, I have broken its mouth and marked its territory as my own.

Our eyes meet. He reads me as I read him. He tries to be aggressive—and he probably is—but any good human animal knows when to fight and when to tuck tail. Call it before the fire gets too hot. Live.

He turns his back on me and walks back into the house.

"You know she's pregnant, don't you?"

Stops. Doesn't turn around. "Naw, she never said nothin'."

"Is it yours?"

"I don't want any more kids." He begins to shuffle off again. "Never wanted the two I had."

"That much is obvious. Where'd she run off to next, then?" I ask, not following.

"Said an old boyfriend would take care of her."

"Name."

"Old boyfriend was his name." He turns around. Stands there, sunlight from the west coming in through a picture window behind him glowing through his emaciated frame as if it were an X-ray.

"In this next room I have a revolver a friend lets me keep. I'm coming back out to shoot you with it."

"What is a felon doing with a firearm?"

"Come back here and find out."

"I don't think your parole officer will like that."

He says nothing. He simply walks around a corner. Maybe a kitchen. Maybe a dining room. I stand there; make sure there is no door behind me he can sneak through.

Seconds are molasses. Infinite. Dragging ass. Let's see what he's made of.

Nothing.

Time ticks. What is probably thirty seconds finds a way to stretch itself out into half a day. The stale cheap smell of his house permeates me. I light a smoke, finish it. Crush it out on the carpet. Grind it out.

Ben doesn't come back out. I step out the front door. Leave.

51

Riggens is on the phone.

"Mr. Buckner?" he asks. I'm accelerating on the highway on-ramp. Time to eat.

"Go ahead."

"Look, I know you don't want to hear this but I think I've got Blane Tapolski dead to rights on the arson."

"It wasn't him."

"Look, I think it was. Remember how I told you he torched some cat's car back in the day? The guy who smacked his sister around?"

"Yeah."

"Well, under the hot lights he let us know that was only the *first* burn job. There are more."

Shit.

"Yeah. He confessed to starting two other fires since then. Another car, then a *house*. And, the house belonged to a girl he tried to date but shot him down."

Shit.

"Really? Did he confess to the Bellview's fire?"

"Not yet. But I plan on another round of interrogation. It's just a conversation or two away."

"Heard from Rudd or Volksman?"

"Sure. I heard from both."

Good. Hold your chin up high, RDB. Here comes some better news. Got to be.

"Shoot," I say.

"Rudd told me that before she met you she heard you were an asshole and she made a bet with a co-worker you'd be better than the rumors. Said she lost fifty bucks."

"Case related? Anything?"

"No."

"Volksman then?"

"He said the pastrami Reuben over at Macotoni's Deli at 5th and Brookside was great but the corned beef Reuben was shit."

"Case related?"

"No."

I hang the phone up.

52

I'm halfway through the pastrami Reuben at Macotoni's when the phone rings.

"Mr. Buckner?" Female voice.

"Yes?" I say, wanting this meal to be interrupted. As further proof that Volksman is a liar and a horrible human being with no intrinsic worth, the pastrami Reuben here *sucks.*

"Mr. Buckner, my name is Belinda Boothe."

Macotoni's is great for all things Italian deli; their hard meats, pastas and imported cheeses can't be beat. I always take a stuffed pepper home with me. But pastrami is, more or less, smoked corn beef, and Macotoni's smokes their own meats. They suck at working a smoker. All I taste is salt and shittiness.

I grab a smoke. Lean back.

"Thank you for calling me back, Ms. Boothe. Has your mother told you about me?"

"She says you're like Dog the Bounty Hunter. Only you have better hair."

I rub my eyes.

"She actually said you cut your hair very close. She said your beard stubble was longer than—"

"Well...anyways," I say. "Do you have a clue where your sister might be?"

"None. I'm sure Mom has told you Delilah flew by the seat of her pants everywhere. She's a scatterbrain who runs from the minutest form of responsibility like it was the plague."

"Can you name any of her friends?"

"None since high school."

"Go ahead with them, please."

"Well, Juliette Marsden would pass for her best friend. Candace Bolivia, Jennifer Blades and Tracy something were other gals she hung out with."

"Boyfriends?"

"She wouldn't commit to anyone. She dated a lot, and to be honest, Mom and I never met half of them, let alone knew their names. She talked a lot about various guys: Eric, Patrick, Randy, Edmond, Paul, Sterling, Travis. We never knew them. Any. By the time she got into high school I was in the Naval Academy anyways."

"Ever hear her mention a Pierce White or a James Dobbins?"

"She spoke of Pierce for a few weeks. I think she was really into him but whatever they had, it didn't last long. I know they got fired together."

"James Dobbins?"

"No. Who was he?"

"He was the boyfriend she got fired with at the next job."

"Really? I know she lost her job—she told me she was fired—but she didn't mention any new boyfriend."

"Huh. Well, it was the same scenario. Different gig, different beau. Same outcome."

"What now then?"

"She called your mom a few days ago saying she was pregnant and scared. Pierce White has been murdered, James Dobbins found dead—although that appears unrelated. He was a doper. Got caught up in doper stuff."

"Do you think Delilah murdered Pierce?"

"I have no idea. The way he was killed would indicate someone with whom he was intimate. Doesn't look right for a stranger murder."

"Oh..."

"Ms. Boothe, do *you* think your sister could kill a man?"

"Delilah...I don't think so. Murder is committing to something."

"Really? She can't commit to anything to the point where she'd put off murder for the simple fact that once it's done, it's done? No turning back?"

"Yes."

"Hmmm..."

"Mom told me about the fires."

"Yes. And I've spoken to the arson investigators and all three of them are centering their investigations on three separate people—one of them your father—and no one seems to think they are connected."

"Dad probably did them."

"Well, even if it was him the investigators refuse to see the glaring connection."

"Why?"

"Because they suck."

"And you think Dad didn't do it?"

"He might have set the fires, sure. I spoke to him and he was rather noncommittal about anything."

"Okay."

"But, even more so, Delilah went to him for help a few weeks ago. Know why she would do that?"

"Out of options. She was out of options. Had to be. Plain and simple."

"Can she not make it on her own?"

"Not really. Delilah was a failure to launch. I don't really remember a time where she lived alone for very long. Maybe between roommates but she'd just fill the void with a boyfriend. She's too much of a social creature. I think she associates surviving with other people. To survive she needs another presence to take care of her. Like an enabler of sorts."

"Okay." I need to start looking for someone else she's living with then. "Your father, he said he gave Delilah forty bucks and sent her on her way. Is your mom not an option to her now?"

"Not if she doesn't have any money. Plus, Mom would just harp on her about straightening up. Always has. Delilah doesn't want to listen to anyone, let alone Mom."

"Alright. So she goes to your father and bums money."

"Really? Dad? She didn't stay?"

"Said an old boyfriend would take care of her. Know anyone?"

"Not Pierce or that Dobbins guy?"

"It might be that Dobbins dropped her off at your dad's. Either way both are dead so if they were taking care of her, they're not now. How would she get money right now, today, you think?"

"Mr. Derne. Or the same way she got it before: playing people's emotions."

"Mr. Derne says he hasn't given her anything. He cut her off. You trust that?"

"Yes. Mr. Derne was always there, but he was old school. Stern. Stern Derne." She laughs an empty chuckle at her rhyme.

"Anything else then?"

"I couldn't tell you. Ever since I joined up I get family updates in snapshots. I get the sanitized versions. It's hard to see things for what they are when you are being told them over the phone. You know?"

"I do."

"About the fires..." Belinda says. "Why won't the other investigators look at one suspect for all three?"

"One guy thinks that Mr. Derne pissed off the mob. He has done work for them over the years that landed in civil court. If his was the only fire I'd at least see where that path takes me but it doesn't make sense otherwise."

"And the other fire? In Delilah's old house?"

"The wife had an ex-boyfriend who is starting to

confess to other arsons. That investigator thinks it's only a matter of time before he confesses to this one as well."

"Well, that makes sense."

"Yeah, but things like that happen. A crime occurs, you attach a suspect to it—even if it is purely circumstantial—you investigate and you find out that suspect has committed other crimes just like the one you are working but the suspect didn't commit *this* crime." I exhale. Long week. "Things like that *happen*. They've happened to me. They're happening now with the fire."

"I see."

Silence between us.

"Is there anything else I can help you with?" she asks.

"Yes." I think of a kind, pleasant way to ask, and then decide on how I always ask things. "Did your father molest you growing up?"

Silence. Different quality than the last one.

Might as well say *yes*.

53

"Belinda?" I have to ask. She hasn't so much as breathed since I brought it up.

"Mr. Buckner, I have no idea how you would get such a—"

"Your mom hinted at it," I say, snorting smoke. "Your dad dodged it like a bull was coming and he was wearing all red."

"Dad...he, uh...we might have...oh, *oh* I wish Mom would keep her damn mouth *shut*! I have worked so hard to get beyond this and I have, I *really* have, and now fucking Delilah has to go and disappear when she knows how worked up Mom gets over her little angel with dirty wings and she starts telling people things and—"

I wait. I light another smoke. Wait more. Her rant ends and time stretches out. Finally I hear her sniffing back small cries.

Whisper, confessional: "Dad touched us a little. I described it to my therapist as 'exploratory.' Nothing more. I think he was...weighing his options. That's all."

"You said 'us.' Delilah too? One of your friends who spent the night?"

"My sister. She brought it up one time. Her experience was the same as mine. No intercourse, no...just, as I said, *exploratory*. I told her to tell me if it happened again. She never did."

Exploratory could mean a few things but I'll leave it alone.

"Tell your mother?"

"No. No one."

"Not a teacher, not a policeman? Not a stranger on the street?"

"I said *no one.*"

"What about her? She tell anyone?"

"Who knows. Delilah has this way of starting to confess things that she thinks in the moment are great ideas and then as the words are coming out she just clams up. Thinks better of it."

"Your mom said the same thing."

"I hate that about Delilah."

"You think your dad got her pregnant?"

"Oh God! Could he have? I mean Jesus, how could she—"

"The timelines don't readily match up but I seriously doubt anyone has told the truth so far. Hell, for that matter Delilah might not be pregnant. But if she is...and if Delilah is as desperate and out of options as you say she is...I don't know her. You do. Could she exchange help from your father for sex?"

"Mr. Buckner, I—"

Cuts off. She moans. I wait.

Belinda Boothe vomits. I hear it splash on the other end of the line. She chokes out the words, "I have to call you back," and hangs up.

Tough thing to hear.

I'll take the puking to mean two things.

One, Belinda worries that Delilah *would* do it.

Or two, she won't be calling back.

54

Clevenger: "RDB, bad news."

"If the news is worse than Volksman saying the pastrami Reuben at Macotoni's was good I don't want to hear it."

I'm paying my bill and he calls. I drop a twenty on the counter and check my watch. Jeremiah will need his car back in four hours and I have one more stop.

"Funny you should mention Volksman," he says.

"Please say Volksman is dead. Please. It'll serve him right for pimping this grotesque sandwich."

"No. On the contrary, his case is solved."

"The arson?"

"Yes. You'll love this."

"Will I really or will I hate you?"

"Hate me. Early this morning fishermen pulled a dead man out of the bay. Paulie Torreno. Executed. Dumped."

"The Andretti Family's torch man?"

"The one and only."

"Unbelievable," I say.

"Listen, Richard—"

"Volksman—who is a worthless piece of shit by the way—lands an arson, pins it on the mob for something that went down decades ago then just happens to find a dead mobster firebug? He's tying all his loose ends with messy little knots and calling the case closed?"

"Why would he not?"

"You know, Volksman—I'll bet money...*good* money—that Volksman would rather find a fall guy and whack his ass to make it a convenient way to close his case."

"Volksman is lazy but he wouldn't gun down a mobster just to lighten his own case load."

"You give him too much credit," I say.

"I know your hand is turning up all jokers but we'll get through this."

"Jesus—well, thanks for the head's up. I gotta go. I'll call you later."

"Hang on, now," Clevenger says.

"Yeah?"

"White's wife has an alibi for the murder. Checks out. Said White went to the doctor to get tested for AIDS and whatnot. Some idiot at the doctor's office mailed him the results and the wife opened the letter, confronted him about it, et cetera. Big fight. She rolled out and went on some huge bender in Vegas. Probably racked up enough infidelity counts to rival a professional athlete. She's on at least eight different casino security cameras.

"She didn't know of any mistresses he kept. I checked with his work place and his friends, and none of them coughed up anybody. Must have learned well getting burned with Delilah Boothe. Bottom line is Pierce White is dead by unknown party."

"Okay," I say.

"Also," Clevenger says hesitantly, "Pinky Meyers got busted on a parole violation three weeks ago. Been in the pen ever since. He's not our guy."

"That was a big to-do about nothing."

"Just thought narrowing your suspect list down would be good news."

"It is. Riggens called with similar news less than an hour ago."

"I heard he pulled in Abigail Bellview's ex-boyfriend for questioning. He confess?"

"Riggens thinks it's forthcoming. Now Volksman."

"Well, you know Rudd likes Ben Boothe."

"Yes. We spoke earlier. He's so dirty one fire isn't going to put any tarnish on his record."

"Rapists," Clevenger says. "As a species they are never going to get better, are they?"

"Sure," I chuckle. "Alright, I gotta go for real this time."

"No problem," he says. I hang up.

A-bomb. What a fucking A-bomb.

The cashier hands me my change and I set the tip down on the table. I start to head out and veer off to the counter again.

The cashier is the diner type: middle-aged, overweight, pleasant-looking, chewing gum. Poofy hair, pencil behind her ear. Apron.

"Ma'am?" I ask.

"Yes, sir?"

"What's better here, the corned beef Reuben or the pastrami Reuben?"

"Oh my gracious, honey." She seems shocked that I wouldn't just *know*, let alone *ask*. "The corned beef. Everyone knows that."

Fucking Volksman.

55

Juliette Marsden was married six years ago and became Juliette Franklin.

Delilah's high school best friend is of average height, weight and pretty. Noticeable, but not stunning. I prefer noticeable as opposed to stunning because I am a man of limited charm and the stunning women expect a lot from suitors that my charm will not produce. Nor do I care to put out that much effort.

Juliette Franklin's cleavage is just the way I like it: exposed, Grand Canyon deep and in my face. She and her husband let me in their door after I tell them who I am and what I am doing. He prepares drinks and Mrs. Franklin sits down next to me. Close enough I can count the freckles on her boobs.

Even if she doesn't know anything this visit will be worth it.

If her husband has a problem with his wife's conduct towards unannounced guests he either doesn't say anything for fear I'll fuck up his world or he doesn't notice.

Or care.

"Yes, Delilah was here three days ago," Mrs. Franklin says as if it weren't a big thing.

Well, I'll be damned. Mrs. Franklin, if you knew how many people I have killed in pursuit of this gal.

"What were you having again, Mr. Buckner?" the husband asks as he sets a fu-fu looking cocktail in front of his wife and her boobs.

"Three Wise Men."

"Just a shot? Want a beer also?"

"No, no beer. But you can put the shot in a glass."

"What kind of glass would you like?" He smirks, asshole-like. "A *shot* glass?"

"A collins glass is fine."

"You want *that* much booze?"

"Yes, I do." I make it a point to turn my attention back to his wife's chest.

He simply turns his back and begins grabbing bottles. Good boy.

"Three days ago?" I ask her boobs.

"Yes. She stayed here for about a week and then left. Just got antsy one day. Upset. It was hard to talk, really. I offered her a longer stay, but she said she was going out of town."

"Say where by chance?"

"Three Mile High, I believe."

"Say where in Three Mile High?"

"No. But she has a boyfriend up there."

"Does boyfriend have a name?"

"Something about Jimmy. Jim. Or John..."

"James? James Dobbins?"

"Yes! Thank you."

"My wife is terrible with names." Mr. Franklin sets the collins in front of me. He smiles and for the first time I can see he doesn't want me looking at his wife the way I am. Which, incidentally, I have not been trying to hide at all.

"I'd hate for Juliette to not be able to help you with your case. I'm glad you're able to jog her memory about those things. I know *I* can't," he says.

"No problem, Mr. Franklin," I say and take a drink. Severely watered down. Cocksucker. "I'm good with getting what I want from women."

He gives me an incredulous stare and I persist, "So don't worry about the case. If there's anything else your wife is terrible at that I want, I'll be able to work out in the end."

"I see..." He draws from his beer and looks to his wife. She looks back and smiles blankly.

"So Delilah came here. Say where she's been?"

"Poor thing. Said her stepdad tossed her out of a place he bought for her, so she went to her real dad and he wanted nothing to do with her. She came here and of course we put her up for the night. She just let her hair down for a few days and then she said thanks but she had decided to move in with her boyfriend in Three Mile High."

"I see."

"Funny," Mrs. Franklin says, thinking hard. "You know, I never remember her mom remarrying. Also, Delilah never struck me as the type of girl to just run around like she's doing, sleeping on couches and moving in with men."

"Well, honey," Mr. Franklin says, "you two have lost touch since high school. A lot can happen to a person to change them."

"Of course," his wife says.

Mr. Franklin looks on, sipping beer. His eyes sneak back at me anytime I lift the watered down drunk to my lips. I wonder if he snuck a little dribble of piss in it. He seems like the kind of frat-house fuck-face who would pull a junior varsity prank like that.

"Delilah isn't that kind of girl?" I ask. "Until you offer to let her live here? *Then* she becomes that kind of girl?"

"Well—" Mrs. Franklin says. The thought seems to block her up. Mr. Franklin looks on, not wanting to talk about Delilah's conduct.

"Mr. Buckner, are you investigating her sexual past or are you making sure she is safe and sound?" he asks. A tell.

I look him in the eye and flash the cards in my hand at him. "Both."

"I see..." And with that he simply sets his mostly full beer down and stands up. "Honey," he says, "I just realized I need to finish with that thing out in the car. I'll be back in about, oh, fifteen minutes."

"Great, baby," he gives her a little peck and takes off. He gets my message.

Now that we're alone: "Did Delilah mention being pregnant at all to you?"

"Oh, Mr. Buckner," she says, surprised. "In confidence but...I didn't think she—"

"She called and told her mother. Her mother told me. Have you told your husband?"

"No, I haven't. I just figured he wouldn't care. He always kept his distance from her."

"Shy?"

"Yes."

"I see. Let me guess: didn't know what to say so he'd just complement her."

"Yes. He was always very nice."

"I bet," I look at her, so clueless. "You seem very nice as well."

"Thank you." Blushes a little. I watch the color rise in her cleavage.

"You are extremely beautiful, I might add," I say.

She giggles. Fans herself. There's nothing better than making a run at an asshole's wife in his own home and coming up roses.

"I hope for the best, Mr. Buckner." Change of subject. All right.

"Her mother. She's very afraid," I say.

"I would be too. What with it being—" She stops, sips her drink. "Will you excuse me, please?"

"Of course."

She gets up and carries her breasts towards the bar. Freshens her drink. While she is away I grab her husband's beer and spit in it. I'd drink it myself but who knows what this guy has. Since he obviously was sleeping with Delilah he's got whatever she gave him.

Mrs. Franklin comes back, sits down. Composes herself. Stirs her drink. It's all clear booze now, no coloring, no fruit, no salt rim, no umbrella. I take my highball glass and knock back the waste of alcohol in it. One swig. We're about done here.

"May I call you Juliette?"

"Please do."

"Juliette, do you have Delilah's cell phone number?"

"No. If she had one she never told me."

"She made a call to her mother—when she said she was pregnant—and it was anonymous. Is your number unlisted?"

"Yes. My husband is an aide to a politician. He doesn't like to be bothered."

"Democrat?"

"Of course."

"I thought so."

I give her my card and stand up. "Thank you for your time, Juliette."

"You're welcome." She gives me a bright smile.

"Thanks for the drink."

"Anytime."

I get my coat. She comes scurrying up to me and hands me a sheet of paper from a notepad I saw under a magnet on the refrigerator.

It has her name and phone number written on it, surrounded by little scribbles hearts straight out of a high school yearbook. Before being her little flirty-note, it was the grocery list. Her hearts have to compete for space on the paper with things like "eggs," "buttermilk" and "stronger fiber pills."

I imagine the fiber is for her husband, who looks like he hasn't been able to shit out that used condom his boyfriend lost up in there days ago.

I give Juliette a smile and open the door.

I walk out and see her husband in the garage doing nothing. The door is up and I walk right in.

"Mr. Franklin?"

He looks at me, straightens and then leans all cool-like against the roof of his non-descript four-door sedan. So tough.

"Yes."

"So, you fuck Delilah Boothe once or twice and then she splits." The look he gives is one that all guilty people who cannot hide their guilt give. I expect more from a politician's aide. Lying convincingly should be the language he does business in.

"I figure the first time was because she was in a terrible place, vulnerable, whatever and you were all cutesy and gentlemanlike."

I walk closer. Right up on him. See the first droplets of sweat on his brow, his upper lip. It's freezing outside.

"But after that, she either felt dirty for doing that to her *generous* best friend or thought it was going to get out of control. She's got a long history of ruining things by sleeping with married men. Too bad you couldn't cash in more often."

"Fuck you, sir," he says as limp-wristed and empty as the devil must have been moments before he was cast down. "Now get off my property."

My hand out. He looks down. I take his cell phone right off his belt. He does nothing. Weak. Thumb through; find a listing in his address book for Delilah. View it, write it down.

I drop his cell phone to the concrete. Look at him. Start to turn around and say: "If you're done with the one inside, I'll take her."

I walk off. He says nothing. I leave. Jeremiah is getting off work soon.

56

It dawns on me and I call Mrs. Franklin as soon as I'm down the street.

"Hello?"

"Mrs. Franklin? It's Richard Dean Buckner—"

"Oh my God, I was hoping you'd call me—"

"I know. We can have sex later. Right now I need you to tell me who's the father of Delilah's baby."

"Excuse me?"

"You had started to say something when I asked you about it earlier. Who is it?"

"Oh, Mr. Buckner...I guess I thought she told her mom and she told you."

"No."

"Well, this is gross but...her dad."

57

Ben Boothe's ramshackle shitbox sits on a small lot in a bad neighborhood and faces a major street.

The tree in the front lawn looks like it was struck and killed by lightning twenty years ago and now the weight of decades of decay are taking their toll. The thing looks mummified: withered and feeble.

I pull up alongside the street. I can't get in the driveway; the police cruisers, the ambulance and the crime scene tape are in my way.

The trifecta: Riggens fingers the Shitski flamer, Volksman fingers the conveniently dead mob flamer, now this. Whatever it is, I know two things: arson investigator Rudd is here and the EMTs are carting out a body bag.

I get out. Approach Rudd. She waves me through the police line, albeit with a sour look on her face.

"He dead?" I ask.

"Yes, he is."

"You do it?"

"No, I did not."

"His daughter? You seen her?"

"No, she did not do it either."

"Did Volksman kill your suspect for you also? Make it an easy case to close?"

"Volksman did not kill the mob goon he pinned his fire on. Please be reasonable, Mr. Buckner—"

"What happened then?"

"Why do you care?"

"I was here an hour ago. Looking for his kid."

"That explains it."

"Explains what?"

"I was here a few days ago as you are well aware. You

come by today, barking about more crimes. I stop by today with his Intensive Supervision Officer while he made a home visit. The ISO requested I come inside with him. Ben knew me from the arson investigation and probably put two and two together. He left the door open, walked into the other room and ate a 9mm. End of story."

"So you are going to pin your arson on him?"

"Parolee gets out, immediately commits another felon— which will be his third strike, mind you—and we come sniffing around from a few different angles. You and me and the ISO. He knows the gig is up, doesn't want to go back inside, doesn't want to run, so he cowards his way out. Signed, sealed, delivered."

I know the look consuming her eyes. Confident. Swimming the deep seas of arrogance. Unwavering. A believer. I cannot tell her anything about her case. It's solved.

I think about saying that his daughter is running around telling people he knocked her up. But I don't. I don't even ask who the homicide investigator is. Doesn't matter anymore.

Rudd adjusts her coat and begins to say something but her face becomes an angry red smear. Her words twist and distort in my ears and melt down into a buzzing sound that goes well with the swirl of color dripping across my vision. I feel my brain go numb and my eyes swell as the pleasant tan of Rudd's face darkens to a brown and to a black. The whites of her eyes spill down her face like popped eggs and runners of cream fall like rain. I hear her voice crawling up from some void towards me, and as it approaches the Big Fry smear slowly inches back to where it hides in my brain.

"Mr. Buckner. I need a statement," Rudd says with her hands on her hips and an impatient look on her face. Scolding mother look.

"What?" I say.

"I'll need a statement about your interaction with Mr. Boothe. A *written* statement. And I'll need it now."

She hands me an official Saint Ansgar PD Witness Statement form. I write, "Sexual predator did the right thing," fold it in half and put it under her windshield wiper.

I leave. Confirming his alibi with the supposed rape victim can wait now.

58

Drop off Jeremiah's car.

Then: a bar. Tie one on out of frustration. Maybe start a fight. Then: home. Then: sleep it off. The next day: Rail to Three Mile High. Cab to a rental car place. Straight to James Dobbin's residence. I park, take a photo of Delilah and walk up and down the street.

The entire neighborhood is bitterly cold and drained of color. Dirty snow and shades of pale gray dominate the street. The cold grips at my ankles where my pant cuffs are wet. It sneaks fingers down my collar.

First two houses, no answer. Next seven, answer the door but not the questions. I lose count after that.

Never seen her.

Didn't know the guy to begin with.

Can't help you.

Can't help you but I'll keep an eye out.

Never seen nobody.

That guy over there is dead. Shot in his own house. Could have been me.

He's dead now?

I thought he was gay. Always has dudes over. Hmmm...the universe is a strange place.

It goes on and on. I pass Dobbin's house on both sides and head to my car. Hour and a half. Canvassing goes like that; either people answer the door at every house with something to say or the neighborhood locks down like an airport when somebody whispers bomb.

Beside my car I trod up into the lawn. I light a smoke and just stare at the home, vacant now. Not a FOR RENT sign posted in front of it. The police tape has been taken down. Now, just...a ghost haven.

A neighbor pulls in to the next house north. The first house I knocked on with no answer. Looks more respectable than who I would think should reside in this place. I go over.

"Excuse me, sir?"

Middle-aged, glasses, bald down to his temples, average trench coat, briefcase, designer knock-off dress shoes, suit that cost him a few hundred, placid face.

"Yes?" He sounds stiff. Like he's readying himself for me to punch him. What the hell kind of neighborhood is this?

"I am looking for a missing young woman. Her boyfriend used to live next door. I was wondering if I could show you her picture? Maybe ask you about them?"

He eyeballs me just enough. A tell: he distrusts any kind of law enforcement look. He doesn't answer.

"She dated the man next door," I say. "Her mom wants to speak with her. Like I said, she's gone missing."

"Oh," he says. "Oh..." Eases up just a notch. He looks at the picture as it's in my hand. I offer it and he takes it gently.

Studies.

"She drives a red, four-door—"

"Taurus. Ford Taurus," he says, nodding. "She would come by here only a few weeks ago. Never saw her before, never saw her after. Only about a week. Thought she was visiting from out of town. Had plastic bags from a burger joint downtown. Melrose Half-Pounders."

I write it down. Then: "I'm glad you know the car."

"I used to own one for years. Hers was a deep red, almost wine. Mine was green. I loved that car."

"Okay. See her with anybody besides the neighbor?"

"No. Never really saw the neighbor. He's dead, right?"

"Yes. Doper. What do you mean you never saw *him*?"

"Well, nothing suspicious, I guess. He seemed like a

keep-to-himself kinda guy, really. Left, came back with groceries, usually from a gas station. Never on a regular basis, though. I don't think he held employment."

"Did he get any regular visitors?"

"None that I took note of, no."

"Okay. But you've seen the girl here carrying food bags. Last week or so?"

"No. That was yesterday, actually."

"Yesterday?"

He thinks about it. Witnesses often give scattered testimony. The worse the crime, the worse the scatter. People who aren't trained to observe every little detail usually don't take them in very well. And even then, sometimes they'll have good information but they'll hold back because when a cop asks questions they didn't ask THAT question.

Finally: "Yes."

He motions to the driveway and carves a vehicle's path through the air. "She drove up, scurried to the front door, knocked, pounded, shouted. I was thinking of telling her he had...you, know, *passed.* But I didn't want to be the one telling a complete stranger. She was just making so much noise beating on the door and all. It caught my attention."

"Make out what she said?"

"No. But whatever it was, she was saying it emphatically."

"Then?"

"She left."

"Remember which way?"

He points to a pair of fresher-looking tire prints in the snow that run from Dobbins' driveway through the man's own yard and into the street. The tires knocked down some kind of sign that was posted in his yard. A roofing advertisement or something.

"She went that way."

I give him my card. Then: "Anything else?"

He studies my card the way he did her photo. "No. But I'll think on it and if anything else comes about I'll call you."

"Thanks," I say and turn around. Flick my cigarette butt into Dobbin's old yard. Get in the car, start it.

The neighbor walks down his yard and rights the sign. Dusts off snow the color of ash and muddy water. His grimace fills his face. Goes in. Just when I start to think about how a decent, respectable man lives in this neighborhood I drive past the sign and see it says he's a registered sex offender.

It fits the theme today. I leave. More important things right now.

59

Melrose Half-Pounders.

I set the photo on the countertop. French fries crackle in the background and create an omnipresent noise. Like the buzz of a hive, the white noise of fryers boiling and meat cooking fill the ears.

A counter guy walks over: requisite pimples and mottled skin belonging to anyone who shuck and jives in a lard-filled fast food restaurant. Scrawny. Greasy, scraggily hair spilling out in tendrils from underneath his ineffective hair net. Defeats the purpose.

His fingernails are long and dirty. He stares at me with the apathetic look that any adolescent has. I look at him. Push the photo across the counter.

"When was the last time you seen her?"

He looks at the picture, thinks. "How do you know I've seen her?"

"Everybody says so. Now spill it."

He regards me with angst-fueled contempt. As if giving me a pseudo-tough guy routine will earn him street credit.

"C'mon, goofball," I say, taking the picture back. "Don't make me punch you so hard the impact pops all your zits."

He looks at my knuckles and sees they've been chewed up with a lifetime of slugging faces.

Instantaneous change in attitude. "She was here maybe a half hour ago."

Bingo.

"Then?"

"She went across the street."

I look out the storefront and see a row of non-descript brick buildings. Look like small warehouses or general office buildings.

"Which one?"

"The one with the stone staircase. Double doors."

"She went in there thirty minutes ago?"

"Yes."

"With anybody?"

"Just her leftovers."

I set down my card and look at him. "I'm going over there. If she comes outside without me, call this number. If you do that for me, I'll come back and leave a bill on the table. If you *don't* and I find out she went this way, I'll come back and leave your teeth on the table. Do we understand one another?"

A nod and I'm out the door.

60

This is what a payday smells like.

Out the burger joint's door and my cell is dialing. Derne answers.

"Yes, Mr. Buckner?"

"Good news. I'm fairly confident I will be meeting Ms. Boothe in about three minutes."

"Really? Thank God. Where?"

I tell him.

"Three Mile High?"

"That's correct. I can ask her if she will come back to Saint Ansgar with me, but if she refuses I can't make her."

"Well, at this time of day I guess I could take the Rail up there. Think she'll be around for another ninety minutes or so?"

"I'll try. If nothing else I can tail her and we can meet up."

"Are you near the Rail station?"

"Actually only about five blocks north. When you get off the train just ask a Rail cop how to get to the Starlight Theatre. It's three blocks south of us."

"Okay. Train station to the Starlight Theatre, then two more blocks north to this address."

"Correct. Right across the street from Melrose Half-Pounders. It's a burger joint. You'll smell it well before you see it."

"Thank you, Mr. Buckner. I can't—I just—" He pauses. "Thank you."

"Yup."

"I'll wire the money while I'm on the train. How's that sound?"

"Sounds like we're getting squared up. I'll see you."

That's what I want to hear. Cash up front. Sometimes things like this don't turn out the way the client likes so they become reluctant to pay. Derne's case went from a simple missing person to some kind of freak show crime spree. I hope I didn't blow my wad prematurely but the thought of this being over in the next ninety minutes makes me salivate.

I walk up the stone steps to the building. In the door. The lobby is nothing special. Plain brown-colored tile. Stairs and blank endless hallways.

On the wall is a directory. Entire floors have the word VACANT next to them. Fifth floor sees a lot of activity.

Friday at 3:00 p.m. AA meets in room 506. Monday at 4:00 p.m. Incest Survivors meets in room 501. Tuesdays and Thursdays and every other Friday, Unity Christian Mission holds prayer vigils in room 503 and 504 starting at noon and continuing until God has listened.

It goes on. No doubt, this building has occupants somewhere.

Today is Monday. Watch says 4:17 p.m. Ben Boothe knocked up his little girl. I make my pick.

61

Elevator out of order: stairs, then.

Five flights later I step out into a dark hallway. There's one room with a light on and I hear some kind of commotion behind the door. I stand outside and listen for a moment. Women conversing. The room number matches up with the directory downstairs. Delilah is in here. I can smell her food. I push the door open and enter to the sounds of voices.

Open room. Table. Chairs. Dozen or so females from all walks of life, trying to enjoy what is left of it. Knowing they are there to tell stories shunned by normal society and to support each other.

A younger-looking female, maybe thirty-one or -two, doesn't turn around. From a seated position I can cull her stats: five-six, one-thirty, black and blue, no known tattoos or scars. Not a dead ringer for Abigail Bellview, but I can see where Benny made his mistake, high or not.

"Hello," one brunette says in a quizzical tone. She's seen better days. The group tries to smile but there is a palpable weight in the air, heavier than a fart in church. Regret. Shame. Disgust. It clings like lead and oil to the atmosphere.

The seen-better-days brunette stares at me for a moment. "How can we help?"

"Gosh," I say and do my best to look uncomfortable. "I was looking for room 501. It's a survivor group."

"This is room 501," she says.

"You're here," another woman says.

The seen-better-days brunette says: "Please come in. We have plenty of time for you to share."

Incest Survivors Anonymous. Incredible.

"Great. Thanks," I say. What the hell. Derne said ninety minutes, right?

62

Almost sixty minutes into it now: "My name is Jennifer and I am an Incest Survivor," the woman next to me says.

I doubt very much her name is Jennifer. She trembles and will not stop staring at her small hands. She isn't bad looking but on the same token she's not great looking either. It could be the situation talking; maybe if I didn't have an idea about what is going to be coming out of her mouth I might find her more attractive.

But as I study her and decide yes, she's not bad after all, she goes and ruins it.

"I'd been sleeping with my first cousin for eight months the first time I got pregnant." A solitary tear runs down her cheek, flushed red as the site around a compound fracture. "I was fourteen."

That's how she starts it off. I wish I'd gotten a cup of coffee before I sat down. Delilah's hamburger aroma is making me hungry.

"The baby was born with several incestual defects. She—it was a 'she'—lived for almost a week outside the womb. I named her Desiree."

I've heard a lot of terrible stories but I've never really been a fan of these types. Listening to ashamed and broken people trying to piece themselves back together, so fragile a sneeze tears them apart; not my scene.

"My cousin never claimed Desiree and my parents never knew about us. They thought I was just a 'common' slut." She adds air quotes around the word *common*. "It would be years before I told them I was no ordinary loose woman."

When Derne arrives I'll pair up the two of them and call my end of the bargain fulfilled. It's settled: dinner at

Melrose Half-Pounders. Then a few days off. Tie one on every night.

"The next one I aborted. I couldn't live with myself knowing I'd put some terminally handicapped child into the world to suffer and die. I thought the choice would be hard...but it wasn't."

Oh God, lady. Finish up already.

"I don't think I'd make a very good mother." She sounds very small saying that.

Maybe I'll stop by that breakfast diner next to the rail station and look for the waitress who gave me the phone book.

"After a while, Elliot—my cousin's name is Elliot—did I say that already? He started dating a girl. A cheerleader. Just a run-of-the-mill high school tramp. Her name was Roberta but everybody called her Bobbi." She says the name in an airhead, California-girl falsetto. Vitriol drips off her tongue with it.

"Elliot dumped me like I was...I don't even know. I felt so *ugly. So damn used.* It was so abrupt. It was an insult after all I did. He paraded around with Bobbi the Cheerleader, taking her to meet the damn family, and I had to just sit there in the background and cry. I had to lie about why I was bawling all the time. I was violated. He didn't care. I had never felt more violated and used."

Jennifer starts to cry hard, enraged. I eyeball Delilah and I can see why she had a lot of dudes sniffing around. Even knowing what I know about her she is still attractive. Already you can see the first faint marks of her hard life wearing on her, like a car left sitting in the desert. It won't take long to start to see the sandblasting and the sun blisters on her.

Jennifer stabs one bolt-straight finger onto the table. "I gave him my virginity." She stabs it again. "I let him finish inside me." A third time. "I carried his babies. I went through all the humiliation of the first pregnancy." A clenched fist now. "I lost the baby...he never even consoled me. Why does that surprise me? He wasn't even there. Just started fucking me again a few months later."

I shift in the seat. The air around Jennifer is boiling with heat rising from her scars. I start to build the gall to excuse myself and leave the structure altogether. I'm the only dude here anyways. I'm starting to think this is a women's only group and they just don't have the heart to tell me. I'll just stakeout the building for Delilah's exit and just when my mouth opens Jennifer cuts me off with her continued rant.

"You know what they say, *a woman scorned...*"

Her face sets hard, decided. "I found them one night."

I hadn't noticed until now that Jennifer has tats up and down her arms. She has long sleeves but in her confession she's been fidgeting, rolling them up to her elbows. She gathers her hair in one fist and her neck is inked as well. I like tattoos but these are ghetto. Looks like prison ink to me.

Prison ink: melted KY jelly mixed with soot, rubbing alcohol and water. They burn candles and collect the soot, then scrape a handful of KY off of their cellmate's ass. Little bit of toilet bowl water and some rubbing alcohol, stir, do whatever it is they do. You get Jennifer's artwork.

The confessor's face settles into a tranquil daze. "I didn't *kill* them. I didn't tell the court this but I was going to. Instead I made Elliot admit to Bobbi the Cheerleader that he'd been with me for years and we'd made babies. I made him cry and tell her that his dad and my dad were brothers. We weren't ordinary lovers. Our babies weren't ordinary babies."

Well, she knows who she is. A lot of people can't say that about themselves anymore. Not honestly they can't.

"*That's* what Bobbi the Cheerleader was sleeping with.

That's what she was parading around with. Whatever she'd done to him *I'd* done first. I wanted her to think about that and then see how pretty she felt."

I look at Delilah and she just has her small chin resting in one of her small palms. Her eyes wet with sympathy for Jennifer the Incest Survivor. Jennifer the arch enemy of Bobbi the Cheerleader. Delilah's eyes flick over to me. She must feel the weight of my stare. She gives me a smile and drops it the way someone does when they're not really smiling but do it anyway. I look back to Jennifer.

"Bobbi the Cheerleader puked. Three times. At gunpoint, I made Elliot call me his first lay. I shot him in the leg. I was aiming for his dick but the gun jumped. He almost died. I already had. I died a long time ago. But I still breathe. That's what he gets for how he treated me. I got eight years for it."

Probably served her time in Happenstance State Prison. It's about forty miles out of town, north. It's a shithole of a women's prison. I bet little, scorned Ms. Jennifer here is much harder than she looks. Eight years in that prison will sharpen a kitty's claws. She might just be hot again, ghetto tats or not.

"Look at me now. Who will want me?" she says.

She is done now. Her gritty eyes search the table for a hidden meaning in the fake wood grain of the surface. Before the group can console her or whatever she abruptly stands up and goes to the drink table. The half-full coffee pot is ancient and long-stained brown. Split patterns of sugar and non-dairy creamer decorates the table.

I look back to Delilah and she is staring at me. I think might she might smell something foul with me showing up, maybe she'll confront me. But she doesn't. Instead it just looks like she is waiting. So is everyone else.

"What?" I ask.

"I think Jennifer will need a minute," the brunette who

has seen better days says. "Why don't you go ahead."

"Oh I—"

"First time?" a rotund, cruel-looking woman asks. She has the air of a lifer in these kinds of things; she's probably been to enough court-mandated AA and NA groups to have the procedures and habits down.

"I was nervous my first time," a cherubic woman says. She looks like she should be crocheting and bragging about her son's high school football achievements, not talking about being in a mutual sexual relationship with relatives. "Just start and it will share itself. You'll feel so much better."

Heads nod in agreement. The rotund lifer smiles. She's missing a tooth. If she keeps goading me I'll take care of the rest here shortly.

I shrug and light a Rum Coast. What the hell. Derne said ninety minutes, right?

63

"My name is Joe Tiller and I am an Incest Survivor."

"You don't have to share last names," the seen-better-days brunette group leader says to me.

"I guess I was around puberty when I began having sex with both my twin older brothers," I say. Over at the table I see Jennifer take a flask out of her jacket and spike her coffee. A lot.

"And we just never stopped. I knew people would look down on us but it felt special. It felt loving. Maybe it felt natural because we were brothers...I don't know. It's not like they would hang out with me when they were around their friends, so the sex was really all I had if I wanted attention from my older brothers. And what little brother didn't?

"Eventually after Ben graduated high school he married a girl. Had kids. Bill and I never cared; neither did Ben. We kept it up, but Ben—a couple of years ago—he killed himself Hemmingway-style."

I'm sure this crowd is used to this stuff. I hope.

"Dropped his wife off at work, took his kids to school, went back home and got out the double-barreled shotgun. Loaded it with lead slugs, put the barrels in his mouth and put a toe on both triggers. Might have named one Joe and the other Bill. Who knows. I'd be flattered if he did, but..."

Stares. Crickets chirping. Mouths open just enough. Off in the distance a dog barks.

"He got both barrels both off. I would have thought as he toed them down the first one would have been all. But no. The slugs went right through the damn roof two floors up. Bill and I told him he paid too much for that house."

I'm having fun now. I might start doing this on my off time.

"And another thing if you all will indulge me: Ben inherited that shotgun from Dad. The bitch of it was, Dad had promised it to me. I guess that's neither here nor there, but still."

Delilah stirs and I keep my peripheral vision on her. It would be my luck that I'm bullshitting my way through an incest confession and she slips away.

"Anyway, Bill and I, uhhh...we kept going but it was strange without Ben's help. Bill and I could pull it off, but we were a *trio*. I have no idea why Ben would kill himself; he had a good job and his kids were too young to be fuck-ups. Maybe it was because he thought his wife was banging the neighbor. She probably was, but then again he was banging us."

I stop and look at my hands. Delilah in my peripheral. Everyone else is staring at me. They want more. Call it the train wreck syndrome. I like the stopping point I've found.

"You're right," I say to the cherubic woman. "I *do* feel better."

The group stirs for just a moment, looks to the woman next to me. She shakes her head *no*. She'll share next time, I guess. Probably doesn't want to follow up the Joe Tiller story. C'mon Derne. Fifteen more minutes or so if he's on the money.

Heads turn. Someone clears her throat. Someone else runs her fingers through her hair to add some bounce.

Delilah takes a deep breath. Begins to speak.

64

"I don't remember the first time I had sex with Dad," she begins.

The thing about sitting at a group therapy table is this: people will either look one another in the eye as they spill their horror show secrets, or they find every last thing in the room to be more interesting. They'll be twiddling thumbs, shoes, cracks in the ceiling, counting twinkles on stainless steel fixtures and appliances. Whatever. Someone will be telling everybody how when they were drunk they got into a fight with their grown kid and shot the motherfucker and one other guy in the group will be counting dirt speckles on the tiled floor.

On the other hand when someone relates to what you are saying, well, they stare right at you. Nod. Agree. Been there, done that. You're not alone.

Most of the group: nodding, been-there-done-that-ing.

Me: twiddling and counting.

"My parents had a horrible relationship. This was when they were together...when my sister and I were young. Ben—I call my father by his first name now—he was in and out of our lives before he was finally just *out*. Mom was a good mom, but she had to work constantly. She kind of became that loving but sad woman who was around as much as she could be...which became less and less for some reason. The next door neighbors became Belinda and I's new folks.

"I don't remember when I started making bad decisions either."

She lights a smoke and I wonder if she knows that's bad for her baby. On a side note the walls need re-papering. Several of the seams are starting to droop and curl.

"When I graduated high school I had had two pregnancy scares but I made it through them. I dodged two bullets, I guess you could say. The first one I told Dad about. The second one I didn't. He freaked enough with the first one. *Is it mine? Is it mine?* He'd grabbed me by the shoulders and shook me while saying that, always looking over his shoulder for someone else to see him. He was always so paranoid.

"Belinda was career driven. That's how she got out. The Navy took her. Even in high school she was a star. Whenever Belinda wasn't around, Mom would say that God gave Belinda her smarts to get by on and I got the personality.

"Friends were never a problem. I just made the wrong ones. I liked thrills and that's a road I should have stayed off. But Dad was always there. I knew it was wrong. I just—it didn't *seem* wrong. Maybe it wasn't. There's two ways to look at it, I guess."

I rub my eyes.

"It seemed like love at first. The attention. I needed it. Ben was never—he touched me a few times but we never—it was just...*clinical*, like he was making up his mind on whether he should do it or not. And only when he was drunk or high. Mom said Ben was a hound...but he only came after his daughters when he was intoxicated.

"I made most of my terrible sex decisions when *I* was intoxicated. I guess I got that from him. I wonder if I'm worse than he is. About those kinds of things."

What?

"But anyways. Sometime in my teens it stopped feeling like love and started feeling like I was auditioning to be a new wife. I had big shoes to fill, that's for sure. Then it felt like obligation. Or a bad habit. Then it was just dirty. So I freaked out and left. Ran around the country for a few years. I made a lot more mistakes. I always do with men."

Wait a second. Now I'm looking at Delilah.

"The next door neighbors were like our parents, so that's why I feel like it was incestuous to sleep with Dad."

She holds her hands up to pause the scene and clarify. "Not Ben, my *real* father. Ben the sperm donor. No, no, no...Elam is Dad's name. I guess I should call him that."

Oh shit.

"After I returned home I decided I was going to take control of my life. I felt scummy for sleeping with Dad—Elam—and what we were doing to his wife, who was always in frail health. So I told him he was paying for my school. I'd earned it. In return I'd keep quiet about our affair.

"Losing your virginity at nine to a man in his forties gets you decent tuition."

Less than five minutes. I'll go meet him outside. Shoot him. She doesn't have to know.

"He shut his trap and paid. I don't know what he said to his wife but they did it. And four years later I had a degree. Then I told him he was buying me a house. We'd had two pregnancy scares, after all. He argued and didn't call for a week, but in the end he did it. I knew he would. I know *him*. And the house...I loved it."

She smiles fondly, the way a lost soul will smile when there is an honest moment of recollection which brings them back to the days when there was a path to follow. Peaceful contentment gracing a sad person.

"As soon as I got into my new job and living in the new house, well, I made another mistake. I fell for a man I knew deep down was just using me. I wanted it to be something more so bad, but thanks to Elam, I look at love in the wrong way. It's my fault too. I need to take responsibility but it seems *preprogrammed* in me. I know this and I still do it. It's like a drug addict loading up a shot, I guess. The addict knows and is joyous as he pushes the plunger."

Delilah has her mother's sad face. Her hair is shorter than the latest pictures Darla showed me. She looks thinner as well. Her hands are elegant. She pulls a tuft of hair behind an ear and swallows hard.

"So, my new job. Pierce was married but we dated anyways. He used me and eventually I confessed to the wrong co-worker. Ellen something. She ratted us out. We were fired. Broke up. Ellen...I heard from another friend that Ellen actually *put down* what she had done in her employee review. To help her out I guess. A raise or promotion or something. Whatever.

"Bitch." Her teeth clenched, Delilah hating this woman for capitalizing on her sin.

"About this time Elam came back around and thought that Pierce was the worst man in the world. I told Elam that Pierce and I broke up but it was like it never sunk in. He never got off of it. Elam hated Pierce immensely. He just didn't let it go. I wonder even to this day if Elam hated Pierce for breaking my heart the way a father would, or if it was jealousy. Probably both."

Delilah wrings her hands together and she looks away for a moment. This bittersweet catharsis seems to heal, but her price to pay is to expose the wounds she hid in the first place.

"Elam started acting very strangely. Even for a secret monster he just got *weird.* He approached Pierce, introduced himself as my father and told him he didn't want Pierce seeing his little girl anymore. They got into a shouting match. That was a long time ago now."

Three minutes.

"I went back to my old job but I was dead inside. And of course I started seeing a bad boy there. I had no idea he was fresh out of rehab. I had no idea he was estranged from his wife. We were caught having sex in the building. Fired. My life was over.

"We did drugs recreationally. Nothing new for me. I clung onto this dirtball even though I knew I shouldn't have, and before I knew it he turned 'recreational' into 'daily habit.' You know how some folks can tie one on and wake up the next day and just go about life like they never did? And others get bowled over and ugly right off the bat? James, the guy I was seeing, he got ugly. He couldn't moderate himself. He dove headfirst into the deep end and held his breath. And that was it.

"I'm sure he blames me for where he's at now. He stopped going to his group meetings to go out with me."

She smiles the way someone does when they know the truth and don't want to say it. So they put up a face and hope the moment melts away. My guess is she would not have been cool with a boyfriend who didn't party. She knows it. But she puts on her face anyways.

Her eyes shimmer beautifully. Tears glaze over them and I hate how the glistening makes her so pretty. It's not that I enjoy her turmoil, but I agree with her mother that not even pain can spoil her allure.

"I don't remember when my downward spiral began, but I remember when Elam told me I could get out if I wasn't going to pay him the mortgage. Now he had me, I guess. I knew how to earn my keep."

She bursts out crying. I look away. Hearing it is enough.

Delilah continues: "So I started sleeping with him again. Elam. I didn't know what else to do. He held my leash and he tugged at it. He knew just when and where and how. Maybe that was when the spiral began. No, it began before that...but it got much faster then."

She calms down some to cry softly. Two minutes.

"I kept it going for a while. Elam wrote me letters—

281

terrible things. He insinuated his wife could die in her sleep and he and I could relocate. He'd sell his company. We'd live happily ever after. He made odd statements. Creepy, veiled things. He started coming by again, not calling, not announcing himself. I woke one night and his car was idling outside. It was like three in the morning.

"I'm sure he did it more than once. I'm sure he was inside the house. But I never told anybody. I never called the cops or anything. Like I said, I make bad decisions. Looking back on it, maybe I should have. But anyone who knows me and who knows Elam...they would side with him. I'm not much of a...oh, I don't know.

"I'm just not *much*. How's that?"

No one says anything different. I don't know why. I don't either. But I don't know the girl. She might be dead on.

"By this time I was drowning my sorrows in booze. I got back into recreational drugs. I think it got the better of me. I don't remember a lot of my life. I remember waking up a lot and knowing I'd had sex the night before. I'd be nauseous from over doing it. I'd have strangers in the house. Even my parties were getting out of my control. Friends of friends of friends would show up. People so far removed from the guest list I might as well have broadcast the party's time and date on the radio. I'd spend most the night meeting the folks who were inside my house, touching my things.

"At one of those parties a guy stayed over with me. I don't remember his name now. All I remember was the guy had a Bugs Bunny tattoo and at some point Elam came in the room shouting. Who knows where he came from. He woke us up. Called me a whore and a jezebel. He threw things. He ran the guy off. We were screaming. I felt like such a raging bitch. Like a harpie or something. I never burned with hatred so much before that moment.

Elam told me he was going to sell the house and I just freaked.

"I don't remember what I said or did...but I think he started to ask himself if I was going to be good enough to be his new wife. I might have put some big dents in those golden happy dreams of us. Looking back on it I imagine he was buried further in some la-la land than I thought. I think he invented an entire world around us. Whatever it was, I needed him to not be mad anymore. I needed to do something. I had no job, I had no money.

"A few days later he came over and we made up. More sex. Big surprise, huh? Then we were kind of on-again off-again and I just started treating myself poorly. I even tried getting back with Pierce but that was so foolish. I was drunk so much during those few months. I think I got old to Elam. I put on weight. I quit bathing regularly. I think I changed something in him...I think he could smell the end on me. Maybe he couldn't put his finger on it...but instinct told him I was rotting.

"I have no respect for myself anymore."

Time's up.

"So I left. Moved in with my mom. Elam would call and my mom didn't know any better. They were old friends. When he told me he sold my house I was so desperate and depressed and on edge and hateful and sick of myself I tried to earn the house back. He used me. I think he got me pregnant. I mean, *I am pregnant*, I assume it is his. I've had sex with other guys since him. But he still sold the house.

"I was so unearthly mad. The word 'fury' cannot contain how angry I was. I think God was upset with me for poisoning my body with such hate and malice. Elam...I was so—unclean. I have felt like trash, but never like this. I had to hurt him back.

"I told Elam I was going to give his letters to the police.

I wanted to make him pay for how bad he destroyed me with that house and how he made me act and how gross and used up and no-good-for-anyone he made me. I just wanted him to go away for good.

"He had a sweet wife, children who loved him. Those kids are my age. Hell, they're a few years older, really. No one else knew about this second face of his. If he and I just agreed to part ways, we could keep our mouths shut. *I* would. It'd be easy. It'd be over. I keep secrets, Lord only knows. I have so many, what's one more?"

Delilah scratches at her hands in some kind of biblical gnashing of teeth outburst. She grabs her hair and screeches. She almost jumps in her seat and looks so uncomfortable, so ready to uncork we all get uneasy. Meltdown.

"I mean, seriously? Right? *Look at me.* Jesus Christ, I let a guy do anal with me and then I gave him a blowjob! *He was supposed to recognize the devotion in that act!* What the fuck good am I? That's something rapists do to women they are trying to degrade and I do it just because it might have kept the sonofabitch around! I did that for attention! I don't share that little juicy tidbit! I can sure keep quiet about fucking my surrogate father for half my life!

"I just wanted him to go away for good. Is that so bad?" The woman sitting next to her reaches out and offers her hand. Delilah snatches it up like it were a lifeline and white-knuckles her grip.

"In all reality I threw the letters away as soon as I'd read each one. I couldn't produce them if the cops wanted me to. But I threatened him anyways. It only seemed right that I held a little power over his head. But, Elam...he freaked like I'd never seen before. I didn't really think about it before the words came out of my mouth—I do that, but most times I catch myself, thank God—so I just said it. To me they were pretty much just words. To him it threatened everything his entire life was built on. Cut and dry. I was the worst thing he could ever face in this life. *The worst.*

"He threatened my life. Said he'd do anything. I know he meant it. He called me his 'little queen' and said he would put me in my throne one day. He just started spouting all this bizarre, creepy, threatening stuff. I was so scared. I ran. And I haven't been back since."

Flashback: Dr. Windslow.

"...I need you to find a certain young lady for me."

"Your daughter?"

"Absolutely not. As it were she was a...mistress."

Somewhere in the corners of my mind dots start to come together and, once again in my life, I become rather disappointed with myself. Sometimes I can see it all, sometimes I miss so much.

"Anyways, Delilah became like she was my own little girl..."

"I don't remember the first time I had sex with my father."

"Well, why do you need a private detective to find a woman who you think will still want to be with you? If she's that in to you she shouldn't be hard to find."

I should kill him now and spare her the looming threat.

I should kill Elam now and spare Delilah the looming threat.

"I do not hunt women for angry, jealous men." I say this and I mean it.

I do not hunt women for angry, jealous men. I say this and I do it.

I do not hunt women for angry, jealous men. I say this and I must un-do it.

I have hunted a woman for an angry, jealous man.

Damn you, Richard. Damn you.

I stand up.

Delilah looks at me and says: "I guess I'm done."

I'm not sure how loud I say, "I'm not trying to interrupt your life story." But I say it. Maybe just to myself. Maybe I want her to read it in my eyes. Either way I hope she can hear me.

The group leader eyeballs me for a moment and then begins the closing prayer. I head to the stairs. Maybe I can head off Derne and take care of this quietly.

Maybe not.

65

A cacophony of women start at the top of the stairs as I'm getting to the bottom.

Something hangs over me. Ominous. It feels like a death shawl. Find the edge of it, the corner and throw it off like a child does when they get lost underneath a sheet they've been playing with.

This thing hanging over me is pushing in my chest, telling me this thing is getting ugly. Unseen until now. This will end poorly. I have to do something to get out from underneath it; a storm cloud roiling with lightning getting ready to strike Delilah. I did this. I need to undo it.

How could I not see that Elam Derne was asking me to hunt down his victim?

The women's noise follows me. Tide. Flood. Now that the confessing is over the loud, pop culture and baking talk has begun.

"Oh no, honey. Use egg wash so that doesn't happen."

"She was married twice before they got together when they were filming...oh my, I forgot already but they were co-stars—"

"Yes. Divide them in the spring or after they bloom or else—"

"This sounds terrible but it works: use hemorrhoid cream for the wrinkles under your eyes—"

I thrust through the front doors and eyeball the street, hoping to clear my skull and get a deep breath of crisp winter air. Things have gotten dark. Bleak. As if the situation has drained the atmosphere here of anything resembling hope.

These are the times I call upon my gun or my fists or my gut instincts to take the wheel. Autopilot. If I can just get my sights on the problem I can beat it to death. Primal. Final.

The snow piled in dirty frozen lumps up and down the road. Each one spilling a shadow that looks like a rock mason who should be wiring me my blood money. The arc sodium lamps buzz like flies getting ready to die and my breath has become a blinding cloud of opaque white before me.

I can't think straight. My heart is rumbling, off-time and deafening. Detonating. So enraged at my own shortcoming it is hard to concentrate on anything else.

This is what blowing up in your face feels like.

This is what they mean when they say "screwing the pooch."

Make it right. Make it right. Make it right.

I need to find Derne before he shows up here. I turn in a circle and realize if I can't find Derne I *can* find Boothe. Fucking idiot. She was right there a second ago. I've walked halfway down the sidewalk when the thought hits me but I do an about face and double time it. Sometimes I can see it all, sometimes I miss so much.

Every car that rushes by I look for his face behind the wheel. Fifties. Thick glasses. Coarse beard the color of bleached sand. Hefty build. Thick. Stocky. He could have been saddled and pulled a cart in his youth. Maybe even now.

Slush and dirt spray up in plumes under tires. The sound is discordant and so loud it fills my entire head. The Doppler effect of engines roaring, each carrying on them the haunted ululating of incoming artillery. I tell myself this all gets fixed with one shot.

I'm only a door away from the Incest Survivor's Anonymous building and I draw out my phone. Dial Derne. I'll head him off, tell him I lost her. She went to the bathroom, whatever. Never came back. Call him in fifteen minutes and say I picked her scent back up. Have him meet me in some alley. Blip him. Send his face through the back of his skull. Go home. Maybe have some meatloaf.

She'll never have to know. She'll never have to know I hunted her down for her demon.

I dial. It rings. Each one slows my heart rate but tightens the tensions of this piano wire I walk out on.

In the background I hear a phone ring. In time. Coincidence. Has to be.

It's not.

I hear the phone removed from a pocket and silenced. Same time I get connected to voice mail. I drop my phone into a pocket, scramble. Race. Scan. Detect. Infuriated. Used. The sound was coming from—

"Delilah!"

The sound comes from where that voice comes from.

I look. Derne, cautiously approaching his life-long victim. She freezes. The look on her face is the exact look a deer had once when I accidently stepped on a dry patch of leaves and alerted it to me. But the deer knew better than to think its life extended out any further. Alerted only to death.

I'm not trying to interrupt your life story.

"Delilah, I—"

She starts to back up. She's crying. Other women look concerned. I draw the .44. Start to move faster. I look where to put my sights. I've always shot better at night. All the women know and no one has done anything to clue them in. Prey can smell this coming on the wind. Alerted only to death.

Derne says through his own tears and clenched teeth: "Delilah, I've always loved you, my sweet, sweet baby. My little queen."

And then he shoots her in the face.

66

The .44 Magnum roars to life.

Before Delilah hits the ground, cold and dead as the world around her, I've got three hunks of lead on fire and flying at Derne.

Miss, miss, graze. He bares his teeth in a hiss of fury and malady. Grabs his thigh. My first two rounds *zing* off into the night. The brick edifice of the buildings across the street harmlessly absorbs them. Thank God. Each round fired in public that misses is a million dollar bullet. I'm moving.

Women scream. The cacophony goes from cooking tips and gossip to lives being shattered. A berserk nympholepsy swarms through the crowd. Frenzied, violent emotion for the one thing they can't have: safety.

Derne turns. Blood soaking his pant leg but it doesn't seem to bother him. Gun in a shaky hand. Determined to ruin everything on his own terms. I make a target of myself. Keep away from the innocents. This is my doing. He fires. Miss me, miss me, miss me.

He sinks those rounds deep into the crowd.

The first woman Derne accidently plugs collapses beside me and I trip on her. Swerve. Eat concrete and dirty slush. The second woman screams on and on forever and while she is filling the world with her sufferings I take a shot and miss and Derne tries to throw a woman out of her open driver's side door and he is trying to get into an idling car but she gnashes her teeth at him and hammers down on the gas and he throws himself onto the sidewalk to avoid her squealing tires. He gets up in a mad dash and empties his gun and chunks of the road kick up and I can feel my face bleeding but no lead in my body I hear the dry click of an empty weapon trying to cough out more than what its belly was full of and I fire one more time and a street lamp goes out I assume I did that now I'm up and I slip I'm not sure if it is slush or blood feels tacky no time he's running limping but making good distance the bastard he's running like a fucking dog who knows what is behind it will set it straight and I don't think I can track him by any blood droplets because the night has settled down and blood looks black at night and the night is black too so it doesn't matter I am running and that woman is still screaming as if as long as she holds that note she will somehow stay on this side of the big white curtain and I know that's not true I've heard that note before and I almost want her to just die because that note is in my head caterwauling now I run past Delilah Boothe and she is just a white female black and blue thin and busty missing her beauty because it's sprayed all over the sidewalk and we're going down the street Derne turns a corner and crosses over into a parking lot and fuck me this is the Starlight Theatre he runs and is swallowed by rows of snow the trucks have plowed up into hedges and before I can gather my thoughts and reload and find where he is in this maze of night and ruined promises I hear metal clink so hollow and cavernous and I know what he's done.

He's gone into the underground runoff system.

I leap to the same manhole and I'll be damned but the first runner of smearing color traces itself down my vision. I scream, "NO," to the Heavens but that call of indignation just spills ten more runners one hundred more runners a thousand a billion down over me and all I see is defiled traces of snow white and death black and Delilah's red mixing as they race through my ruined brain and streamers of my seething rabidity soak the runners in volcano crimson. Snow white gives way to a shiny black and the black gives way to another shiny black and the red of Delilah's poor ending gives way to the shiny black but my tempest stays.

I fall over onto the parking lot. Guns clatters away. Stomach turns, from the smear or the outcome I don't know. I cough, vomit. Grab my head, shake it out. At some point the smear goes. On my feet. Armed.

The manhole cover is hastily put back in place. Askew. I move it, drop in. No hesitation, no fear. On the ladder, three rungs at a time, flying down. If he's lying in wait at the bottom he'll realize it is the biggest mistake of his life. I get on solid ground, scan while moving. He's not waiting. He's running. I'll find him.

This is what fury leading up to brutal revenge tastes like.

67

First leg of the hunt is a feeder line to the main artery.

Inky black darkness layers this place. Sac cloth draped over these brick and concrete burrows. Every edge of brick, every crack in the concrete, every imperfect corner interrupts the solid caliginous surface. This tunnel is bone-dry except for the thin trickle of moisture running down the center. Round concrete conduits, eight-foot diameter, around one hundred years old.

The place is a labyrinth. Any sound is a ghost, playing with echoes. I stand silent. Listen. Spectres run their fingers through the liquid shadows down here, pooling in the corners and giving off faint susurrations. I hear something: heavy breathing distorted by the plumbing we are inside. Maybe something bigger has already eaten him.

Come spring the mountain runoff will flash flood these tunnels and the water will be scraping the ceiling. These eight-foot feeder tunnels lead into the twelve-foot diameter arteries, pour out into the river somewhere.

Here and there a body will wash up miles away. Homeless, mostly. Vagrants camping out because the place is better than a cardboard hovel in the snow. Kids playing down here will sometimes get lost. It's sad when they wash out.

But this spring it will be an incestual child molester.

Teasers of arc sodium light spill down through the manhole covers; next to nothing. Something moves. Quick. Scratching noises. Feet hammering down. I fire, twice. Double tap. Deafening. Move. Gun empty. Spent brass in my palm then to my pocket. Speed loader on the move. New rounds in. Ready to perforate. Flashes of manhole light almost make things worse. I stop. Hold my breath. Hear someone groaning through clenched teeth. Movement. Metal crashes to the ground. Dropped gun. His. I run to the sound, open fire. Boom boomboomBOOM*BOOMBOOM!* Muzzle flash gives me glimpses like the flash of a camera in a haunted house. Each expulsion and Derne is still, caught in flight. The next he is positioned differently. Chunks of the tunnel exploding from the wall. Even after the gun blasts stop echoing the sound of pebbled concrete settling continue. Reload again. Stop. Listen for anything louder than the ringing in my ears. Like being in the war all over again. Shadows get deeper and then thin out, formless objects crawling on the walls and floor and ceiling all around us. The trickle of water thickens, widens, no light from a manhole. My heart has stopped beating. My lungs do not work. All I smell is gun powder. No blood. All I see are shades of night hiding my prey. My skin buzzes with electricity. I stalk. One hand on the wall. I lean down, hand to the floor, palm out. I find the trickle, move away from it. Feel for splashes. This goes on. I find one. I explore, find warm and tacky splatterings. He's losing blood. I follow it, one hand with the gun forward but tucked in close, one palm reading his bleak future on the tunnel. Small tunnel, six-foot diameter. We go. Him not too far ahead, a game of silence and distance now. He must not know I am following but he must think I am close. He's moving. He slips. I almost shoot. Somewhere in the absolute darkness ahead of us he is faltering. I creep closer. He regains his feet, moves ahead. Straight lines. We go. Ahead, light filters in from above like spears of angels coming down from the heavens. He pauses. So do I. Bathed in the gloom, my eyes adjust enough and I squat down into the black embrace. Umbrage, a camouflage in this cavernous hunting ground. I can start to make out the weak, watery light playing small twinkles on his glasses.

He is afraid to move even though every instinct in his bones and muscles and heart are screaming *run motherfucker run up that ladder and back onto the street run* but he stays still. See if I am on his tail. Make a mistake. We wait so long, measuring each inhale and exhale to hide them from the other that by the time he makes his move I am calm as a clam in clear blue water. He cautiously rises and limps to the ladder.

Climbs it painfully.

Reaches for the manhole.

"Derne," I say.

So startled, he falls. Regains his feet and starts to bolt away deeper in the runoff system.

My cylinder has six fresh shots. All I need is one. Raise the gun. Deep breath. Hold it. Let half out. Relax the grip. Squeeze, squeeze, squeeze, surprise. The barrel barks.

Direct hit.

Derne goes down, his right foot missing at the ankle.

I never said it would be a headshot. Not this one.

68

I don't think I hear the gun fall from my clenching fists and strike the bone-dry concrete because of the shot echoing in here.

"I don't remember the first time I had sex with my father." Playing over and over in my mind. The tear falling to the table.

Every bad decision has a birthplace. This man coils and slithers around in the sewer, writhing. Grabbing. Soiled in blood. Squealing through clenched teeth.

I grab a handful of the tight, curled weave of hair resting on the back of his skull. Clench. Raise. Swing. His face becomes a battering ram into the tunnel wall. The concrete gets a load of Derne's facial bones and tissues.

All I can really see is Delilah, a year from now, holding her baby. Her smile fulfilled and beaming down, her fingers splayed open and her child's miniature hand reaching up to palm its mother's. The small, perfect affectations of innocent life towards their parents.

Delilah smiling, her face flashing back and forth between her youthful beauty and a hollow cavern of splattered brain matter and cartilage. At some point I see her dead body go limp like a marionette with its strings cut and the baby falls, and ash pours out of the empty blanket swaddling the child.

Every terrible thing in this world has a birthplace.

My shoulder is tired from swinging but I do it anyways. A chunk from the tunnel corner breaks loose and rolls off into the pooling shadows, leaving small blood-prints like a rubber stamp gone haywire as it tumbles and rolls.

I see Delilah, Darla and Belinda wearing their matching sweaters on Christmas. Three women trying to recover from an unfair position in life. I see Delilah losing her virginity to a boy who said he loved her as a way to get into her pants and I see her praying he means it because that is all she needs. I see a young girl looking at herself in the mirror every morning and asking herself why her daddy left her and why her new one won't. I see her watching her own lips move as she mouths the question *was it something I did?* I see the tears fall in response.

I see the seeds of spiritual cancer planted and sown in the life of this woman. This soon-to-be-mother, now faceless and soaking wet, lying in the red snow of some foreign city surrounded by people who will treat her clinically as they scoop her up and take her somewhere where they can refrigerate her and dissect her before exclaiming to the world she died from being shot through her beauty.

I stop swinging when the bones in my fingers hit the corner.

Between my fingers, clenching and pulsing with unsatiated rage, remains small tufts of what used to be hair, now matted and tacky-wet. A fragment of the back of Derne's skull the size of my palm.

It's all over.

Nothing left to do now except wonder how I will answer for what I have done when asking for admittance at the Pearly Gates. That conversation with Saint Peter will be an uncomfortable one, for sure. At some point my fingers unclench enough for the handful of Derne's facial remains to fall free. His body slumps. Decapitated. I turn around.

Gun in hip holster.

I leave. Done here.

69

Whiskey washes it all away that night.
The morning brings with it an end. Bathed in sadness,
but an end.

EPILOGUE

Delilah's body had cops crawling all over it before I handled Derne.

They might have heard the gunshots, but we were blocks away and underground. That had to play hell with the sound.

Most of the women in the group had scattered to the wind, besides the dead one and the one still trying to sustain that horrible note to keep her on this side of the curtain. She kept it up for three days before she lost her voice in the hospital.

The one thing about an anonymous group like the Incest Survivors is getting names. Witness lists, accounts of the violence, who did what, where did they go, how did it happen, blah blah blah. Entries on report forms left blank.

A few of the women stayed with the shooting victims or came forward later. As far as I can tell no one brought me up, maybe because I was there to help. In their eyes. I did fight the man murdering one of their own.

None could have known I'd been the one to draw the monster to their front door. Keep it that way.

They did describe Derne.

Forensics and crime labs vary greatly from department to department. Both Saint Ansgar and Three Mile High share a lab, centrally located in Saint Ansgar. It is in the Stone Age. My bullets were either not found or traced to me. I'll keep holding my breath on that one.

Three Mile High police had traced Derne's bank account transaction and the phone records to me.

Yes, he hired me to find her.

Yes, I found her.

Yes, I told him.

No, I did not know he intended to murder her.

No, we have not spoken since.

No, I do not know where he is now.

All technically true. The location one I lawyered a little bit. Sure, I know where we disappeared into, but I have no idea where in there we wound up at.

Yes, I do not know where he is now. In Hell.

Then the next question: would I mind coming down for an interview and polygraph? No, I don't mind.

On the way I call Jeremiah on his personal cell. I ask him a question to which he answers: "Of course the patients here take blood pressure medicine. You name it: Metolazone, Metoprolol Succinate, Lisinopril, Felodipine. I got 'em all."

"Toss me down some."

"Which one?"

"I don't care."

Ten minutes from the station house I swallow a handful too many of the pills. I don't check the quantity; I don't check the medication itself. I'm sure it's a cocktail of all of them.

Lying is easy. I did it to IA all the time. The polygraph: stare a single dot on the wall, breathe in and out in a measured pace, even voice, chemically assisted heart rate, chemically assisted vasodilators. Set your baseline readings by telling little white lies on simple questions. Creates wiggle room.

Four hours later they give me a pat on the back as I walk out the door. I get home, struggling to hold in the side-effect diarrhea. I finish with that mess right before I vomit from the pills. It'll take days to realign my system.

Darla and Belinda were crushed. Small parts in both seemed to expect some kind of horrible ending. But to see it arrive on the wings of a family friend, to learn truths too ugly to contemplate...it scars. Darla couldn't help but have that look in her eye when she saw me last. The *this is your fault* look. I don't blame her. Some of it is.

In the wake of the murder, all hell broke loose. Clevenger leads the Saint Ansgar-end of Derne's investigation. He tied it into Pierce White's murder.

It didn't take long.

Derne's life was flayed open after Delilah's murder and in Derne's glove box Clevenger found a tiny receipt for a storage unit outside of town. Paid cash.

Warrant.

The place was small. Six by six. Two cardboard boxes and a wheelchair belonging to Derne's frail wife. In one box were second-hand nonfiction books about the greatest arsonists of the twentieth century. Fire Science 101. Other evidence that lays all three torchings squarely on Derne's back and must have sent Riggins, Volksman and Rudd through the roof. Good. Fuck all of them for not listening to a real investigator.

The other box contained self-help materials on things like incest, self-esteem, what one book's title called "An All-Consuming Crush." Pyschobabble label for obsession. Stalking. Things to help him temper himself with his feelings for Delilah.

Get out of your own way. Life coaching made easy. Three simple steps to overcoming what you can't change. Take charge! When a parent's love goes too far. Surviving the demons of incest.

And then, at the bottom of the box, were fiction books. Far more titles than the self-help books combined. Erotica fiction based on incest. Seedy shit printed in basement presses. Clevenger said the worst was when he leafed through the self-help books they were pristine. No bent corners, no book marks. No notes. But the erotica, they were scribbled to the point where some passages were unreadable.

The wife's wheel chair: apparently a throne Derne had retro-fitted to put his new wife into. Nails hammered through it so the points would impale when she sat. The title LITTLE QUEEN scrawled across the back. *He threatened my life. Said he'd do anything. I know he meant it. He called me his "little queen" and said he would put me in my throne one day.* Through the back of the chair, right where her heart would be, the knife he used to carve up White. It was still caked in blood.

Maybe the chair was a fantasy; something he needed to build in order to get it out of his system like those letters people write telling off folks and then they never send them. Obviously Derne was far more disturbed than the world around him knew. I sniffed this guy hard and couldn't scent this.

Either way, the throne was cast aside for the shoot-her-in-the-face-in-front-of-a-bunch-of-witnesses plan. Good for Delilah.

The dope, just a red herring. The men who ruined their lives for Delilah, a red herring. The drug dealers who took the dump truck load of shit Delilah brought with her when she their lives, red herring. Ben Boothe, red herring. It goes on.

Wrapped up now.

Not the way any fairy tale book would end it, but life chose this one.

I'm not okay with it. But I don't get to decide.

A month goes by, each second lags like they were stills in the memory of dementia; just snapshots of life, disconnected, lazily passing by the mind's feebling eye. Another month. More cases come and go. Then one day phone rings.

"Howard, how are you?" I ask.

"Very fine, Richard. I see you've been gallivanting, pissing off the locals again." His voice, charred by years untold of smoking filterless cigarettes, grumbles across the line.

Howard Michigan retired from Saint Ansgar PD a few years after I signed on. He was what went for an FTO when I graduated the academy. Then, seventeen years later when I was labeled "unfit for service" by the PD, he was the private investigator who showed me these ropes.

He still has an office but he barely takes a case. It's just as well; no one comes to him anymore. They've been coming to me for years.

"It was a case. Fuck Derne. He can be upset."

"Derne? That guy who mowed down some women up in Three Mile High?"

"Yes. Why? Who are you talking about?"

"Windslow. Dr. Marcus Windslow."

I am Dr. Windslow and I need you to find a certain young lady for me.

Your daughter?

Absolutely not. As it were she was a...mistress.

Why do you want the mistress?

To rekindle, I suppose.

I sit up straighter and lean into the phone. "*You* know Windslow?"

"Yes. After he hired me to find his ex-girlfriend he cussed you out up one side and down the other. I swear, Richard—"

"How much?" I ask. Fury emanates like heat snakes on a sunbaked road.

"Oh jeez, he went on and on. He hates you—"

"No. *How much to find the girl?*"

"Why? Jealous?" Howard makes a laughing sound; it is a burble in a backed-up drain.

"*How much?*"

"Slapped down a cold two grand. Said one grand was for looking into the broad, the other was for keeping his comments about you a secret." More laughter. "I told 'em *no problem.* I even called you a cocksucker just to gain his trust. Hope you don't mind, buddy."

"*No, I don't mind.*"

My revolver comes out, I look at the cylinder. Six fresh ones all packed up and ready with their dance cards.

"I feel like I should toss you a couple Benjamins just for doin' whatever it was you done to send the poor bastard my way."

Almost under my breath: "He waited a few months. I wonder if he tried to hire anyone else first, or if he just gave it some time to cool off."

"What? Who cares? Why'd you turn him down anyways? He try and write you a check?"

Why do you need a private detective to find a woman whom you think will still want to be with you? If she's that in to you she shouldn't be hard to find.

Will you take the case or not?

No. I will not take your case. But I will be keeping an eye on you. If Denise Carmine, white female, age thirty-two, brown and blue, five-foot-eight, one hundred and thirtyish, divorced, no children, drives a white Ford sedan turns up beaten or dead, I'll remember you.

"We had an understanding and he welched on me."

"What was the deal?" Howard asks.

"The girl. Let me guess: Denise Carmine?"

"That's her!" Howard says with a chuckle. "Jeez, Richard, I don't know how you passed on two—Richard? Richard?"

I hear him shouting my name through the phone. I put my overcoat on, close the office door behind me.

This one I can stop.

His door is solid oak. Stained a deep red, almost brown. The knocker is heavy brass; a ring dangling from the mouth of a lion. Bold. Decisive-looking. I like it. I just might take it with me. Four raps with the lion and I hear his voice on the other side.

"Just a moment. Just a moment, please."

I keep knocking.

The door opens impatiently.

"Mr. Buckner," he says, surprised. I step inside without an invitation.

I take the knocker with me when I leave.

POST SCRIPT

I've lived with RDB since early 2006 or so. That's longer than I've lived with my children. Not because I'm a deadbeat dad or anything; my kids are just younger than RDB.

I read a book called *Shadows Over Baker Street* edited by Michael Reaves and John Pelan that was a short story collection about what would happen if Sherlock Holmes entered the world of H.P. Lovecraft. Sounded intriguing. I was sold on the concept of Holmes's superior logic versus the nightmare insanity of Lovecraft's domain. It was worth it the cover price.

A little while later I read *Kiss Me, Judas* by Will Christopher Baer. All I could think about was the narrative voice. One of the few times in my life since Chuck Palahniuk's *Fight Club* (yeah, I'm one of those guys) where I just gripped a book as hard as I could and knew I needed to *write like this*. I loved the voice. Loved it. Needed to be like it.

So my plan was to use that voice (at the time I had no concept of noir or hardboiled as terms) and write a story about some gritty, brass-knuckles PI who was thrust into a nightmare world where his police logic didn't help. Hardboiled detective versus pure evil.

My wife Donna helped me name the man Richard Dean Buckner. We were sitting in a California Pizza Kitchen and mulled it over dinner. My dad told me all about .44 Magnums and how cops worked. I mixed my home town of Kansas City, Missouri, and the eastern side of the San Francisco Bay area for Saint Ansgar.

And then I pitted RDB versus a resurrected demon-thing that was trying to make Earth its new hell.

No one touched it.

No one.

I don't even think I got the courtesy of a form rejection. I think I just got tossed, un-opened, into the slush pile. Deflated, deterred, upset, I cried into my pillow for weeks. I probably cut myself too. Sure, the book was full of plot holes and inconsistent logic (where were you then, Chuck? Benoit?), but it had a freakin' .44 Magnum shooting a monster! Rejection to a story so great was tantamount to absolute bullshit from the universe itself.

So I wrote another book about other people doing other things. And then another book, about more people doing other things.

But I never forgot about that dude. The only guy I knew that was badass enough to get swallowed by a hulking, tumorous demon just so he could get close enough to her beating heart to stuff it with dynamite.

And one day, I figured RDB might do better in the real world, so I started writing about that. I wound up writing this book. This was 2009.

Beat to a Pulp published the first chapter of this book as a stand-alone story and I am eternally grateful. I used the pen name Derek Kelly for reasons I can't really remember now. BTAP editor and founder David Cranmer did for me what no one else had done: given me the deep-seeded satisfaction of making RDB relevant to the crime world. That was such a blast to my waning dream of being published that I kept up the fight. It was rejuvenating. BTAP was nothing to mess with, and if they liked RDB, others might as well.

I did a couple of RDB short stories and was honored by having them published at Crime Factory issue #7 again under the name Derek Kelly and Shotgun Honey under my own name. He's appeared in Crime Factory #12 and *Two*

Bullets Change Everything, a split I did with Chris Rhatigan and put out through All Due Respect Books.

So, thanks to God.

Thanks to my wife Donna, who, since I first asked her out on a date back in 1995 until right now, has been the sun around which my universe revolves. She has given me the greatest gifts I could ever receive in the form of our little babies and without her, I would be absolutely nothing.

Thanks to Billy Porter and John Regan for being my first readers ever.

To Randy Foster, Mike James, Bob Macon, Jarrod Wood, Mike Aude Alink, Kurt Reinhardt, Edmond Carrillo, Bob Kirk, Travis Marshall, Darlene Santiago, James Gregg and the other cops I've worked beside and learned from, thank you for your input and war stories.

To my brothers in Zelmer Pulp. Brian Panowich, Chuck Regan, Issac Kirkman, Chris Leek, Gareth Spark and Benoit Lelievre. We did it, and we keep doing it.

To Craig and Emily McNeely, Andrew Hilbert and the Weekly Weird Monthly gang, Chris Rhatigan and Mike Monson over at ADR Books, Joe Clifford and Tom Pitts (we all know you're a couple), Ron Earl Philips and the Shotgun Honey lineup, Brian Lindenmuth and the Snubnose Press peoples and everyone else, thank you.

To Eric Campbell and the Down & Out Books crew, like I keep mentioning every chance I get, this is a real honor. Thank you.

To the other writers I have had the pleasure to be published beside and spoken with here and there, I know you all worship me as a living god and follow my every move, so here you go. Chapter One in the Bible of Ryan. You're welcome.

And to you, loyal reader. Thanks for being interested in a guy I wrote about when I wanted to write about killing a demon. If this book doesn't catch your fancy, there's something wrong with you, but just keep buying all my stuff. Eventually you'll find something that clicks.

ACKNOWLEDGMENTS

I wrote this book before I became a policeman, so I relied on my father, who stood between society and its underbelly for over thirty years, to answer questions and guide me along as I wrote. I always wanted the book tuned slightly higher than reality—maybe up to 110%, because normal *anything* isn't entertaining enough—and I felt comfortable where I landed. It's exaggerated here and there. Mainly the violence. Whatever is written correctly, my father advised me on. Whatever wouldn't fly in real life is squarely because of me.

ABOUT THE AUTHOR

Ryan Sayles has over two dozen short stories in print, anthologies and online, including the Anthony-nominated collection *Trouble in the Heartland: stories inspired by the music of Bruce Springsteen.* He is the author of *Subtle Art of Brutality, Warpath, Goldfinches* and *That Escalated Quickly!* He is a founding member of Zelmer Pulp. He was in the military and is currently a police officer.

OTHER TITLES FROM DOWN AND OUT BOOKS

See www.DownAndOutBooks.com for complete list

By Richard Godwin
Wrong Crowd (*)

By William Hastings (editor)
*Stray Dogs: Writing from the
Other America*

By Matt Hilton
No Going Back
Rules of Honor (*)
The Lawless Kind (*)

By Terry Holland
An Ice Cold Paradise
Chicago Shiver

By Darrel James,
Linda O. Johnston &
Tammy Kaehler (editors)
Last Exit to Murder

By David Housewright &
Renée Valois
The Devil and the Diva

By David Housewright
Finders Keepers
Full House

By Jon & Ruth Jordan (editors)
Murder and Mayhem in Muskego
Cooking with Crimespree

By Andrew McAleer & Paul D. Marks
(editors)
Coast to Coast (*)

By Bill Moody
Czechmate
The Man in Red Square
Solo Hand
The Death of a Tenor Man
The Sound of the Trumpet
Bird Lives!

By Gary Phillips
The Perpetrators
Scoundrels (Editor)
Treacherous

By Robert J. Randisi
Upon My Soul
Souls of the Dead
Envy the Dead (*)

By Ryan Sayles
The Subtle Art of Brutality
Warpath (*)

By Anthony Neil Smith
Worm

By Liam Sweeny
Welcome Back, Jack (*)

By Lono Waiwaiole
Wiley's Lament
Wiley's Shuffle
Wiley's Refrain
Dark Paradise

By Vincent Zandri
Moonlight Weeps

(*)—Coming Soon